UNDER A CLOUD

LUV LUBKER

HISTORIUM PRESS

THIS BOOK IS DEDICATED TO

My Mom, Jaleen Lubker, who taught me my special research methods, and asked strange questions I went searching to prove wrong, only to find they were true.

My readers of my first book, whose kind praise has encouraged me.

My family and friends, whose love and praise supports me on my journey.

The Emperor Frederick III, "Our Fritz", who wished to make the world a better place.

THANKS TO:

My Mom, Jaleen Lubker, who taught me how to find things I would never have thought of. My brother, Alex Lubker, for proofreading my book. And of course all my family and friends, for all your love and support

Tom Buk-Swienty and Rayne Hall, whose books helped me enormously in my research in matters about which I repeatedly cried, "I don't know how to write about this!"

The other authors and researchers, who have written about so many fascinating people, and spent so much time, effort, and money to publish the wonderful collections of letters and diaries, which I know from experience take years to transcribe.

To the Royals themselves, for living such interesting lives and leaving us the legacy.

And particularly to The Empress Frederick, "Vicky", for making the best of her life and writing her story.

NOTES ON THE GERMAN LANGUAGE

Much of the dialogue of this book is supposed to really be in German. I specifically mention when people speak English, outside of the English Royal family.

"chen" at the end of names or words is a diminutive in German, such as "Lenchen" as a nickname for "Helena".

I tried to use words which are more known or obvious from context, such as "danke," for "thank you", "Ich," for "I", "du," for "you", "ja" and "nein" for "yes and "no" and so on, or have the phrases repeated in English.

Pronunciation notes – the umlauts: ä is pronounced how English speakers say the letter "a", so "bäker" in German is pronounced similarly to "baker" in English, where as in German the "a" would be more of the "awe" sound. Ö and ü add a sort of soft "r" sound with them; it is difficult to describe. "ß" is an "s" sound, where as "s" is a "z" sound in German, and "z" is "tz".

CHARACTER CAST

In England: The Royal Family

Queen Victoria, Vicky's Mama

Prince Albert, the Prince Consort, Vicky's Papa

Uncle George Cambridge, Queen Victoria's cousin

Alix, Princess Alexandra of Denmark, later Princess of Wales,
Bertie's wife

Vicky's siblings

Bertie, the Prince of Wales, future King Edward VII

Alice

Affie, Alfred

Lenchen, Helena

Louise

Arthur

Leopold

Beatrice

In Prussia – The Royal Family

Fritz's Papa, Helmkin, King Wilhelm I of Prussia

Fritz's Mama, Augusta, later Queen Augusta of Prussia

Vivi, Fritz's sister, Grand Duchess of Baden

Prince Charles, Onkel Karl, Karly, uncle to Fritz

Marie, Princess Charles of Prussia

Fritz Karl, son of Prince Charles, cousin to Fritz

Marianne, wife of Fritz Karl

Mariechen, Ebi, Annchen, Louischen, daughters of Marianne

Anna, daughter of Prince Charles

Lotte, Fritz's cousin and closest friend in the family, died before Vicky's engagement

Addy, daughter of Prince Albrecht

Wilhelm "Willy", Charlotte "Ditta", Henry, Siggy, Vicky and Fritz's children

Aunt Elisa, Queen Elisa, Dowager of Friedrich Wilhelm IV

Aunt Adina, Grand Duchess of Mecklenburg Schwerin, Prince Charles's "best sister"

Onkel Albrecht, Prince Albrecht, uncle to Fritz, brother of the King and Prince Charles

Other Royals

Louis of Hesse, Alice's fiancé and later husband

Aunt Feodora, Queen Victoria's half-sister

Feo, Aunt Feodora's daughter, wife of George of Meiningen

George of Meiningen, Feo's husband, Lotte's widower

Uncle Ernst, Duke of Coburg

Princess Christian, mother of Alix, later Queen Louise of Denmark

Prince Christian of Denmark, father of Alix, later King

Oscar, King of Sweden and close friend of Fritz

Tsar Alexander II of Russia, Fritz's cousin

Franz Joseph, Emperor of Austria

Victor Emanuel III, King of Italy

The Bey of Tunis

In Prussia: The Royal Household

Wally Paget, nee Hohenthal, formerly Vicky's lady-in-waiting,
now in the diplomatic corps in Denmark

Valerie Hohethal and Hedwig Brühl, Vicky's lady-in-waiting,
Wally's sister and cousin

Count Seckendorff, Vicky's former page

Emma Hobbs, Vicky's English nurse

Georgianna Hobbs, Vicky's English housekeeper

Rosa, Vicky's maid

In Prussia: Political and Wartime

Otto von Bismarck, Minister-President

Albrecht von Roon, Minister of War, Fritz Karl's former governor

Von Heydt, Minister of Commerce

Sir Andrew Buchanan, British Ambassador to Prussia

Friedrich von Wrangel, Commander-in-Chief

Falkenstein, Chief of Staff

Gablenz, Austrian Commander

POINT OF VIEW KEY

 – VPR, Victoria Princess Royal, Vicky

 - FW, Friedrich Wilhelm Prince von Preußen, Fritz

 - Queen Victoria, Vicky's mama

 – PC, Prince Carl/Charles

TABLE OF CONTENTS

**The Crown Prince of Prussia and Prince Wilhelm
at Balmoral Castle – October 1863**

PRAISE FOR "UNDER HIS SPELL"
(Book One of the Rival Courts series)

What Goodreads and Amazon reviewers are saying....

"Loved it. You got this perfectly right. It's a fantastic read. Amazing love story of Queen Victoria's first daughter Vicky during the first part of her marriage. The amount of research done is just outstanding. The way things are described and details is top notched. You feel like you have gone back through time and seeing and touching things first hand. This is one of my favorite historical periods, so I felt that I knew them and now see more of their stories. Thank you for letting them speak again." - Leah A.

"Such a personal account of a courtship and love. Queen Victoria of England's first-born, The Princess Royal Victoria (Vicky), left a happy family and court for intrigue and vice in Prussia's court. Only the great love she shared with her husband, Prince Fritz, sustained them both through their first years of marriage. I had no idea court life could be so hard. Also, I could tell Lubker used real documents, letters, etc. to write this fascinating tale. I'm so glad I read this book." - Victoria S.

"Royalty at its finest! This story transcended me to a place of noble and palatial surroundings, namely Balmoral and Osborne. I thoroughly enjoyed learning the characteristics of the royal family of England. I fell in love with the Queen and King and how their lives differed from Prussia's and other Monarchy. They genuinely loved each other, unlike most royal marriages. I was also enamored by Princess Vicky and her lover, Prince Fritz. Their characters were similar to the King and Queen of England." - K. Estrada

PROLOGUE

Neues Palais, Potsdam, July 5, 1862

"Tell me everything! Everything! You will not have peace until you do." Fritz embraced Vicky carefully as she tried to throw herself into his arms in her usual impetuous greeting. He didn't want to risk hurting her or the baby when she was so close to the birth.

"London is looking very nice," he said, smiling, "and the Exhibition is going very well."

"But how is everyone? And how is Alice? And how did Mama tolerate her departure?"

"Alice was as calm and serious a bride as you were," he said, kissing her and sitting down. "Your Mama was – as well as can be expected, I suppose."

"How I wish I could have been there, for everyone's sake. I still can't imagine Alice as a wife," Vicky said, snuggling in his arms.

"Your Mama gave me this to give you. It is Alice's note written the day after, so you can see how happy she is." He kissed Vicky. "We made a good choice, I think."

"Yes. Louis is a good young man. And Alice will have such a much easier home than we do. But you haven't told me about the wedding! How was everyone?"

"Your Mama wept as you can imagine; indeed, everyone did, except Alice herself. Louis had tears in his eyes the whole time.

Only Bertie did not break down until the goodbye came. Alice told me afterwards she was thinking of Papa the whole time, but the tears simply would not come. You will see how much she misses him, and you, in her note."

"I do wish I could have been there, for Mama's sake, when Alice had to leave. She appreciates your presence so much, Fritz; you have been such a support and comfort to her, in these months since Papa's death," Vicky said, looking up into her husband's face. She blinked, and realized he had tears in his eyes too. "All of us love you so dearly, and I was glad to let you go to support them."

Fritz swallowed, trying to find his voice, but he only held Vicky closer to him, as the memories of the past seven months flooded over him. Life had changed more completely than he had thought possible.

PART ONE:
MOURNING

CHAPTER ONE

TO LIVE AGAIN

Windsor Castle, December 23, 1861

Fritz looked about the room, remembering the first time he had slept – or rather spent the night – here, nearly four years ago. He felt tears come to his eyes as he thought of his father-in-law, the man who had always listened to him more attentively than anyone ever had before, always read and answered his letters in so much detail, always encouraged him to stand up for his own opinions. The man who had made the British monarchy what it was.

He took a letter from his pocket and read it over again.

"*Mein Schatz[1]*, how I long for you more than ever now, now when I know Papa is no longer of this earth, that I will never again know his kind words and looks and never have another kiss from him, and never say good-bye. I can imagine how Mama longs for him, as I do for you, but now she will never know the joy of meeting again in this world. We must learn to live again without him, but that is the hardest lesson, at first, as it will seem wrong to cease to mourn deeply for one whom we adored as we did him.

"What you say about Bertie is soothing; I had felt that Mama was much upset in that quarter, and I am so very glad you say that he and Papa had reconciled before he came home. I know you will always give my brothers the best possible advice they can have from anyone but dear Papa, and I kiss you in gratitude.

---

1 My darling

"I am so thankful you are with Mama and all my family. She writes so touchingly of your kindness and I see by your letters you feel how she overwhelms you with affection.

"But it is so lonely going to bed each night alone, and I long for your return more than words can express.

"*Deine Frauchen,*[2]

"Vicky."

Fritz pressed the letter to his lips, returned it to his pocket, wiped his eyes, and left the room. He would have another long, serious talk with Bertie before he left for London, Dover, Germany, home, and Vicky.

The evening before, his mother-in-law, Queen Victoria, had talked with him long into the night. She had taken him to see the room where her husband had died, which was to be kept as a memorial for him. She had also shown him all the papers concerning the recent scandal about her son, Bertie, the Prince of Wales.

"He was so concerned about Vicky," the Queen said through her tears. "He said on her birthday, and repeatedly, 'If only nothing happens to Vicky'. Fritz, you know how much he trusted you, and how much I trust you. Take these letters to show Vicky. She must know everything. And I am writing my will again; it is so complicated now, with having to leave things to specific people. Before, everything would have been under his direction, if I died." She paused, trying to control a burst of sobs. Fritz put his hand on her shoulder, and sat down by her side. She leaned her head on his shoulder and burst into tears again.

Finally, she became calmer. "Fritz, if I die while the children are still young, I want you and Vicky to be in charge of their education, you and Vicky and Alice. Of course Bertie will have to be officially, as he will be King and would be the natural guardian of his younger siblings, but he agrees with me on this matter. Show

---

2 Your wife

Vicky all of this. He – he, Vicky –" She shook her head, and burst into tears again.

"Mama, I will do all you wish," Fritz said, putting his arm around her and kissing her cheek. "He did – and you have done – so much for me, of course I will do all you wish. And –" He paused, thinking. "I hope that Vicky and I can spend some time away from Berlin this year."

The Queen nodded, wiping her eyes. "That is what he would wish for you, too."

Kronprinzen Palais, Berlin, December 23, 1861.

Vicky had sat listlessly at the window where she usually sat busy with her writing or painting. Now she sat, doing nothing, her handkerchief dragging the floor as she let her hand drop, her other hand resting on a stack of photographs of Papa. Today, in London, his funeral was taking place. Her heart went out to her mother and siblings, and she longed to be there, or for Fritz to be with her. His tender heart would be aching now, witnessing her mother's overpowering grief.

Something outside caught her eyes, and she looked down. A Royal carriage had just driven up; the horses were stamping in the snow. She saw the monogram on the carriage, and shivered. Was Prince Charles coming to her place, during her terrible grief for her father? She looked about. What could she do if he did? The footman jumped down from the back of the carriage and disappeared. The carriage was too close to the building for Vicky to see the door open and – Vicky shivered again, as if someone had thrown open the window and let in the swirling snow.

She hurried to the door and locked it, but knew that would do nothing. Prince Charles was a locksmith. Then she turned back to the window. Everything was still; the groom had taken the horses. It was not to be only a brief visit.

Where could she go; where could she hide? She heard steps now, a man's steps, in the next room. She heard someone trying to open the door. She suddenly couldn't see the room, or the door. It was as if she was back in the laundry, Prince Charles' hand gripping her shoulder, her chemise – her only garment – half torn, and his hypnotic green eyes staring into hers.

Kronprinzen Palais, Berlin, December 25, 1861.

Fritz hurried upstairs and into the sitting room, looking about. Vicky wasn't there. She hadn't been at the station to meet him, but he hadn't really expected her to be.

He opened the bedroom door. "Vicky?"

"Oh, Fritz, you are home?" Vicky raised her head, looking at him from under a heap of blankets. He stepped forward as she sat up.

"Are you well?" he asked, taking her in his arms and kissing her.

"I don't know," Vicky sighed. "As well as I can be, I suppose. But how is poor Mama, and everyone? What do you have to show me?"

"Your Mama is terribly sad, of course, but she is so brave, and carries on as well as she can. Alice looks very pale and thin. Louis, too was at the funeral, but sometimes I doubt if Alice will go in a few months. I do not see how she can be spared."

"I have thought the same thing," Vicky said, hiding her face against his chest. When she looked up, her eyes were filled with tears. "How I wish I could go to Mama now. I cannot bear this," she sobbed. "I don't see how I can learn to live again, without Papa. He was everything – of course, Fritz, you are – but – he –" Her voice trailed off into sobs, and Fritz realized he too had tears in his eyes.

He lay down by her side. "I have many things to show you. Your Mama gave me papers she wishes you to see. And I have spoken very seriously with Bertie, and he seems to take it in as we could wish, and is certainly very sorry at having so deeply upset his Papa. But we will speak of these things later, if you wish."

"Oh, no, they are everything to me; I wish to know everything. How did everyone stand the funeral? Poor Affie and Leopold are still not home."

"Uncle Leopold is looking very aged. Uncle Ernst is terribly sad, and poor little Arthur's sobs broke all our hearts, if they were not broken already. Bertie tried to stay strong, but he was very pale, and I could see he shed a few tears. But Vicky, how are you feeling? Did anything happen while I was away?"

"I feel as well as I can, as I said, with this horrible grief, and you being away, and being so sick. And they tried to make me go to the Christmas dinner at the Schloss tonight. I wouldn't go, and said I was ill, and that was why I wasn't at the station to meet you." She looked up at him. "Your Mama didn't wish to go, either, but – oh, and Aunt Marie came to see me. That was very interesting."

"What did she say?"

"She came – it was the day of the funeral. Prince Charles was away that day. You know she has never spoken to me much, and always seems to avoid me a little, but she was so touchingly kind. She said she wanted me to know her real feelings and how much she supports us, though she cannot show it usually, and how much she grieves for Papa and for his hopes and dreams for Germany. She and your Mama are both very disgruntled over being required to appear at everything, when they consider themselves in mourning. Your Papa hasn't even acknowledged my letters, or come to see me."

Fritz looked away. He had hoped his father would be supportive to Vicky while he was away, but he could never know what his parents would do.

Vicky thought of that moment, two days before, when Princess Charles – Fritz's Aunt Marie – had come to see her.

The moment of terror when she thought it must be Prince Charles had been terrible. She had stood petrified as the lock turned and the door opened.

"A – A – A – Abbat," she gasped, as Fritz's cousin stepped into the room. "I – I – I – thought it was – someone else – why where you in – that – carriage?" Her voice came out broken and shaky, as relief flooded her.

His face looked very sympathetic, as he stepped forward and took her hand and kissed her cheek. "I am so sorry," he began. His face and voice were so like Fritz's. Vicky threw her arms around him and burst into tears.

"I am so sorry," Abbat said again, patting her back and guiding her to a chair to sit down. "I can imagine how you must have felt. I'm so sorry I didn't think of it." He knew what had happened to her at the hands of Prince Charles. Vicky and Fritz were working to have him appointed to be, in the necessary circumstances, Regent and guardian for their children, if something happened to both Fritz and the King during Willy's minority. Otherwise Prince Charles would naturally be, as he was next in line for the throne after Fritz's children.

"I am so sorry about your father," Abbat went on. "I meant to come before, but have not been able to. I – I know what it is to lose a parent, though not in the same way." Abbat's parents had been divorced when he was quite young, and both lived away from court. He had never seen his mother again.

Vicky nodded. "My Papa knew what you went through, you know. His parents were separated when he was five." She thought of something which had occurred the year before, after Fritz's parents had become King and Queen.

They had never gotten along particularly well, and had, for years, often lived apart, Fritz's mother keeping her own court in Koblenz, where they had lived when he had been Governor of Mainz, in the Rhineland. But after their succession, their quarrels had grown more serious than ever.

"No, no, Mama must be Queen!" Fritz had come in repeating the words to himself again and again, after going to tea with his parents.

"What do you mean? Why wouldn't she be?" Vicky had asked.

"They are talking of a legal separation – not just in fact but legal, Vicky – and I know if they do this, Onkel Karl will find some way to make it so she won't be crowned Queen, or convince him to divorce her, or – *ach*!" He shook his head, walking rapidly up and down the room, biting his lip. "She must be Queen," he repeated. "Otherwise – everything is lost! We may as well not exist! Without her, Papa would give himself up to them entirely – of course not consciously – but – *ach*! What can we do?"

Vicky had felt helpless in the face of such a question, but it was – thankfully – never brought up again. Fritz left to go to tea with his parents the next day with a very grim face, but came back quite joyful.

"Papa doesn't think of a legal separation – and everything is quite peaceful today. Papa was even affectionate to her, which he has not been for some time."

Vicky looked up at Abbat and took his hand.

"Thank you, Abbat. I understand what you mean. But why were you in – that – carriage?"

"I was visiting Aunt Marie. Onkel Karl is away. She is here to see you, too. She was already going to see you when I came to see her, so I joined her."

"She is here?" Vicky asked.

Abbat nodded, kissed her cheek again, and went to the door, opening it.

Princess Charles appeared in the doorway, dressed in deep mourning. Vicky realized that Abbat, too, wore a black armband. She glanced at him, touched her arm in the same place, and gave a sad smile and nod, which he returned before he went out.

Vicky curtseyed deeply, and held out her hand. She wasn't quite sure what to make of this visit from Princess Charles. Fritz had always said she was kind, and supported them, and so had Marianne. But Vicky couldn't help feeling that Princess Charles had always ignored her, even snubbed her. But perhaps it was only because she was hiding her true feelings, which she probably didn't dare to show in front of her husband.

"Vicky – may I call you so?" Her voice was gentle as she spoke, and she took Vicky's hand. She looked so much like her sister – Fritz's mother – only she wore a wig of a dark blond instead of very dark brown. Her expression was also much gentler than her sister's.

"Yes. Have you –" Vicky wasn't sure what to say.

"I have come here to say how much I feel for you, and mourn your father's death. He was a very fine, honorable man, whom I admired immensely, as my sister does, but you can imagine I cannot show this very often."

Vicky nodded. "*Danke*[3]."

"I – I – May we sit down?" Vicky nodded, and went to the sofa across from the window.

"I share your feelings so much, I cannot say," Princess Charles went on. "You know my brother went to college with your father, and they were good friends."

"Of course."

"I have always admired your father, and he has done so much for this country. I – I wish to thank him – to thank your mother – for allowing you to come here. You and your Fritz are our hope – our beam of light. You can imagine how hard it is for me –" She paused, her face changing, and Vicky realized she was trying not to cry. Vicky's heart melted.

"Thank you," she said, taking her hand. "You share our grief – I was never sure what your feelings were; you have spoken to me so little, though Fritz and Marianne always say you are kind."

"Of course I cannot show my feelings when – he – is here, but I do. I do – so much. I want you to know that," she said, wiping her eyes. She rose to leave.

"Thank you again, Aunt Marie," Vicky said, curtseying once more. "It makes it a little easier to learn to live again, knowing there are more here who care, who share our grief and our hopes."

---

3   Thank you

CHAPTER TWO

SHEEP WITHOUT A SHEPHERD

On board the Victoria and Albert, *February 14, 1862*

Vicky watched as the yacht drew near to the shore. She thought she saw a carriage waiting, and when she alighted, Alice and Colonel Ponsonby were waiting for her.

"Vicky!"

"Alice!"

They fell into each other's arms, and Alice led her back to the carriage.

"How is Mama?" Vicky asked. She looked up when Alice didn't answer, and they both burst into tears. Vicky was glad it was a closed carriage.

Finally, the carriage started to move. "I almost dread the meeting," Alice said. "Mama has longed for you to come, but it will be so – so –" Her voice was drowned in tears again, and Vicky put her arm around her.

"Are you quite well, Alice? You look so thin," she said, kissing her sister's cheek. "I can't help thinking –"

"I have had a long watch at the bedside," Alice said. "Louis is very kind and understanding and will not object if the marriage must be delayed. But I long for it – for him – and to have some happiness to cling to. He is so much to me, even more than before, of course. But there will be no kiss from Papa at my wedding."

Vicky nodded, wiping her eyes. "You will perhaps be able to be much in England the first years, as your place is not finished." Mama had paid for a new Palace to be built in Darmstadt for Alice and Louis, one which would belong entirely to them and have modern conveniences, so that Alice should not have the difficulties Vicky had in that way.

Alice nodded. "We shall go to Darmstadt for a few months after our marriage, but come back to Mama, as we shall have to live with Louis' parents, and their place is rather small, I understand. It will make the transition easier for us all." She paused. "Dear Papa was so worried about you, the last few days before –" She burst into tears again.

"Mama wrote that he spoke of me repeatedly. That he was worried some fresh trouble was about to come upon us. I wonder if he suspected anything specific, besides a change of government."

Vicky looked up, seeing the castle ahead. "We are nearly there. Dear Osborne, I am so glad to see it again, but without Papa." They both burst into tears again.

The carriage finally drew up at Osborne.

"Oh, Mama!" Vicky threw her arms around her mother as soon as she entered the room, both bursting into tears.

Vicky tapped at the door of her mother's bedroom. "Vicky?"

She opened the door. Mama sat on the edge of her bed. Vicky thought she looked so touchingly young and pretty in her mourning cap. On the bed, next to her nightgown, lay Papa's red dressing-gown and coat. Little Beatrice sat on the bed, looking at Vicky.

"Dear Mama," Vicky said, taking her mother's hand and kissing her cheek as she sat beside her. Mama covered her face, and Vicky realized she was crying silently. She put her arm around her and said nothing.

"I don't know what to say," Mama sobbed, "and I don't know how to help you. I know you and Fritz need him so much, more now than ever if we can say that." She turned to kiss Vicky's cheek. "Fritz was so kind at the funeral. He is my support, now, and must be, with Stockmar unwell and Uncle Leopold too." She stopped, struggling against her tears. "When they – I don't know what we will do."

"I know what you mean, Mama. Fritz needs support more than ever, with our situation as it is, and it is not growing easier. But I am so thankful to be here, Mama. I have felt so cut off and far away. You need me too."

"I don't know what I shall do when Alice goes," Mama said. "I sometimes feel as if I must forbid her to marry, but I don't wish to ruin her young life. But I must have someone with me, and Lenchen's tears will only set me off again, and Louise is too young."

"You can let Bertie help you," Vicky said gently. Mama looked up sharply, her expression changing. "No. He is not fit to yet. He will go to the East. It is better we are not more together than we are." She spoke crisply and without a trace of a sob in her voice now.

"You have forgiven him, haven't you? You don't hold him acc –"

"No, I know he is not responsible for Papa's – he is not, but –" Her face twisted as she struggled against tears again. "I cannot have him always with me. I must have one of you girls here."

"Baby is here," Beatrice said, wriggling between Vicky and Mama. She reached up to pat Mama's cheek. "Poor Mama sad, Baby is here, Baby makes Mama happy."

Vicky smiled, but felt tears start to her eyes again.

✳ ✳ ✳

Osborne, February 27, 1862

Vicky sat on the terrace with her easel and paint, but sat unmovingly, watching the wind in the trees. Papa had laid out the landscape at Osborne so beautifully, but everything connected with him made her cry. That meant everything here did. Osborne was so inextricably connected with Mama and Papa's love for each other, every little detail was extremely personal. She took a letter out of her pocket, pressing it to her lips and unfolding it to read over again.

"The children sit at my feet, playing sweetly together as I read the papers and even when Schleinitz comes to speak with me. There have been no new troubles since your departure, only the ones which you know of. Give your Mama my tenderest love, and all the *Geschwichter* too."

Fritz did not sound too low in the letters she had received so far. Vicky was glad. She had been concerned about leaving him just now, as he had so often been very depressed over the political situation in Berlin.

"Mama?" Vicky said, rising as her mother and Alice came towards her. "I have had another letter from Fritz."

Mama glanced at her, sitting beside her as Alice went on. "I have heard from him too. He sounds as if he is in a little better spirits."

Vicky nodded. "There have been no major difficulties since the opening of the Landtag[4]. We weren't going to attend, as we are in mourning, but Prince Charles tried to forbid Aunt Marie and Marianne from going. My Papa-in-law then commanded 'all the Princesses' to attend, so I had to too. I was glad to see him overrule, or rather rule as he should. He is the King, after all.

---

4   Parliament in Prussia

Prince Charles pushes his opposition further and further." She paused, looking at her mother. Mama looked interested and absorbed, the sad look having left her face for the time. "Willy had a nosebleed on his birthday, which lasted for some time, but the children have been very well besides that. Just fancy, he is three years old already! And I wasn't sick on the passage, in spite of everything."

"How has Fritz been? His letters have not been at all cheerful until this last one."

Vicky sighed. "You know how difficult his position is, my poor darling. He is still required to be at the councils but to never speak. And Prince Hohenzollern's resignation is looking quite certain now. I don't know what is to become of us if Bismarck becomes Minister-President."

Mama looked serious. "I shall write to Uncle Leopold about it. I have been intending to, but he has not been well."

"Fritz's will was completed the day before I left. That is a weight off his mind, to know that if anything happens Abbat will be in charge of the children and of my affairs, and not Prince Charles." Vicky shuddered. "Fritz writes that Sanny – Grand Duchess Constantine – is in Berlin," she said, changing the subject. "She is always kind, like Michael and Cecile are, and not proud like Olga." Vicky had met several members of the Russian Imperial family, many of whom were very proud and haughty, but a few of them "came off their high horse" as Fritz said, when one got to know them.

"You haven't met the Emperor yet," Mama said, smiling slightly. The Emperor Alexander was an old friend of Mama's, Vicky knew. He had been in England before Mama and Papa were married, and if he hadn't been the Tsar's heir or if Mama hadn't been Queen, they would have married.

Vicky shook her head. "No. But it is likely I shall some time soon. They speak often of the prospect of his visiting Berlin."

Windsor Castle, March 6, 1862

Vicky squeezed her mother's hand before she got out of the carriage, stopping to look up at the castle. She sighed a long, shuddering sigh. She was here at dear Windsor, the home of her childhood, but – without Fritz, and without Papa. It had never been so before. She hurried in, heading toward the rooms she knew she would be given.

As she entered the suite, she paused, looking about. This had been her and Fritz's honeymoon suite. Vicky smiled as she sat down on the sofa where she and Fritz had sat, hand in hand, too shy to speak to each other. She went to the bedroom, remembering their conversation that first night together, when he was unsure of how to speak to her, not wishing to associate their love with the coarse, vulgar language he had often heard, or the endearments he had only ever heard in sarcasm or in inappropriate situations. She sat down on the bed. Fritz was always so kind, so tender, so patient. She thought of the second night. She would write to Fritz before she went to bed.

Berlin, March 11, 1862

Fritz sat at his desk, reading papers. He picked up one with an official seal from the King on it.

"Papa, Ditta wants –"

"Hush, Willikens, Papa must concentrate," Fritz said, bending down to stroke the children's heads before he went on. He began to tear open the envelope when a scream pierced the air.

Charlotte lay on the floor, flailing about and shrieking. Wilhelm shrank back against Fritz's leg, looking alarmed. Fritz sighed. He bent down, took Charlotte's wrist, and made her look at him. Tears poured down her cheeks, but she smiled as Fritz picked her up and cuddled her in his arms. "Papa," she said, reaching up and touching his cheek.

He kissed her, and rose to ring the bell to call the nurse. "Can Ditta be quiet and let Papa read?" he asked. She nodded. "Come here, Wilhelm," Fritz said. Wilhelm ran to his side. Soon, Mrs. Hobbs came in and took the children. Fritz went back to the desk, taking up the letter again. He had opened it and was just starting to unfold it when there was a tap at the door, and Georgiana Hobbs burst in.

"Your 'ighness, your little Princess 'as a tantrum hagain, hand you know she won't calm down for hanyone but you," she said. "Hemma begged me to fetch you."

Fritz paused. He had difficulty understanding the Hobbs sisters' cockney accent, and had to think through what she had said. He shook his head. "I must read this," he said slowly in English. "Charlotte said she would be quiet for Papa. Tell her so."

Georgiana looked uncertain, but turned to leave the room. "I must have no interruptions," Fritz said in German, then repeated in English, "No interruptions."

He turned back to the paper, glancing over it before settling down to read it thoroughly. This was indeed urgent. Prince Hohenzollern had resigned from the post of Minister-President, and Papa had introduced Prince Adolf Hohenlohe as Provisional Prime Minister before the Council meeting which Fritz had not attended.

Berlin, March 17, 1862

"Papa, you must settle the government according to your own feelings, your own judgement. Don't let them manipulate you! This must not be! You must not bring back those men you have been free from for the last four years! You are the King! Don't let your judgement be clouded by the councils of those who are untrustworthy!"

Fritz looked at his father. The King sat with his head in his hands.

"Fritz," he said slowly, "your words are true, and I will do so. Prince Adolf is of the same views as Prince Hohenzollern, and things will go smoothly. Thank you for your words of encouragement." He rose, briefly patted Fritz on the shoulder, and left the room. Fritz sat still, feeling rather stunned. Papa rarely thanked him for his advice. It was much more likely for him to be screamed at for daring to counsel his elders.

"Fritz, I hoped you would be here," his mother said, entering the room. She sat down where Papa had sat a moment before. "I heard what you said to Papa, and am very glad he took it as he did. I only hope he means it, but I am afraid he does not – or rather –" she looked sharply at Fritz, and then away again, "he will be manipulated into forgetting all about it and appointing the people *they* wish for." She rose, walking up and down the room, murmuring anxiously to herself.

Fritz rose, taking her arm. "Mama," he said, "we will do all we can, and can only pray and trust in God's Will. His Will be done. That is all I can say. We have come through so much, we can face the next storm."

"But if they bring those men back, then they will be sure to take Bismarck, and as soon as possible." Mama snatched her arm away, turning and covering her face. "And that will be a tragedy for the country, for the whole of Germany. And I can do nothing about it. He says my opinion has absolutely no value," she said, her face twisting.

Fritz stared at his mother, realizing she was trying not to cry. It seemed strange. He had only ever seen her cry two times that he could remember, once when his sister, Vivi, had fallen out of a window when she was very small, but had been caught by a passing guard and was uninjured, and once, during his first private conversation with her after Wilhelm's birth, when she spoke of her pride in her grandson and her gratitude to God for letting Vicky and the little boy live.

"Mama," he said, putting his arm around her, "You know he doesn't really think that. He does value your opinion, and know you see the situation in a truer light than he does. It is only –"

She turned, shaking off his arm and hurrying to the door. He could only catch a few words of what she had said, but knew it was something about Onkel Karl.

Berlin, March 18, 1862

Fritz shook his head again, staring at the card he held. His efforts had failed. Papa *had* brought back the men into government who had left four years ago. All but one were supporters of the Kreuzzeitungpartei, of Manteuffel, of Bismarck – of Onkel Karl.

He thought over the events of the day. He had received this news at seven in the evening. Mama had been extremely upset, but he had had to go to see Papa, and to meet the new ministers. All had met him gravely, coldly, returning his bows very stiffly.

Fritz sat on the edge of his bed, and then knelt down to pray. How were they to make it through this new web? He lay down, taking a letter out of his pocket.

"Mein Schatz,

"I sit writing to you from the room where we spent one of the happiest moments of my life – when you first pressed me to your heart as your wife. My heart beats wildly at the thought of that – but I cannot help feeling sad here, when I think of poor Mama and how lonely she is without Papa. She is so alone, and she longs for him as I do for you. She sleeps with his dressing gown spread over her. Everything seems so strange without him; we wander about like sheep without a shepherd, and though the sun shines and the flowers bloom, it seems, as Mama says, to still be the midst of winter in our hearts.

"Kiss the children from Mama and say how much I miss them. I long to be with you in our nest, and wake from dreams that I am in your arms, that I rest my head on your shoulder as we talk, and you are there to kiss and cuddle for as many hours as we wish. And I wake – lonely, but not so dreadfully lonely as poor Mama must always be.

"*Auf wiedersehen, mein Schatz, mein Engel*[5],

"*Deine Frauchen,* who will love you – 'till death do us part.'"

He had already read it many times, and he pressed it to his lips. It would still be some time before Vicky came back. If only she was here, she always knew how to comfort him during difficult times like these. But he was glad, for her sake, that she was not in Berlin during this time. It would not have made things any easier in reality.

Berlin, March 22, 1862

Today was the King's birthday. *May Gott bless Papa and protect him, and guide him to do his heart's true desire, to serve and guide his people to unity, to be a wise shepherd to the country. May Gott protect him, and guide him to make the right choices!*

---

5 Goodbye – literally "Till we see again", my darling, my angel,

Fritz lifted Charlotte and Wilhelm into the carriage and climbed in. A few minutes later, he was at the door of his parents' Berlin Schloss.

"*Alles Gute[6]*, Papa," he said, kneeling as he kissed his father's hand. He turned to Mrs. Hobbs, who curtseyed and set Charlotte down. Fritz took Charlotte's and Wilhelm's hands, leading them up to his father.

"Großpapa don't look old!" Wilhelm said, looking up at him. Fritz stifled a laugh, glancing at his parents' faces, but both had laughed at his remark, and Fritz joined them.

"I suppose he thinks I am a whole year older today than I was yesterday," Papa murmured to Fritz, ruffling Wilhelm's hair. "*Kommt her, Kinder,*" he said, lifting them to sit on his knee, and patting their heads. Charlotte soon slipped down.

"Goßmama give – Ditta – someing?" she said slowly, looking up and smiling. "*Goßmama gebt mich etwas?[7]*"

Fritz glanced at his mother, trying to show his alarm in his eyes. She caught his eye, and shook her head.

Fritz bent to pick Charlotte up again. "You haven't given her things before, have you?" he whispered in his mother's ear.

"No, Fritz, I am very careful with them."

"Why does she expect it, then?"

"You know she is very good at wheedling what she wants out of people," Papa laughed.

"You should not say such things before her," Fritz said.

"As if such a baby could understand such things," Papa muttered. "Fritz," he went on, "I do want to thank you again for what you said a few days ago, and I'm sorry things haven't turned out the way we hoped. I will try to be strong at the next council."

------

6 Every blessing
7 Grandmama give me something?

CHAPTER THREE

IS IT TRUE?

Karlsruhe, April 1, 1862.

"Fritz, I am so glad to see you."

Fritz kissed his sister's cheek and shook hands with his brother-in-law, Fritz of Baden.

"You are looking very well, Vivi," he said, as they gazed at each other.

"You are not; Fritz, you look pale and tired," Vivi answered, taking his arm. Everything was beautiful in the park here, where spring came much earlier than in the north.

Fritz sighed. "I have been very lonely. And we have other troubles, as you know." *And more you don't know of,* he thought, and sighed deeply again.

"I know," she said, squeezing his hand. "Vicky will meet you tomorrow, will she not?"

"*Ja.* After a month and a half's separation! That is a long time for us, you know."

Vivi nodded. "I know your political troubles are worse than ever now. I wish Papa would come here. He is always in a good humor when he is here."

Fritz nodded, not speaking. Papa had never confided in Vivi as he did in him, although in many ways he was closer to Vivi than to Fritz. His usual manner with her was much less formal. But Fritz knew there were reasons for the King's good humor when in Baden, and he didn't wish to encourage him to go there.

Aachen, April 2, 1862.

"It is so good to be back," Vicky said, throwing herself into Fritz's arms as soon as they were alone in the train. It was the longest they had ever been parted since their marriage. "Of course, I was very sad to leave Mama and everyone, but I have been longing for you for too long now," she whispered.

"How is she?" Fritz asked.

"Very sad, of course. But she is able to do business with Alice's help. I still don't know how she will manage when Alice leaves." Vicky looked up at Fritz, wiping tears from her eyes. "I wrote you about how she sleeps with Papa's dressing gown over her. It is all so sad, and the thought of it made me miss you even more."

"Vicky," Fritz said quietly, "have you received any letters from Stockmar? Or any strange letters?"

"Yes," Vicky said, blushing. "I received some very impertinent letters from the Grand Duchess of Mecklenburg-Schwerin. I burned them at once. I didn't think they were worth keeping."

Fritz nodded. "That is what I suspected. Stockmar has sent me several letters – from many people who are interested in us in a kindly way, as well as the malicious ones – asking if it is true that I have fallen in love with this or that lady and you have gone to England for a divorce." Fritz sighed, rolling his eyes.

Vicky shook her head. "It is just like when I fell down the stairs and Papa came to visit. Everyone said *you* were responsible for my fall, and Papa came to patch up matters between us. It is such absurd nonsense."

Fritz took a letter out of his pocket. Vicky glanced over it. "It is the same tone as the Grand Duchess's letters were in. What business do they think they have, asking such questions?"

Berlin, April 15, 1862

"Is it true that you have come into opposition against your father the King?"

Fritz sat still, not speaking, looking up at the ceiling. What should he say? It would not be wise to tell the Minister-President that he was in opposition to the King, and yet, what could he say when the question was asked so bluntly?

"I will not – commit myself in opposition unless something really unconstitutional is done," Fritz said slowly. "And I am *not* in opposition to the King. I may not agree with the Government, but I am the King's first and most loyal subject." He looked at Prince Hohenlohe seriously. "But when I am asked what my opinion is, I will not fail to give it. You know how seriously I take these questions."

"Everyone knows about it; Uncle Ernst, Vivi and Fritz of Baden, and many others speak openly of it," Vicky wrote to her mother. "It is no secret. But I can hardly believe it, from my first impression of Princess Christian. She seems so nice and lady-like. I don't like to believe things like that of her."

Vicky had been reading letters from Wally, her former lady-in-waiting who had married Augustus Paget, a junior member of the

British diplomatic corps who was now Minister to Copenhagen. It was through her that Vicky had contact with the Danish family, over the question of Bertie's marrying Princess Alexandra, or Alix as they called her. Wally often wrote to her sister, Valerie, who was now Vicky's lady. It was a welcome connection to Vicky, as Prussia and Denmark were on hostile terms politically.

The latest letters spoke of rumors of Princess Christian's having illegitimate children. The stories, according to many sources, seemed to be quite true, but there were also stories that Princess Christian's niece had told the story, Princess Christian's sister having some old grudge against her, and poisoning her children's minds against their aunt. Vicky had, at first, believed this story. Vicky wished to know the truth of the matter, before Bertie married into this family.

"Princess Christian does also know about Bertie's unfortunate story," Vicky wrote. "Uncle George has told her. Wally found her reading his letter and much upset at the idea of you and Bertie being on bad terms, as she was concerned about Alix's becoming Bertie's wife if you and Bertie are estranged. Wally told her of your letters to me where you have praised him so highly, so she feels more at peace on the subject."

Fritz sat on the bed, reading softly but loud enough for Vicky to hear his voice well. He read from Thomas Erskine May's history in English. "The growth of the influence of the crown, at a period in the history of this country when government by prerogative had recently been subverted…"

Vicky sat on the floor with Charlotte on her lap, facing away from the bed. She picked up an apple from a bowl of fruit. "What is this, Ditta?"

"*Obst*," Charlotte said, reaching out to take it.

"Good, it is a fruit, but what kind?"

"*Obst,*" Charlotte said again.

"Papa reads his English very well now," Vicky said. "Can you tell me what this is in English, Ditta?" She still held the apple out of Charlotte's reach.

"Papa!" Charlotte struggled to get out of Vicky's lap. Vicky let her go. Charlotte walked a few steps before she fell. She crept forward on her hands and knees, gripping Fritz's leg to pull herself up again. She threw her head back, laughing up at him, her face beaming with smiles.

Fritz stroked her head, letting her take his hand in both of hers. "Ditta," he said gently, "go to Mama and tell her what that is." He spoke slowly in English, pointing at the apple and turning her around to face Vicky again.

"Apple," Charlotte said perfectly clearly, turning and smiling up at Fritz again.

"Tell Mama," he said again.

Charlotte sat down, and crept back to Vicky. "*Obst*," she said, reaching for the apple.

"What is it?" Fritz asked again.

"Apple."

"Very good!" Vicky picked her up, giving her the apple. Fritz went on reading.

Vicky turned to look at Fritz. "She creeps and crawls so well." She smiled at Fritz. "Willy never did of course, with his arm." She looked down, an odd expression crossing her face. There was a knock at the door.

"Schleinitz says he must speak with your Highness," Valerie said, looking at Fritz.

Fritz nodded, putting the book down. He rose. "I will send Mrs. Hobbs," he said to Vicky. She nodded.

Vicky sat on the floor, still holding Charlotte. She picked up a figurine of a small bird. "Can you tell me what this is?"

"*Vogel*," Charlotte said.

"Very good. Now, tell me what these are." She spread out a variety of figurines, photographs, and fruit. Charlotte picked up a large photograph of Fritz.

"Papa," she said, looking about and beginning to cry.

"Hush," Vicky said, kissing the top of Charlotte's head, but keeping her facing away from her as she hugged her. She was relieved when there was a tap at the door.

"'ere he is, yer 'Ighness," Mrs. Hobbs said. She entered the room, carrying Willy.

"Please, take her, Mrs. Hobbs," Vicky said, rising and putting Charlotte in the nurse's arms.

"Hobby!" Charlotte said, a smile immediately returning to her face.

"Why's she called so?" Willy sked, putting his arms around Vicky. "Papa your husband."

Vicky laughed. The children called Mrs. Hobbs "Hobby" or "Hobbsy"; Willy had confused the word "husband" with these nicknames.

"*Mein Gemah*[8], Willy," Vicky laughed. "Papa is my husband. *Gemahl*. Hobby is Mrs. Hobbs' nickname, as Willy is yours." Vicky turned to Mrs. Hobbs. She kissed Willy, and set him down. "Go with Mrs. Hobbs, Willy," she said. She turned, sitting down on the bed as the door closed.

She sighed, leaning her head on her hand. She hoped Fritz

---

8   My husband

would come back before it was too late. She thought of changing to be ready to go to bed, but she shivered. She didn't feel like undressing right now.

"Fritz!" Vicky started awake as he slipped into bed beside her. She lay on the bed, fully dressed.

"Are you feeling well?" Fritz asked, kissing her forehead. "I did not mean to leave you alone with her," he said, looking at her seriously.

"*Ja*, I feel quite well. I was able to have her with me a few minutes, after you left, and I didn't feel uncomfortable. Only – when I said she creeps and crawls so well. Fritz, I have never told you," she said, turning uneasily to face him. She rose, going to her dressing room. "Let me change, and then I will tell."

She returned a few minutes later, wearing her dressing-gown as well as her night-gown.

"I thought you said you were feeling well," Fritz said, looking at her seriously.

"I am, but – I want to feel comfortable, so I can speak of things."

He nodded, putting his arms around her as she lay down.

"Fritz, I was able to be with her, without hearing your voice, and without having Willy with me too. And I don't feel – you know. Perhaps I shall be able to overcome this struggle. But, Fritz," she whispered, laying her head on his shoulder, "when she does things – just ordinary, everyday things any little child might do, like creeping – but which Willy never did because of his arm – I feel such a burst of pride, as I haven't had a child do so yet. But –" Her voice broke, and she hid her face against Fritz's chest. "It feels so – wrong – to be more proud of her than of him!"

"It is not wrong to be proud of your children – all of them," Fritz said, soothing her and kissing her forehead. "I am proud of her. Every day, she does something new, and I feel so proud of her."

"I want to be proud of *our* children, Fritz. I – I don't want to be more proud of – of her – than of your son."

"She is our child, Vicky. You know I have always called her so."

"*Ja,* you are so good with her, about showing her the affection I can't give. It must be hard sometimes –"

"Vicky," Fritz said, making her meet his eye. "Is it really true that you think I do that out of duty?"

"Of course!" Vicky seemed surprised at his question. "You must love our child more than her. Why wouldn't you?"

"Vicky, don't you believe me when I speak of her? She is my daughter. I love her just as I do Wilhelm. There is no difference for me."

Vicky looked at him, her eyes filling with tears as she hid her face again.

"Please, do not speak of this more, if it upsets you," Fritz whispered, kissing her forehead.

"No, no, Fritz, don't – you said you would listen if I needed to speak about it!" she sobbed. "But I don't wish to burden you with–"

"I only meant, I thought you were glad you were feeling well, and wished to remain so. I did not mean I did not wish to listen to you, if you feel you need to speak." He rubbed her back and kissed her forehead. "Tell me everything," he whispered.

"Please, don't whisper. Speak aloud, so I can hear your voice." She hid her face against his chest again. "I do, usually – Fritz – I do know you love her. I only –" She sighed. "I have to let these thoughts out, when they are there. Otherwise they float about and torment me endlessly. I usually do write them to Mama, as I do not wish to always tell you, as I know how deeply you feel it. But – I must, sometimes." She snuggled closer to him, pulling his arm around her. "It is – so hard to find the words, to express what I really mean. And these thoughts are so entirely separate from my usual being. But yes, I am thankful I was able to be with her without you having to be there."

Fritz kissed her forehead. "I am always glad to be with you, of course. But I do see that she is more attached to Mrs. Hobbs than to you. I wish it was possible for you to spend more time with her, when I am not present."

April 29, 1862

"Affie." Fritz smiled as he embraced Vicky's brother who had come to meet him at Dover.

Fritz was on his way to the opening of the second Great Exhibition. He sighed as he thought of the plans he and Vicky had made less than a year ago. They had spoken of the hope of being together at the opening of the Exhibition, with Wilhelm. The first Exhibition had been where they met when Vicky was only ten; it would have been so special to be at the second with their son. But now, so soon after Prince Albert's death, neither the Queen nor any of her children would be at the opening. Vicky would not accompany Fritz. It would be a rather melancholy event, rather than the joyous one they had anticipated.

But in the last two weeks, his father had been extremely inconsistent in saying whether Fritz would go to the opening at all. He had said he could, and then he said he must not. Fritz had made plans to go a little later, when he was in England for Alice's wedding. Finally, the King again said he should go, as his representative, but Fritz would have to pay for the journey himself, in spite of representing the King.

Windsor Castle, April 29, 1862

"*Auf wiedersehen*[9]," Fritz said, bending down to kiss his mother-in-law's cheek. He embraced Alice, kissing her cheek.

"*Auf wiedersehen, Fritz,*" everyone said, as they came up to embrace him. The Queen had been much better than he expected, and able to say goodbye without crying. She and her children were going to Balmoral. Fritz would leave for Buckingham Palace at the same time.

That evening, he lay alone in the same bed he had before his and Vicky's marriage. He thought of that time. How nervous he had been! He was unable to sleep for the two days he was in England before the wedding. Over four years had passed since then. Now, again, he lay there, sleepless, but for very different reasons.

He thought of Vicky. It was too bad that she could not come to the second Exhibition, one of the last projects of her dear father. How was she feeling? His thoughts wandered back again, even further back. Today was the eleventh anniversary of when they met, two days before the opening of the first Exhibition, when she was ten years old. He smiled, thinking of her as she was then. She had been such a charming, fascinating child.

He had begun to doze at last. In his dream, he had seen Vicky as she was then, ten years old, but also, with her, instead of her siblings, Wilhelm and Charlotte were there. That didn't make sense, and startled him awake.

---

9 Goodbye – literally "Till we see again"

*** ***

London, May 1, 1862.

"*...open!*" The Mayor of London finished his speech and the trumpets sounded.

Fritz stood on the dais with the Queen's aunt and cousins, the Cambridges, Prince Oscar of Sweden, and the city officials. It was so strange to not see the Queen and Prince Albert and the children. His thoughts went back again to the scene of eleven years ago, and tears sprang to his eyes as *God Save the Queen* was sung. It seemed as if he must see Prince Albert, the creator of all of this. The sight of the Queen weeping during his previous visit to England appeared in his mind. He struggled not to give way to his emotion.

*** ***

Berlin, May 7, 1862

It was half past eight. Fritz jumped out of his carriage and hurried into the Palace, without stopping to freshen himself after the dusty carriage ride. He must see the King.

Thankfully, all was going comparatively well, and his father was in a pleasant mood.

"Papa seemed very pleased to meet me, and asked all about the opening," Fritz told Vicky. She smiled up at him, lying with her head in his lap. "He even took interest in my description of what I saw."

"I am so glad Mama was better, and not quite so sad," Vicky said. "I don't look forward to Alice's departure for her."

Fritz nodded. "I missed your Papa so much," he said, leaning down to kiss Vicky's forehead. "It simply did not feel right to be there without all of you – and particularly without him."

Tears came to her eyes, and he stroked her cheek. "My speech was taken well. No one seemed annoyed by my bad English."

"No, they have written to me that your speech was particularly good, and your – different use of idioms simply made it more interesting."

"Oh." Fritz frowned. "I suppose that is their way of saying it was annoying."

Vicky sat up and shook her head, kissing him. "No, Fritz. They appreciate your learning English more. They meant what they said. Everyone praises your English, when I am at home. You know that." She lay back down again. "And they – the government and many others – say they have always liked you for my sake, but this time they like you for their own." She smiled up at him, reaching up to touch his cheek. "They love you. They love you as you deserve. But what did you see? You haven't told me."

"Everything is still arriving, as at the first Exhibition, you remember. But I saw the English display in general, the Austrian machinery, and our steel products and weaponry. They were much admired by the British soldiers. I saw the Parisian upholsterers, and French bronze work, and our porcelain, very like that for our wedding." He smiled at her. "The Brass church adornments from the middle-ages fascinated me. Then the Chinese, Japanese, and also the American displays were not completed yet, and I also saw the agricultural machinery, but I do not know enough about them to describe them."

Vicky nodded. "Bertie was fascinated with the machinery at the first exhibition."

Neues Palais, Potsdam, May 1862.

"Is it true that Bismarck is still to be in Paris? He causes so much trouble there," Vicky said as Fritz came in.

"Yes. But it is also true that he was at Glienicke the other day, when I went to the dinner there. Onkel Karl and he are hand-in-glove. I saw them whispering together, just as I did fourteen years ago, when I first saw Bismarck."

Fritz frowned as he took out his diary and unlocked it, opening it to read over what he had written in the last few days. He smiled as he came to the day – a couple of weeks ago - when they had moved again to Potsdam. Vicky had found a four leaf clover just outside the entrance to the Neues Palais. Fritz had pressed it in his diary.

They have proposed Fritz Karl! – to become Minister-President! Fritz wrote. He shuddered. Fritz Karl in any position of power was something he dreaded. He knew that he stood in the way of Fritz Karl becoming King – unless the threats which had been made were carried out and Fritz was disqualified to be the heir – but still, Wilhelm came in succession before Onkel Karl and Fritz Karl.

But becoming Minister-President was not a matter of succession. Fritz prayed Fritz Karl would not receive the appointment. It was said that Prince Hohenlohe was thinking of resigning. *But which is better,* he thought, *Fritz Karl, or Bismarck?*

CHAPTER FOUR

THE HONEYCOUPLE

Osborne House, July 1, 1862

Fritz stood near Bertie, watching as Alice came in on Uncle Ernst's arm, followed by her bridesmaids: Louis' sister Annchen, Lenchen, Louise, and little Beatrice. The Queen sat in an armchair, surrounded by her sons. The temporary altar had been set up under the family portrait by Winterhalter from when Lenchen was the baby. On another wall was a portrait of Fritz himself with Vicky, Wilhelm and Charlotte. He felt a tear trickle down his face as the Archbishop began to speak. If only Vicky could have come. Everyone missed her terribly.

He wiped another tear away as he glanced around. Everyone wept except for Alice. The Archbishop himself had lost his wife recently, and the tears poured down his face as he read. The Queen burst out sobbing at the words "till death do us part", and Affie sobbed dreadfully through the whole ceremony. Alice stood calmly, pale but serene, her face seeming to glow when she glanced up at Louis as the rings were put on. Louis' eyes were filled with tears as he kissed her.

Louis' parents, Karl and Elisabeth, came up to embrace their new daughter-in-law, and Fritz watched as they embraced the Queen. He stepped forward and kissed Alice's cheek, embracing her. "Vicky –" He meant to say that Vicky sent her the embrace, but his voice choked as he met her eye, and he only embraced her again. Alice looked up at him gratefully, nodding, but she, too, was too moved to speak much.

Fritz took the Queen's arm as everyone went into the Horn Room, where all the furniture was made with deer antlers from Balmoral, to sign the register.

Fritz watched as the carriage began to drive away. How would the Queen manage without Alice? Several people suddenly ran forward to pelt the carriage with rice and slippers. Fritz took one, smiling slightly. He ran forward and tossed the shoe, hitting Alice in the head. She caught his eye, smiled and waved, and took Louis' hand and kissed it.

"May they be as happy as we are," he murmured, and turned, finding Bertie standing behind him, struggling to keep back tears. Bertie was the only one besides Alice who had not given into emotion during the ceremony. Fritz put his hand on his shoulder, and Bertie glanced up at him.

"Fritz, I – you know what Mama said, just after Papa's death," Fritz waited for Bertie to steady his voice. "I didn't mean to do anything which upset Papa so much. You don't think I am –"

"No, Bertie, you are not responsible for your dear father's death, and your Mama does not think so, either, really. It was only the feeling of annoyance exaggerated in the first moment of grief. She has praised you to Vicky and to me, and said she wished you to know it."

Bertie looked up at him, tears brimming in his eyes again, as he shook Fritz's hand. "You know I am to go on a tour to the East." Fritz nodded. "But I hope to be with you if you and Vicky do go on your Italian idyll, which Vicky said you had planned."

Fritz nodded. "We would be very glad to have you, of course,

Bertie." He paused. "Have you thought about Princess Alix?"

"Yes, and – I am very grateful for the trouble you and Vicky take about my affairs. I understand the trouble it could make for you both, for Vicky to suggest such a marriage. But yes, I have thought of it a good deal of late, with what Papa wrote and said to me. You have seen everything, haven't you?" Bertie's face flushed.

"Yes." Fritz looked at Bertie seriously. "I hope you take those things to heart, and mean what you say in your apology. But I will not scold you. I know how you feel, just now, with Alice leaving."

"Yes," Bertie said, turning away and running a hand across his face. "Alice was always my – my confidant, and Lenchen is still so – young," he said, not looking up. Fritz remembered Bertie's words back at the first Exhibition, when Bertie was only nine and Lenchen five. "She's such a baby," he had said about Lenchen. Fritz knew his thoughts about her had not changed.

"Vicky has been very well, but uncomfortable, as you can imagine," Fritz said, kissing the Queen's cheek before they sat down.

"Yes, you must wish to hurry back, Fritz. She first told me on – on that dreadful day." The Queen took her napkin and covered her face, shaking with sobs.

"Mama," Fritz said gently, moving his chair so that he sat next to her. She leaned her head on his shoulder.

"She first wrote me on December 14th, that she was expecting another little one, and she was the end of the second month. So the new little one may be any time."

Fritz nodded. "I hope things will go well for us this year; the political horizon is looking stormy, as you know. Bismarck may be on the other side, and if he is, my duties will only grow heavier if he becomes Minister-President."

The Queen nodded. "I cannot advise you as – he – always did. I – I feel so helpless in many matters. You know how much he dealt with foreign affairs and how well he understood everything." Her voice broke again. "Fritz," she whispered, taking his hand. "There is something I feel I must say. I didn't wish to, for fear it might hurt you, but I must say it to someone, and there is no one else." She looked up at him. "As disappointed as I was for Vicky not to be at her dear sister's wedding, I felt almost – glad – to have only seen you separately. You were at the – the funeral; she came afterwards. Now you are here, again without her. I miss her indescribably, but – I – I don't want to be jealous of you – of seeing your happiness. This has been hard enough, as you can imagine, with Alice."

Fritz nodded. "*Ja,* Mama, I understand," he said, putting his arm around her. "And I am very grateful for your delicacy of not saying it to Alice. Her wedding and the beginning of her new life has been buried beneath enough clouds, as it is, without her feeling as if her happiness were a burden to you." He put his arms around her, and kissed her cheek. "*Gute Nacht[10]*, Mama."

"*Gute Nacht,* Fritz. Thank you so much for being the support you are to us all. You – you are the only man in the family I can speak to of many things now. Uncle Leopold is –" she trailed off and covered her eyes again. Uncle Leopold had not been well enough to come to the wedding, and they were all worried about him.

"Mama, please don't upset yourself," Fritz said.

There was a knock at the door, which opened, little Beatrice running in. The Queen's face brightened a little as she lifted her onto her lap.

"Mama still wearing her sad cap," Beatrice said, looking up and pulling one of the strings which ran from her mother's

---

10 Good Night

widow's cap. It fell forward, over her face.

The Queen laughed, straightened her cap, and looked up at Fritz. "Baby is my comfort." She sighed. "But she cannot be my strength and assistance, yet. That is what Alice has been, these last months."

"Fritz, I want to ask your advice about something." Affie stood with the croquet mallet in his hand, looking up at Fritz. "Do you think it is possible for me to have Coburg managed by a Regent?"

"You are so young, Affie, you do not need a Regent yet," Fritz said, taking his arm.

"But there is the question of the Kingdom of Greece, and you know they wished for Uncle Ernst as the King of Greece, so that I would become the Duke already. But I don't wish to leave the Navy. I love it, Fritz! I don't wish to go to Coburg. I would – you know, Fritz, my ambition is to become an Admiral. I am only a Lieutenant still, now. I've only been in the Navy for four years. I don't want to give it up!"

Fritz nodded. "I am not sure what the country – the countries would think of it," he said. "For you to be an English Admiral and a German Duke at the same time? But you know the question of Greece is changed. Uncle Ernst did not wish to be King. So it may be many years before you have to become the Duke." He paused. "Did Mama tell you what she asked me to do?"

Affie shrugged. "What?"

"She has arranged for me to be the guardian for the Coburg property if Uncle Leopold dies – until you become the Duke. You know Uncle Leopold holds the property – your part of the fortune and certain possessions – in trust for you, as Uncle Ernst does not manage his finances well."

"That is splendid!" Affie shook Fritz's hand vigorously. "I wish *you* could be my Regent, but of course you have your own duties."

"I would love to do any service I can for your Papa's country," Fritz said, "and I watch your progress, too. Vicky is very proud of her sailor brother," Fritz smiled.

"Bertie is to be sworn in to the House of Lords this year, after his birthday. I won't be for three more years, at least. I don't mind it. I prefer the deck of a ship to the parliament buildings any day," Affie said, swinging his hat on the handle of the croquet mallet as he walked away.

London, July 2, 1862

"The Exhibition looks wonderful," Fritz said to the Queen. "All the displays are complete now, and look beautiful."

She smiled. "Albert would be so proud of it. I am so grateful to you, Fritz, for being at the opening, as none of us were. He would have been very pleased. How did the cattle show go?"

"Wonderfully. I bought some new riding horses, which are on their way to their new home. I wish I knew more about the farms."

Fritz stood on board the yacht, waving goodbye. Lenchen smiled, waving again before turning away. She was so like Vicky in her manner. He would soon be with Vicky again, to tell her all about the wedding. Fritz almost wished he had stayed until Alice and Louis left for Germany, but then again it was better he did not.

Then the Queen would have to say goodbye to him after she did to Alice, and it was easier this way.

"The Queen was quite well, and Alice looked beautiful in her wedding dress," Fritz said as he sat down. He glanced at his parents and across the table at Vicky. He had arrived at the station at nearly eight in the morning. Vicky and the children were well. There had been a reception today of the Persian ambassadors. It was the first time that there was an official Persian representative in Berlin. Most of the men spoke no German; one spoke English, so most of the conversation was carried on through an interpreter.

Fritz sighed as his father showed him a paper. There were more rumors about the state of his and Vicky's marriage, also calling Fritz dissipated, weak, without enough nerve to declare what side he took in politics.

"I shall never betray your trust, Papa," Fritz said, trying to speak calmly. He sat in the council room at Babelsberg, near his father, and across the table from Albrecht von Roon - the Minister of War, who had formerly been Fritz Karl's governor – and the other ministers. "You know what my views are, but I believe in you, and that you will do the right thing by the country. I will never oppose *you*, and I will not speak this year, publicly, on politics."

"*Danke, Eure Hoheit*[11]. You will keep your word on this, I know," Roon said stiffly. The King didn't answer. Fritz sighed,

---

11 Thank you, Your Highness

cringing inwardly. Had he really just given a promise that he would not speak publicly on politics this year? Why had he said this? Roon stared at him, but Fritz didn't meet his eye. He recognized the intense gaze.

"But the military question is still unsettled," the King said. "I will not give in to the two year service. It must be three. It always has been, since before I was born, and I will not change the tradition."

"But the Landtag refuses the funding," Fritz said. "The parliament knows what they are doing. The army does not need a reform. You just said that the tradition does not need to be changed. We do not need a bigger army. Our peacetime army is already so large."

The King shook his head. "The reform must take place. There is always the danger of another revolution. We must have a Minister-President strong enough to bring it through."

"This is more likely to cause a revolution! You mean a man brutal enough to force –"

"You promised you would not oppose me," his father cut him off, glaring at him. "I am the King, and I know how to rule my country."

Fritz began to shake his head, and then froze. He could not shake his head to a statement like that. He rose, nodding stiffly to the ministers.

"I shall leave you to your business, *meine Herren*," he said, and left the room.

He slept in a little cot that night, at Babelsberg, not having time to return to the Neues Palais. In his dreams, he was a little boy again, sleeping in a cot with a thin blanket, never warm enough, never feeling well. He woke, his face wet with tears. He wiped his eyes. He wished his father would listen to him. But he had made a promise to be silent on politics. He had already been hardly allowed to speak at the councils for two years, now, when he was; he made this promise. He shook his head, feeling like shaking himself. He did all he could to please his father personally. Last month he had gone with the hunting party, and actually shot six hares, showing off his shooting skills to please his father. He shuddered. He hated killing the little creatures.

Now, he wondered how he could remain on pleasant terms with his father. He felt as if there was a gag being drawn tighter in his mouth. He could hardly speak to him anymore. The King called everything Fritz spoke of a "revolutionary" plot. Fritz's close friends and advisors were criticized in the same way. Onkel Karl was trying to remove Uncle Ernst from his Prussian regiment because of a speech he had made in Frankfurt, supporting the Landtag's stand against the military reform. If such things were done against other sovereigns…

Fritz felt very much alone.

CHAPTER FIVE

A NEW LIFE TO LOVE

Berlin, August 14, 1862

"A second son!"

Fritz felt himself beam with joy as he jumped from his carriage and ran to greet his father, who was reviewing a cavalry brigade.

"What is the fuss about?" the King asked.

"A second son!" Fritz said again, throwing his arms round his father. "A fine boy, and Vicky is stronger even than last time." The men cheered at his words. The gun salute began.

"I must leave you, and see my grandson," the King called to the men. Fritz smiled. He was glad to see his father was in a friendly, informal mood.

✳ ✳ ✳

"Here he is," Fritz said, holding the little boy up proudly for everyone to see. All through the day, everyone in his household, their families, and his parents' households had come to see the new Prince.

"He is a fine child," Fritz heard repeatedly. He smiled and nodded to everyone. No one said this little one was small, as they had about Wilhelm, and of course Charlotte. Vicky had been so sensitive about it.

"Our boy is so strong, he wins everyone's praise," Fritz said as he gently placed the baby back in Vicky's arms. "No one can find fault with him."

Vicky looked up at him, and then down at the baby. Her face glowed. "I feel so well, Fritz; it is so wonderful to feel so strong this time. And he is such a precious little man." She kissed the baby's forehead, pressing him to her heart.

Berlin, August 16, 1862

Fritz blinked, and turned towards Vicky. Her eyes were open.

"How did you sleep?"

"Very well. And Baby did too, Mrs. Hobbs said. She was here an hour ago, to say how well Baby is doing – he is certainly thriving. I feel so proud, Fritz, to have another little son, and such a splendid one." She paused, looking into his eyes and smiling.

Fritz took her hand. "*Ja*, but remember, Vicky, Wilhelm is still the heir."

Vicky smiled. "I know. But I can't help feeling so proud to have given you and the country a perfect little boy, at last." Her smile faded. "I wish our hopes for Willy's arm had proven true."

"He is our son, our dear firstborn. You have always thought him perfect, have you not?"

"Yes, Fritz, but – don't you feel it?"

"*Ja*, but I do not wish to play favorites with our children."

Vicky shook her head. "Willy is our firstborn, as you say – that cannot change." She sighed, and tears suddenly sprang to her eyes.

"What is it, *meine Frauchen*?" Fritz gathered her in his arms, drawing her close to him.

"Today – today is – it is a year – since – I saw Papa," she whispered, with a catch in her voice.

Fritz did not speak. He nodded silently, kissing Vicky's forehead, as his thoughts went back a year. Today had been the day they had left England, the last goodbye to his father-in-law, though they certainly had not suspected that at the time.

"Baby will never know him," Vicky whispered, trying to keep the tears out of her voice. "Willy and Ditta at least saw him, and he carried them about, and Willy remembers him, but –" She burst out crying.

Fritz soothed her, but he realized he had tears in his own eyes. It was a great, unspeakable loss, that their children would never know Prince Albert.

"I was going to say, what should we call Baby, when the thought came," Vicky whispered. "I'd love to call him Albert, but there are already two Albrechts here."

"I have been reading about Prince Heinrich, the brother of Frederick the Great," Fritz said. "Papa speaks of him, and his memory of him, which is quite remarkable, as Prince Heinrich died in 1803. I would like Heinrich to be one of our boy's names."

"Henry," Vicky nodded. "And he must have Wilhelm, for your Papa. I like that. Albert Wilhelm Henry. If only – Papa could have seen him." She murmured the last words as tears filled her eyes again.

Friedenskirche, Potsdam, August 17, 1862
Fritz nodded to the clergyman as he entered the church. The man

nodded back, not bowing as he often did to the Princes. Fritz always made it a rule that he did not receive any personal homage in a church. He felt it wasn't right to be given earthly homage within the church, besides if it was one's coronation or something like that, where one received the blessing and was anointed. Here, in the church, they were all human, all equal.

He glanced at the Royal pews, pausing in surprise as he saw Onkel Karl and Fritz Karl as well as the King and other Princes.

There was to be a special prayer of Thanksgiving for the birth of the new Prince, and for Vicky's blessing. This happened after every Royal birth. But Fritz had not been present at the one after Wilhelm's birth; it had been during his two days of sleep after being up all night with Vicky. He knew Onkel Karl and Fritz Karl had absented themselves then. They had been present at the prayer of thanks for Charlotte's birth, but Fritz had ignored them then. That hadn't been a compliment to him.

But now, as the clergyman began to speak, everyone rose, bowing their heads, remaining silent. After Charlotte's birth, the Royal pew had been full of talk and chatter during the prayer; no one had retained a respectful silence.

Fritz stood, his head bowed, his hand on his heart. *Thank Gott for blessing us with a healthy second son, and for blessing Vicky to be so well.*

The prayer was over, and the choir began to sing. Fritz remained standing, tears flowing down his face at the sound of the beautiful voices.

As everyone went out, Fritz Karl stood at the entrance. As Fritz passed by, he glanced at him, gave a very brief smile, nodded and patted Fritz on the back as he went out.

"I thought you would have called him Albert; I certainly expected it, and I think your Mama-in-law did too." Fritz read his mother's letter aloud to Vicky a few days later. "I am so thankful, as you too must be, that our beloved Vicky is so well and strong this time."

"I told Mama she may call him Albert if she wishes to, but he shall be known as Henry here." Vicky stroked the baby's head. "Look at him, Fritz. He is so strong and alert. He looks about as neither of the others did at this age."

Neues Palais, Potsdam, August 28, 1862

"The budget must be given, or I shall have to give everything up." Fritz shook his head as he read his father's letter. His father was still insisting he must have the army reform, but the Landtag still refused the funding.

"Fritz, what does your father say this time?" He jumped at the sound of Vicky's voice. She had been in their suite for the most part still since Henry's birth. This was the first time she had come downstairs.

"He –" Fritz winced. He had a severe sore throat, although he didn't feel unwell in any other way. He showed her the letter, shaking his head and putting his hand to his throat. Fritz picked up a piece of paper. "We should go to see the new reception rooms," he wrote.

"Have you really given those orders to have the paintings changed?" Vicky smiled as he nodded. They were having more rooms at the Neues Palais redecorated, and the paintings removed and replaced with others. The ones which had hung there Fritz considered indecent and improper subjects to have displayed before their guests. "They do not offend me, Mama and Papa had such things. I don't mind it," Vicky went on.

Fritz shuddered. "They are disgusting," he wrote.

Vicky shrugged. "Mama is ready for the trip to Brussels and Gotha, to meet Alix and to meet us before we start on our travels. I can't wait to hear what she thinks of Alix. I hope she will love her, and that Bertie's marrying Alix will give her a new daughter to love, now that Alice is away as well as I."

Fritz smiled, taking Vicky's hand. He rose and embraced her. He touched his throat again, and shook his head. Vicky leaned her head against him. "I'm sorry your throat is so bad, Fritz. I hope you will not be ill, so we may go on our tour."

Berlin, September 7, 1862.

"*Auf wiedersehen*," Vicky called. Fritz looked up at her, blowing another kiss before he closed the door.

Vicky sighed, turning to go back to her boudoir. The King had left, Baby's Christening was delayed, so they had not been able to go to meet Mama as soon as they had hoped. Officially, Vicky was still "in childbed" until the Christening, even though she had been out and about for nearly three weeks now. But she wouldn't go out driving now that Fritz was gone. Fritz was going to see Vivi and her baby, who had been born a few days before Henry. Hopefully, all would go well when he and the King returned.

She picked up a letter lying on her desk, opening it slowly. It was from Fritz's mother. Vicky hoped it would be a pleasant one.

She glanced over it. It was pleasant in itself, the Queen being in good humor, but she was asking them to go to Baden for her birthday. Vicky sighed in frustration. They must go to meet Mama and the others in Gotha. Mama would take Willy and Charlotte back with her to England, and they would go on their trip to the Mediterranean. After Bertie's engagement took place, Alix would probably go to England for a few weeks, to get to know the family better, while Bertie would join Vicky and Fritz on their trip.

✳ ✳ ✳

Reinhardsbrunn, September 15, 1862

"Mama! It is so good to see you!" Vicky cried, embracing her mother. "And so good to hear how much you like Alix already, and that Bertie's proposal went perfectly smoothly. Is it settled that Alix should be with you while he is with us?"

"Yes, Vicky," Mama said. "Alix shall come to us for three weeks."

"I am so pleased you will have a new daughter now that Alice and I are both so much away."

Mama's face changed. "If only Papa had met her, too, I would feel so much more pleasure in this," she murmured.

Vicky took her hand. "Papa would be very pleased with Bertie's marriage, Mama."

"But everything – I think of your wedding, and how much he is missed, and it makes these weddings an agony to me."

Vicky remained silent. She didn't know what to say. She missed Papa so much, she knew Mama did even more. "Here are the children," she said, as Fritz came up with Mrs. Hobbs and the little ones.

"Grandmama!" Willy looked up and smiled at the Queen, while Charlotte hid her face behind Fritz's leg.

"Charlotte is very shy still," Vicky said, taking her hand and leading her toward the Queen. "Come, Ditta."

Charlotte looked up at the Queen, but didn't speak.

"They will get to know Grandmama soon enough; never mind their being shy," Mama said to Vicky, stroking Charlotte's head and taking Baby Henry in her arms.

"Mama," Fritz said, kissing the Queen's cheek.

"Fritz, you look tired," Mama said.

"Yes, he has had to go about and back and forth so much, and travel at night, he has had so little rest," Vicky said. "Fritz, do get some sleep as soon as you can."

"We are to go to Switzerland, and to Palermo, perhaps down to Tunis, to Malta, Naples, Rome, Florence and Venice. We did not know if we would be allowed to go to Northern Italy, as the King has not acknowledged the Kingdom of Italy, but this far is approved. We shall go through Austria on the way home."

Mama nodded as Vicky spoke. "I hope the journey goes well for you and you will not be recalled to Berlin."

"We may keep Bertie till my birthday, may we not, Mama?" Vicky smiled at her mother, and glanced up, taking Fritz's hand. "And we will be so grateful, Mama for your giving us the yacht."

The Queen shrugged. "I have no use for it right now. Fritz? What is the matter?"

Fritz had turned away during the conversation, seemingly absorbed in other thoughts. He went to the door. "I thought I heard someone coming."

There was a tap at the door, which Fritz opened. A footman set an envelope on the table by the door and bowed, and Fritz closed the door. He took up the envelope, his face changing as he read it.

"Papa says my presence in Berlin is necessary, I must go to Berlin," he said, taking Vicky in his arms as he spoke. He sighed. "I wish I could stay here with you," He bent down to kiss the Queen's cheek and shook hands with Bertie.

"You must go if your King needs you," Bertie said. Fritz nodded, leaving the room.

"Feo, I am so happy to see you. How is your baby?" Vicky greeted her cousin in the hallway. Feo was one the daughters of Aunt Feodora, Mama's half-sister. "George?"

Feo's husband nodded briefly. Vicky waited as Feo went into the next room, coming back with a nurse and three children.

"I'm so sorry Uncle Fritz left today; he would have been so happy to see you," Vicky said, sitting down and taking the hands of the two elder children, Bernhard and Elsa Marie, the children of George of Meiningen with his first wife, Fritz's cousin Lotte. Lotte had been Fritz's closest friend in the family growing up, and he called Bernhard and Elsa his niece and nephew.

George was rather stiff and formal, and Vicky remembered Fritz having said he was never very fond of him, but he attempted to remain close to him for the children's sake, and now that George was married to Vicky's cousin, they really were closer. Also, Feo's sister, Ada, was married to Fritz Holstein, who had been Fritz's closest friend at college.

Vicky remembered her first ball in Berlin, at Prince Charles' estate at Glienicke. Fritz had disappeared, at the same time as Anna. Vicky had felt jealous of Anna at the time, although she knew Fritz knew she was really his sister, rather than his cousin, she couldn't help it. But Fritz had gone to meet George, wishing her to see the children if he had brought them with him. He hadn't. Now, she was finally meeting them, but Fritz wasn't there.

"Come, Feo, come and see my little ones. And let me make your baby's acquaintance," she said, taking the little boy from Feo's arms. Feo and the elder children followed her to the room which was being used as the nursery.

"Mama!" Willy cried, running to her as she opened the door. Charlotte sat in a chair, asleep, holding a large book. Henry was on the floor, crawling towards Mrs. Hobbs.

"They are such nice little people," Feo whispered to Vicky, picking Henry up.

"Come and meet Aunt Feo," Vicky said, leading Willy forward.

Charlotte yawned, stretched, and opened the book. "Pretty bird. What?" she said, gazing at the pictures of parrots and other tropical birds in a picture book Vicky had taken from Papa's old library.

Bernhard knelt on the floor by the chair. "These are parrots. This is a red and green macaw," he said, pointing at the caption of the picture. He turned the page. "Here is an African grey. My Mama had one of these," he said quietly. Vicky saw his eyes fill with tears. She looked at Feo.

Feo watched her stepson showing Charlotte the pictures. "He was so fond of his mother, poor boy. He wasn't even four years old when she died, but he will never forget her. He is very fond of me, though he doesn't like to call me Mama. Elsa was only two."

Vicky squeezed her hand. "Are you really – is George –" She wasn't sure what to say.

Feo sighed, but smiled. "George was so much in love with her. But we are quite happy together. He doesn't think I am clever enough, though I take interest in everything, as my Mama always encouraged us to. But Ada is so much cleverer than I."

"I hope to see Ada and Fritz some time soon. Particularly now that Bertie is marrying Alix of Denmark. I do feel guilty there, sometimes. Fritz Holstein is such a nice fellow, and Fritz and I have always supported his claims to Schleswig-Holstein. I believe him to be the rightful heir."

"Oh, yes, he certainly is. Bernhard supports his claims passionately," Feo smiled. "Do your children talk politics to you as mine do?" she laughed.

"Not so much. Though Willy is certainly very aware of who is who and who to bow to, and so on. Their eyes and ears are wide open. The King – my father-in-law – always speaks of anything in front of the children. Fritz and I don't like it. We don't want them to have strange ideas in their heads, which they may or may not understand. We are careful what they listen to, though we do have them present at our meetings with diplomats and ministers whom we agree with, as Mama and Papa did with me. I wish Mama had done so with Bertie more."

Reinhardsbrunn, September 19, 1862

The Queen sat in her room after breakfast, gazing at the painting of Vicky's wedding. Vicky had been such a calm, sweet bride, and Albert had looked so young and well leading her down the aisle. It had seemed as though he must live to see the marriage of many grandchildren, as well as children, being only 39 when William was born.

She laid the picture down, and took up the photographs of Alix. Bertie's bride. Bertie was doing much better, she reflected; his journey to the East had gone very well, now he was engaged to be married, and he would go on the journey to Switzerland and Italy with Vicky and Fritz while Alix came to England to get to know the Queen and the rest of the family better. Fritz's company and example always did Bertie much good. Albert would certainly approve of the plan.

She laid the pictures down, taking up her pen to begin writing a letter, when there were footsteps in the next room. The door opened, and Vicky hurried in.

"Mama! Oh, Mama, I don't know what to say. Fritz writes that the King wishes to abdicate!"

CHAPTER SIX

TO RULE MORE THAN EVER

Potsdam, September 18, 1862

Fritz met von Heydt, the Minister of Commerce as he stepped out of his carriage outside the Neues Palais. The surprise showed plainly on the man's face; he had, apparently, not expected Fritz's return.

"Papa – the King sent for me," Fritz said. "We are still to go on our journey, I hope."

Von Heydt nodded. "There have been several very stormy council meetings," he said, following Fritz as he hurried in. "We did not know he had sent for you. The ministry is divided, and the King still insists on the army reform. But the Landtag still will not give the funding. All is in the same state as before."

Fritz nodded. "I must be on my way to Babelsberg in the morning."

"I hope the King will not be harsh with you."

Potsdam, September 19, 1862

Fritz bit his lip anxiously as he drove to Babelsberg. Why had his father sent for him without the Ministers' knowledge? What was going on now?

He jumped out and hurried in as soon as they were near Babelsberg.

"Papa? You sent for me," he said, as he entered his father's study.

"Yes, Fritz. I am glad you came, and that you had not departed yet. Let us go for a walk," the King said, rising and embracing Fritz. He had sat at his desk, his head in his hands, looking much older than when Fritz last saw him.

"I must abdicate if the Ministers insist on not giving the funding for the reform. I cannot go on with the change in the army. It means more to me than anything." Fritz looked up to see tears in his father's eyes. "For 33 years we have had the three year service. I cannot change it for a mere whim of the Landtag. Everything is prepared for the abdication. I only needed to speak to you first."

Fritz stared at his father. "But, Papa, you must not! I mean, it is not a good precedent for the King to abdicate over a Ministerial crisis! This must be solved a different way."

"Yes, I have tried to, but there seems no way. Everything is ready, and you need to sign the papers as well as I."

Fritz glanced sharply at his father. "No, Papa. The heir does not sign the abdication. I will not do that."

His father shook his head. "I said, Fritz, you must sign the papers! It is not the abdication, but simply some papers I wish you to sign. They are only some little matters; it will only take a moment."

Fritz shook his head again. He knew it was a trap. "Let me think over this for a day, please, and write to Vicky. She must know what is going on. And –" *We will not be able to go on our tour, if we become King and Queen just now.* He would not mention that. His father would only call him selfish if he did. But he knew, he knew he must not sign the papers.

Fritz hurried inside, leaving his father standing on the lawn, staring after him. "Fritz! You must obey your father and your King!"

"I am your most loyal servant," Fritz muttered to himself as he hurried to his rooms. He would serve the King far more wisely by not signing these papers, and by convincing his father not to abdicate.

Babelsberg, September 20, 1862

"The King must not abdicate! It is only a plot, a coup," Fritz said to Schleinitz, one of the few Ministers he believed he could trust. "You know the stories which circulate in the Government and all the Feudal party. They wish to pass over me, and make Onkel Karl King, or Fritz Karl, or they are making me sign papers which will make one of them Minister-President, or limit my power somehow, when I do become King. And by 'limiting my power' I do not mean it the way my father does. He means increasing the parliamentary powers. I am for parliamentary government, but with a wise Minister-President. By limiting my powers, I mean they wish to have me under Onkel Karl's spell, or make me promise to never tell Vicky anything, or something absurd of that order. I will not do it, and Papa must not abdicate! He said he would not if I would not sign the papers, so that is safe."

Schleinitz nodded. "Yes, it is a plot to put you in their power, and make you answerable for their mistakes. You are right, in this instance, to resist the King."

Fritz nodded. "I am very glad you think so."

Reinhardsbrunn, September 22, 1862

"Papa agreed not to abdicate, and to find some other way to solve the army reform question," Fritz told Vicky and the Queen. He sighed. "I am so thankful we did not fall into that trap."

Vicky looked up at him. "I thought we would be the King and Queen tomorrow," she said, smiling as she took his hand. "I didn't think of the possibility of *that* being a trap." She frowned. "How I wish –"

"*Ja*, Vicky, I know. But, I really do not believe I am ready for such a thing," he said, hesitantly. "And I do not feel it right to take the reins as long as Papa is still alive. It is not a good precedent for the King to abdicate over a Ministerial crisis."

The Queen smiled. "To change the government is better, you think? I don't know –" She paused, smiling slightly. "I changed the government during the bedchamber crisis, but I was a foolish young girl, when that happened, and I did it over my own selfish whim, not for the country's good. Fritz, you say you are not ready. I believe you are. You doubt yourself too much."

"But I have so much to study and learn. I do not know nearly enough."

"You know more than you think. You would be a good King. And you have Vicky to help you." The Queen smiled at her daughter, and looked at Fritz again. "One must be prepared for it at any moment. Do you think I thought I was ready?"

"You were only a young girl, Mama," Vicky said. "I would excuse your mistakes on that account."

The Queen nodded. "Some people did. Some choose to say the Sovereign should know how to serve their country, no matter what age they are. But you are ready, if the time comes soon, Fritz. I know you are."

Fritz shook his head. "I have had so little experience speaking with the Ministers, since I am not allowed to speak at the councils."

The Queen nodded again. "You have learned the valuable lesson of listening very thoroughly, without speaking. That is a very important lesson for a sovereign to learn. I still have not."

Reinhardsbrunn, September 23, 1862

"Fritz, what is the matter? Are you ill?" Vicky had opened the bedroom door, to see Fritz sitting on the bed, holding his head in his hands. His face looked pale, his expression horrified. "Fritz, what is it?" Vicky asked again in alarm, kneeling down on the floor beside him.

"This," Fritz said in a choked voice. He thrust a telegram into her hand. It was from one of his friends and advisers, Duncker. "Bismarck-Schönhausen has been made Minister-President," it read.

Vicky looked up at Fritz, feeling that her face wore an expression of horror. "No," she murmured. "It must not be true. It can't be."

Fritz shook his head. "I never thought *that* would be Papa's way of solving the Ministerial crisis. I just – I guess I refused to believe it would come to this." He met Vicky's eye. "Your Mama spoke of changing the Government. I did hope it would be so, but I hoped Papa would bring back Prince Hohenzollern, or some other wise man. I knew Bismarck had been mentioned, but I just – I believed Papa when he said he would never take him." Fritz's voice broke. "Now everything is lost!"

"No, Fritz," Vicky said, standing and embracing him. "*You* are not lost. You would have been if you had signed those papers. We still have each other, and we must find a way out of this net. We will not return to Berlin for some time," she said. "Isn't that a relief?"

"*Ja*, although it gives them time to make plenty of mischief before our return."

"Put thoughts of politics out of your head until our return." She kissed him, stroking his brow.

"But Papa, what will he do? Onkel Karl will rule now, really, and more than ever before. How will Mama take this news? Bismarck is one of her greatest enemies! *Ach!* Why does this have to happen? Prince Hohenzollern was such a good Minister-President, and his time let me have hope for the country! Now there is none!"

"Fritz," Vicky whispered. "Please. Think of what I said. You promised you would enjoy this tour. You have long wished to go on a long expedition, you said, and to show me Italy! You will do so now."

He looked up at her, trying to smile. "*Meine Frauchen*," he whispered, leaning his head against her breast, "you are my only comfort."

CHAPTER SEVEN

LIFE'S FIRST JOURNEY

Burg Hohenzollern, Oktober 8, 1862

Vicky gazed up at the mass of clouds above them as the carriage continued up the mountain. "Oh! It is like magic!" She squeezed Fritz's hand. "Have you seen anything so beautiful?" A castle had seemed to appear in the midst of the clouds.

Fritz shook his head. He seemed speechless, and Vicky glanced up at him. His eyes were filled with tears.

The Burg Hohenzollern – a castle jointly owned by the Prussian dynasty and the Sigmaringen family, a Catholic branch of the Hohenzollerns – stood on the top of the Rauhe Alp, which rose straight up three thousand feet.

As they drove on, they all gazed upwards. They were approaching the battlemented walls of the castle, and when they were still at a small distance, Vicky could see the castle above, with many pointed, flag-topped towers.

The entrance to the castle was different from anything she had experienced before. There was not a spiral staircase, but a spiral road, which they traversed still in the carriage. Passing through the first tunnel-like gate, they came to a battlemented wall with another arched gateway. On the third layer, Vicky realized they had finally reached the top. She looked out over the trees, mostly golden but with the occasional brilliant red, like rubies scattered over gold plate or a glass of wine amidst the gold-ware at a banquet. The view from the castle was just as lovely as the view of the castle itself, the mist clearing by the time they reached the top.

The "ground" level of the castle was what had appeared the top of the battlements when they were near to the castle wall, but now the castle rose above them. Inside, the castle had high vaulted ceilings, making her think more of a church than a castle. There were also tunnels, reaching down below the foundation of the battlements into the heart of the mountain itself.

Oktober 15, 1862

"I am *so* tired," Vicky groaned as she lay down. They had gone on an expedition in the Alps which lasted sixteen hours. Vicky hadn't realized how unused to climbing she had become, though it had been five years since she was last at Balmoral.

"Tomorrow we go to Zürich," Fritz said. "What do you think of the Burg?"

"It is so splendid, and like a fairy-tale, looking as if it were built on the clouds." She turned, trying to find a comfortable way to lie down. "I am so sore from climbing. I don't know how I will manage on this trip." She looked up. "Our host was so kind, and his sons are so nice. I never really got to know them so well in Berlin."

Prince Hohenzollern, the former Minister-President, had been present to greet them. Vicky had met his sons, Leopold, Karl, Anton and Fritz, in Berlin, but they were usually on guard-duty or in some other position which did not allow much conversation. Leopold, the eldest, she knew best, as he had married Antoinette of Portugal, a Coburg cousin, a sister of King Pedro, who had married Leopold's sister Stephanie in a wedding by proxy shortly after Vicky's arrival in Berlin.

Oktober 18, 1862

"*Alles Gute[12]*, many happy returns," Vicky whispered as Fritz woke her with an embrace. It was his birthday. Vicky rose and opened her trunk. *Where are they?* She was sure she had packed her presents for Fritz in this particular trunk. She sat down, thinking. Then she shook her head. She had left her presents behind in Berlin.

She hurried into the next room, finding a pretty vase she had bought in Bern the evening before, which Fritz hadn't seen. She hid it in her nightgown, then hurried back to get dressed.

When she was finished, Fritz was talking with Bertie, so she hurried to find some flowers, filling the vase before Fritz and Bertie came into the dining-room.

She sat down, waiting. She saw Fritz go into another room, but Bertie came to join her, laying on the table several letters. Vicky glanced at them and smiled. They were from Mama and the *Geschwister.* He also took out of a bag he carried a triple picture frame.

They had said goodbye to the Sigmaringens on the 16th, going on to Zürich. Their arrival had occurred under heavy storm clouds, and they hadn't been able to see a trace of the Alpine scenery.

Yesterday, after their arrival in Bern, they had visited the grave of Aunt Julchen, Mama's aunt, who had been married to Grand Duke Konstantin of Russia, but had lived in Switzerland after their divorce.

Fritz hurried in with a grave face. "Bad news from Berlin," he murmured to Vicky as he sat down to open the letters. He glanced at the flowers, noticing the vase. He looked up at Vicky with a small smile. He took a case of small photographs out of his pocket,

---

12 Every blessing

holding it up to the picture frame Bertie had given. "We can have our pictures in this, in memory of this tour," he said, smiling at Bertie. He continued reading the letters.

It was time to go. They hoped to be in Geneva tomorrow. Vicky watched Fritz as they boarded the train. He looked so tired. She wished they could have stayed in Gotha longer, so he could have been better rested before their journey began.

Fritz had slept on the train on his birthday, so Vicky had spent the time talking quietly with Bertie and answering letters. Bertie had received a letter from Princess Christian, saying that Alix must be back in Denmark by her birthday. This contradicted what she had promised Mama, that Alix should visit for three weeks.

"Let it alone, and see if she writes to your Mama," Fritz had said to Bertie before he fell asleep. Vicky agreed with this advice.

"Yes, Bertie, ignore it."

"But would that not be rather rude of me to ignore the letters of my fiancée's mother?" Bertie asked uncertainly.

"Her letter is rather rude, and it seems very strange that she should write to you, while you are traveling, and the arrangement had been made with Mama. I shall write Mama and tell her. Please, just leave it. It will come right."

On the 24th they had arrived in Palermo. Fritz had been emotionally excited to show them this place, where he had been the year before his and Vicky's engagement. They had visited the place where he had stayed at the time, and also an old monastery, leaving with bits of beautiful mosaic in their pockets.

Most of the buildings here were of very Eastern architecture. The orange groves, aloes, cactuses, fig trees, heliotropes, date palms, all the vegetation was such as Vicky had never seen before outside of a hot house. They often stopped to breathe in the sweet, almost overpowering scent of the brightly colored flowers, and to watch the swarms of butterflies and bees. The gaudily painted donkey and mule carts, embellished with red dyed feathers and harnesses covered with glittering, jingling bells were also very striking. In the towns, they often met these carts, driven by boys or young men who were dressed for the heat – or rather so nearly undressed Vicky felt shy of looking at them.

She had begun to take sketches of the views which were most striking to her eye.

"You are sure you do not need more time?" Fritz had asked her. She had only been sitting a few minutes when she put her sketchbook away.

"Oh, no, that is plenty. I can finish them later," she had assured him. "You remember my pictures from Balmoral. Most of those were done this way."

"How do you remember the details? Every color is perfect, and the shadows, the drops of water. How do you do it?"

Vicky smiled up at him, meeting his gaze. He stood looking down at her, his eyes expressing his admiration, just as they had when she first showed him her artwork at Balmoral, a few days before he proposed. She shrugged and shook her head.

"It is so easy. I don't know what the fuss is." She laughed. "Bertie, I didn't think you knew so much about art as you do. You knew every artist at the galleries we saw."

Bertie shrugged, turning his face away. He had always professed ignorance and boredom when Papa and Mama had attempted to speak with him about such things. "I know. I – I don't usually find it so interesting, though I do know it quite well. But you make it so interesting," he said to Fritz.

"No, it is she who makes it interesting," Fritz said, smiling at Vicky. "I know so little myself, my company could not possibly make it interesting."

"No, that is not true," Vicky and Bertie both said. Vicky took their hands, smiling up at them. "You have both learned so much about art, I am proud of you."

They dined at a hotel overlooking the sea, palm fronds waving in the window. As they ate, Vicky saw another English ship come into the harbor.

"There is the *Doris* with Sir Leopold McClintock," Bertie said. "We are to go aboard her, are we not?"

"Yes," Vicky said. "But I hope the wind does not come up too much." The sea was beginning to look wild.

Tunis, Oktober 26, 1862.

Vicky gazed around her with fascinated eyes. Everything was so different from anything she had experienced.

They had gone on board the *Doris* the night before, which had turned in its route to Tunis. They would set foot on African soil the next day. Vicky had not been able to sleep, but lay awake, listening to Fritz snoring, and thinking of what they would see the next day.

In the morning, they were all given white cloths to tie around their hats, as a shelter from the hot sun. It was extremely hot, the thermometer at 108 degrees, but Vicky was surprised to find it did not seem overpowering. More overwhelming was the glare of the sun beating down from a deep blue, cloudless sky on the pale sand. There was little but sand and rocks, though her eye occasionally found some relief in the green palms and cactus.

Mr. Wood, the English Consul greeted them on board the ship and accompanied them. Mr. Wood's house was built in eastern style. There were palms all around the house, to afford some shade, but hardly any other vegetation.

Later, they wandered about in the ruins of Carthage, gathering broken bits of mosaic near the water cisterns. The old walls stood tall around them, ending in tumbled piles of sandstone. In the distance were more trees than Vicky had seen anywhere since they crossed to Africa, the blue sea, and faintly visible on the horizon – the mountains of Palermo.

Tunis, Oktober 27, 1862.

Vicky looked out the window of Mr. Wood's house. A fancy carriage pulled by eight mules waited outside. Many men surrounded it on beautiful Arab horses – some in Turkish uniform, some in plain short trousers with white burnouses and embroidered jackets, their chests and legs bare.

One of the Bey's brothers or cousins waited for them at the palace at La Goletta. Vicky tasted the sweets and coffee, but she could eat little from excitement. They reentered their carriage, and the mules took off at a tremendous pace, covering them with dust.

Vicky counted a herd of sixty-three camels which lay about or stood drinking at a fountain just outside the town. The pace finally slowed as they entered the town, and they were able to look about. Tall men in white turbans and burnouses, the women in short jackets, tight trousers with bright burnouses and black veils covering their faces.

The carriage stopped at a small bazaar in the town. There was a constant jabber of conversation between buyers and sellers, of which Vicky could understand nothing. At many of the stalls, the women sat cross-legged, working busily with colorful cloth and beads. The men lay on the ground, smoking long pipes, sitting up and calling out whenever someone passed their stall.

Fritz smiled at Vicky as she bought some colorful Tunisian cloth. "Do you feel you know more about Tunis now?"

She smiled back, nodding. "It is eleven years since I said I wished I knew more," she said, remembering her words at the Exhibition. She had known so much about almost all of the displays at the Great Exhibition, but very little about the Tunisian one. The rich colors of the fabrics had attracted her notice then, too.

Finally, the carriage drew up at the Bey's town palace. The building had a plain, square, white front. Vicky felt rather disappointed at first, but they drove through a door. There was another white wall above, with an open porch with bronze columns and arches, a green decorative rail and lion statues on each side of the stairway.

The Bey's uncles, cousins and brothers waited at the door, but Vicky's gaze was drawn to the architecture before it was to the people. The arches and columns continued, in grey, rose, tan and light turquoise-blue. Unusual symbols intertwined with what looked like fish decorated the walls and floor in a beautiful mosaic. A fountain stood in the middle of the room.

"*Willkommen[13]*," a strange voice said, and Vicky realized the Bey himself waited at the top of another staircase. They all stepped forward, and he gave Vicky his arm, leading the way into an immense throne room through two rows of people kneeling on either side of the room. There were several more arches with beautiful mosaic; the floor looked like a checkerboard; all was white and grey stone except for the magnificent bronze throne and its red canopy, and further up, the walls had red and green designs Vicky couldn't make out. Four chairs with cushions of the same

---

13 Welcome

shade of red were placed and they all sat down.

Conversation had to be made through an interpreter, as the Bey spoke little of any European language. Vicky thought him handsome with his black beard and black jacket, red fez and scarlet trousers, his jacket covered with stars and decorations.

"My brother Prince Alfred visited the late Bey, and my mother the Queen sends her greetings," Vicky said. The interpreter passed the message on, and the Bey smiled slightly and nodded. "May I meet the Princess?"

He nodded again, and they were led into another room. With Mrs. Moore, Mr. Wood's sister, as an interpreter, and Hedwig, her own lady-in-waiting, Vicky entered the harem. The room she saw was very pretty, with a dome shape and a window nearly in the top, the walls of rose and blue mosaic. She had been told that the Bey had only one wife, Lilla Bembey. A small wooden door opened, and a woman appeared in a short pink and white jacket, tight gold trousers and a blue scarf or veil wrapped round her head and throat, but not covering her face. Her feet were bare, her hands and arms covered with rings and bracelets. Her black hair was cut short and brushed forward, almost into her face.

"Princess – Prussa?" she said in a low, sweet voice, sitting down with her legs folded beneath her. There were many other very pretty girls in similar dress of different colors, and without the volume of jewelry.

Vicky talked with her for a few minutes through the interpreter, and then another door opened. As the smell of coffee wafted in, she realized she was quite hungry. Some unidentified sweets and very bitter coffee were served, and Vicky joined Fritz and Bertie again. As she came out, the Bey was investing them with his order – taking the diamond stars out of his pockets simply wrapped in paper - hanging a black sash with thin red stripes over their shoulders, and giving them each a jewel encrusted saber.

Tunis, Oktober 28, 1862.

The passage to Sicily was horrible. The paddle on the *Osborne* was broken, and the rudder damaged as well. The Doris took her in tow, and the ship rocked horribly.

"It is too rough to land here; we must make for Malta," Vicky heard one of the men cry. She groaned. They must face the rolling sea still longer. She didn't know how many times she had been sick.

"The coast is beautiful." Fritz had entered the cabin. "It is an oasis in the desert after being in Tunis. I wish you could paint it." He put a hand on Vicky's shoulder. "Is it so very bad, *meine Frauchen?*"

On board the Osborne, *Malta, Oktober 30, 1862.*

Vicky sat trying to collect herself to write to Mama. In the last day she had been so severely seasick, she felt as if she had been turned inside out. But what they had seen had been so fascinating, and she had been over a week without writing to Mama.

In the port of Valletta, it appeared as if a warship were waiting to meet them, but it turned out to be only part of the fortification of the port. The fleet were absent or in another bay.

Sir Gaspard Le Marchant, the Governor, received them kindly. Vicky tried to shield her eyes from the glare as they drove away in a carriage. The glare was even worse here than in Tunis, everything was white rock, white rock roads, white rock walls, white rock buildings.

But the garden of San Antonio palace was a gorgeous oasis, overflowing with flowers of every description. Jasmine, verbena, roses, chrysanthemums, violets. The air was heavy with the sweet scent, and Vicky laughed to see bees lying on their backs on the ground, humming. Above them was a tree with trumpet shaped flowers which rained nectar at every breath of wind.

"It is so beautiful, I can't feel sick anymore," Vicky said, looking up at Fritz. He stood speechless, stunned with the view and smell of so much beauty, and seemed unable to speak.

Several more scenes stood out in Vicky's memory as if she were looking at a moving, colored photograph, or as if she had painted the scene several times. She did begin many paintings, but not as many as she wished.

"I wish I could paint everything, it is all so lovely," she said, after she and Fritz returned from the Blue Grotto in Naples. They had lain down in a little fishing boat to get through the entrance, and were quite drenched, but it was well worth the drenching. Vicky hadn't imagined anything could be so intensely blue; the water and the roof of the cave were the same deep shade.

In Malta, she had made the acquaintance of Uncle George's son, Mr. FitzGeorge, who was not a Prince, as Uncle George's marriage had never been acknowledged by the Queen. The young man reminded her strongly of a mixture of Louis of Hesse and Bertie.

From Berlin, she heard there was a new British ambassador, but she wasn't exactly pleased. She had felt Sir Augustus Loftus to be a real friend, who gave Mama a correct interpretation of Berlin politics, and she knew Sir Andrew Buchanan was extremely pro-Danish, which could not bode well in the current Berlin atmosphere. She had also heard that he barely spoke any German, but she didn't know the truth of that, and thought that surely Mama would not allow a man who spoke no German to be appointed.

She and Fritz had continued to receive news from Berlin throughout their trip. Fritz was always in a state of alarm when they received the messages, fearing that they were sent to recall him to Berlin. But they never were, and Vicky tried to encourage him not to read all the papers, but to leave Berlin on the other side of the Mediterranean, though she had been deeply concerned at the imprudent speeches the King made, and Bismarck, too.

Shortly after their departure, Bismarck had made a speech, declaring that no parliament or speech could solve the problems of the government or of the country, but iron and blood would be their redemption. Fritz had looked very grave over this, but there was nothing they could do.

In Rome, they met the Pope, a good natured, jolly old man who laughed after almost everything he or anyone else said. Vicky was allowed to go down into the crypt, where ladies were never permitted.

After Vicky's birthday, they parted with Bertie. "I am so glad to have had him with us for so long," she wrote to Mama. "He has been so kind, and we have been so happy together. There has never been the slightest disagreement. I find he knows much more about art than we thought, and was quite interested in the galleries we visited."

Bertie's wedding would be soon. Vicky smiled and hugged herself at the thought. They would surely be at the wedding – Mama would expect it – and indeed, Bertie had already asked Fritz to be his best man. Alice and Louis were also in England already – she was expecting her baby soon after Bertie's wedding, and was to have the birth in England.

Vicky wondered at this. For a Princess to be allowed to have her firstborn – the potential heir – in her own country was very unusual. Vicky couldn't even get permission to have *any* of her children in England. Prussian Princes and Princesses must be born in Prussia, her father-in-law said.

Genoa to Milan, December 8, 1862

Vicky was sorry to say good-bye to the sea, though she had been so seasick, just as she had been sorry to say good-bye to Rome, where they had become completely covered with flea-bites.

A few nights ago, the day they had left Rome, she had been dreadfully sick again. Fritz came to her cabin where she had preferred to be alone.

"Vicky," he whispered, "is there anything I can do to help you?"

"Oh, no, I don't want to be a bother to anyone. That is all I am capable of being just now," she groaned.

Fritz turned to go, but then turned back again, bending over Vicky to kiss her forehead. Suddenly, he clutched at his own stomach, and hurried away. *Poor Fritz.* He had never been seasick, even when all the rest of their party was.

Now, it was time to say good-bye to the sea for the rest of the journey. They reached the Apennines mountains. There was a tunnel running through. Vicky had wondered how they would cross the mountains, hoping there would not be a long carriage drive going up and down, up and down, which would probably have made her feel seasick again.

The carriage entered the tunnel, and they sat in darkness for eight minutes, trying to look about by the light of the lanterns the coachman had attached to the front of the carriage, but it was so very dark here.

Vicky felt a blast of cold on her face. She shivered, and leaned against Fritz, wishing she had a muff for her hands.

Finally, there was light ahead. As they reached the end of the tunnel, everything looked white ahead.

"What is that? It is so white."

Then she realized – it was snow. They had driven for eight minutes, leaving the rocky heights of Genoa with its pretty villas and the blue sea, and come out in the depth of winter. She shivered again. Most of the trees stood up naked under a blanket of snow; a few still retained their leaves, trapped under a sheet of ice, not yet undressed by the hot passion of the sirocco wind. The horses balked at first as they came out of the tunnel, but soon plodded through the deep snow.

Venice, December 10, 1862.

The song of the gondolieri and the night birds wove together melodically. The gondola glided through the water, and there was a splash of the paddle as Fritz looked up at the moon. Here, it was cold, but not snowy. It was a cloudless night, quite bright enough to see the beautiful old buildings and bridges as they paddled about.

Vicky took his hand. "It is like a beautiful dream, is it not?" she murmured.

"It is quite enough to make one forget one's troubles," he answered. "I have not thought of Berlin today, until just now."

"Please, don't continue to. We will be home soon enough. We are already on our way north. I could tell today, it felt so cold after being so spoiled with the warm south in November."

"Where do you hope to be on the 14th?" Fritz asked gently, putting his arm around her. The first anniversary of her father's death was approaching, as well as their return to Berlin.

"I suppose we will be on our way to Vienna then," she said, leaning her head on his shoulder. "How Papa loved Italy," she said softly, to herself.

They had left Verona in the morning, after visiting Juliette's tomb.

At Milan they had met the Crown Prince of Italy – the son of King Victor Emanuel, who had been one of England's allies in the Crimean war, but who Fritz disliked.

"He is far too much like Onkel Karl," he had said. "I do not want you to become any more closely acquainted with him than necessary." Vicky remembered meeting him when he came to England as an ally; she had thought him an odd man, but not unpleasant. He was very short, not much taller than Mama – there had been jokes in the papers about "the little allies" as the Queen, Napoleon the Third and Victor Emanuel were all so small.

His son, Umberto, was a pleasant companion. He was rather gruff and abrupt, but Vicky soon realized it was his way and that he meant to be friendly. He was actually rather shy.

In his company, they had gone to the top of the Duomo – the Milan cathedral.

Vicky gazed into the distance at the snow-topped mountains of the Alps. "This must be the finest view in the world," she said, but could hardly get her words out, her teeth were chattering so much with the cold wind.

On the train to Vienna, December 14, 1862.

A whole year, Fritz thought. He had only woken a moment ago, roused by the sound of a sob from Vicky. He looked at her; she still appeared to be asleep, but tears ran down her cheeks.

"Papa! Papa, don't leave me," she called out. She reached out and seized Fritz's hand. "Papa, please! Why must you go?"

Fritz put his arm around her, gently kissing her forehead. He felt her tremble in his arms, but she finally opened her eyes. "Fritz? Where are we? Oh." Her face changed, but she began to sob again. "A whole year without Papa; poor Mama," she murmured. She turned away, and seemed to wish not to speak or rise.

They had spent the previous evening at Miramar, visiting Vicky's cousin Charlotte and her husband, Max, the brother of the Emperor of Austria.

Vienna, seven o'clock, December 14, 1862.

The train drew up at the station. Vicky held Fritz's hand as they waited for it to stop screeching and groaning as it came to a stop.

At the snow-covered station, the Emperor Franz Joseph stood waiting for them, in Prussian uniform. There were no crowds, no decorations, no red carpet. It was a quiet reception, "in honor of the sad day," as the Emperor said when he shook hands. Vicky studied him. He looked much older than he was – he was only thirty-two, a year older than Fritz, but his face was wrinkled, and there were strands of grey in his red hair. He was not so splendid-looking as she had expected from his portraits, and was shorter than she expected, too. But he seemed a kindly gentleman, and was very friendly with Fritz.

The rooms at the Embassy were very gorgeous, with plush carpets and brocade wall hangings. Soon, their Majesties arrived.

The Empress entered the room on her husband's arm. Vicky tried not to stare at her wonderful hair, which was worn long, part of it worked into an intricate web. A Hungarian fashion, she had heard. The Empress Elisabeth supported the Hungarians fiercely, although her mother-in-law considered them the Revolutionary force in the Austro-Hungarian Empire. The Empress's tutor had been a Hungarian artist, whom she had been very close to.

The Empress's face was not quite so pretty as her portraits showed – portraits often did not tell the truth – but she was very kind. Vicky could not understand how she could bear to wear her clothes so tight – she had an impossibly tiny waist. Vicky often left her corset loose, only tight enough to give a slight form to her dress and figure.

"*Auf Wiedersehen!*" Fritz called to the Emperor, and Vicky waved. It had been a pleasant, friendly visit. Vicky had tried to become better acquainted with the Empress, but she was shy, and spoke in a very soft voice, difficult to hear. When alone in her own boudoir, she had become a little more talkative, but Vicky found it difficult to find any topic of conversation. She didn't sing, draw or play, and she spoke little of her children.

Something Vicky could at least partially understand was her passion for equestrian activities. She was disturbed if she couldn't go out and ride for at least three hours a day, which was, of course, impossible in court life, when it also took three hours to care for her hair at the beginning and end of the day.

The Austrian Imperial family was very large, and there were so many families it was difficult to keep track of everyone, but there were a few Vicky had already met at the manoeuvers in Potsdam, the Archduke Leopold and of course, the Emperor's brother Max, Cousin Charlotte's husband.

"Mama has written about the preparations for Bertie's wedding," Vicky told Fritz as they sat in the train. "She asks that I should come to England towards the end of February, to hold a reception in her stead." The Queen, being still in deep mourning, was not participating in the festivities.

"That should be easily done. I know my father will not refuse a request like that."

"She wishes me to do the honors, as Alice cannot just now. Alix's two uncles – the Duke of Glücksburg and Fritz Hessen will be there – and Anna."

A strange look crossed Fritz's face, and he took Vicky's hand. "I hope she will behave herself."

PART TWO:
INTERLUDE

CHAPTER EIGHT

HASTE TO THE WEDDING

Kronprinz Palais, Berlin, December 19, 1862

"Mama!" Vicky knelt over Willy's little bed in the nursery. She and Fritz had gone there immediately on their arrival. Morning sunlight poured in through a distant window where the white curtains had not been drawn.

Vicky threw her arms around her little son, picking him up and receiving his kisses. "Did you miss Mama?" she asked, sitting down on the floor.

"Papa!" Vicky heard Charlotte say sleepily as Fritz bent down over her bed.

"Mama, I don't want you to ever go away again," Willy cried, kissing her cheek again.

"Hush, Willy, we must go and see Grospapa and Grosmama, but we will be back. We aren't going away for long this time."

"Ditta not want Papa go," Charlotte murmured sleepily, and Fritz lifted her up, stroking her head and rocking her.

Willy clung to Vicky's arm. "Are you not still tired? It is before your time to get up," Vicky said.

Willy shook his head. "Mama's here, can't be tired," he said, but he leaned his head against her, blinking sleepily.

"Don't you wish to say good morning to Papa?" Vicky prompted. Fritz had laid Charlotte back in her bed, and sat down on the floor. Willy ran to him, and Vicky leaned over Charlotte's bed. She slept peacefully. Vicky smiled, but didn't bend down and kiss her.

She went into the next room. Mrs. Hobbs sat in her chair asleep, holding little Henry. Vicky gazed at him. He had grown so much during their absence. He would be quite a little stranger, having been only two months old when they left Berlin. But it was gratifying that Willy had recognized her in the first moment of waking up – and that Charlotte had known Fritz, she being so young. She often wondered how attached the children really were to them, as they spent so much time with their nurses during the months in Berlin.

Berlin Schloss, December, 1862

Vicky took Fritz's arm as they entered the big hall where the dinner was at the Schloss. They were late, the dinner was already over, and everyone was sitting or standing about in groups.

Near the door, at a small table, a man sat, reading the paper. Vicky looked at him for a moment, realizing he was Sir Andrew Buchanan, the new Ambassador. Mama had sent her his photograph, but it must have been taken several years ago. He had quite grey hair, and his face looked much aged compared to the one in the photograph.

"Oh, look who's here," she heard Fritz Karl's voice loudly, even though he stood at a table quite a distance away. "It's Fritzch and his bitch," he said, in English.

There was a burst of laughter from that table, where Fritz Karl had seated himself once more. Wilhelm of Mecklenburg-Schwerin and his mother, Fritz's aunt Adina, the Dowager Grand Duchess sat at the other side. Also Prince Charles, the Duke of Brunswick, and several others. On the table stood several –mostly empty – bottles of wine or champagne, and many empty glasses.

Fritz Karl rose again, and came toward Vicky and Fritz. He continued to speak – in English, but Vicky could not understand him. No Englishman would ever dare to address her in such a way, she knew. She was too unversed in improper language in English to understand most of his words.

Sir Andrew looked up at him, his face plainly showing his horror. He rose, but at the same time, he met Prince Charles's eye, and stood still, finally sitting back down without speaking.

"You should take it as a compliment that I am learning your language," Fritz Karl sneered, speaking in German again, and turning his back on Vicky.

"Excuse me, but that is not my language. I – I don't know any of those words," she retorted in German, trying not to stammer as she searched for her words. "Except for the first one. And I am not *eine Hundin*[14]," she said, looking him straight in the face as he turned back, though being careful not to meet his eye. "Would you care to explain yourself? You thought you were speaking my language, but you must not have been, as I could not understand it."

"It – it was only a joke," Fritz Karl muttered, his face flushing, and turning away, as Sir Andrew finally rose and stepped toward him.

"No," Sir Andrew said. "Explain yourself to the lady, your Crown Princess. And don't pretend you don't understand me," he snapped as Fritz Karl shrugged and began to turn way. He stepped in front of him again. "Do not make a joke at her expense, which she does not understand, when you say you are trying to compliment her."

Fritz Karl's face grew even redder. "I – I –" He turned away again. "I cannot explain in English, and it – is - not proper conversation in company," he said, lamely.

---

14 A female dog

"Then why did you think of addressing her so?" Sir Andrew went on. "Apologize, sir."

Fritz Karl muttered something, and turned back to the table again.

"She said she is not a dog, and she is not *eine Katze*[15], either. I will not soil my lips with the word I have often heard you use. Be ashamed of yourself, sir."

"*Danke*," Fritz said to Sir Andrew. "I am glad to see we have your support."

"Is it really true you did not understand him?" Sir Andrew asked Vicky quietly.

"Yes. I only know enough to know that it is – improper language. My parents never allowed me to be exposed to such things. I have only had the misfortune to learn such things in German."

Another burst of laughter came from the table. They were still laughing over what Fritz Karl had said. There had been several rhymes in his "*willkommen Sprochen*[16]", but they did not rhyme at all when repeated in German.

Kronprinzpalais, Berlin, December 1862.

"Oh, Vicky, I am so ashamed at such moments as what happened yesterday evening," Marianne said, sitting down by Vicky's side. Marianne had come to Vicky and Fritz's private dinner the next day, bringing her little girls. "I felt ready to sink into the ground."

"You have nothing to do with it," Fritz said.

---

15 A cat
16 Welcome speech

"Oh, yes, I have. I am 'Princess Friedrich Karl'; my name is his. I cannot disassociate myself from his behavior." Marianne's voice trembled.

"But people know you do not approve. They do not blame you for it. Why would they? You are not responsible for his vile behavior," Vicky said, taking her trembling hand.

"I know. But – oh, Vicky, he – he speaks so in front of the girls. It is so – so –" She broke off, her face flushed with emotion. Vicky put her arm around her and felt her tremble all over. Vicky looked at Fritz. He leaned his head on his hand, his face flushed. His whole manner reminded Vicky of how he acted when he and Papa were first telling her about Prince Charles.

"Aunty, will we go with you to Potsdam?" Ebi ran to Vicky's side, gazing up at her with wide eyes. "I – I don't want to go to Glienicke."

"She keeps asking about that, and saying she doesn't want to go to Glienicke," Marianne said. "But she won't say why. I – I don't know what to tell her. I cannot change things," she said, her voice breaking off again, as she burst into tears.

"He's *our* baby," Willy cried, pushing Louischen away as she tried to look more closely at little Henry. Louischen shrank away.

"But Mama said we can call you brothers and sisters, Willy," Mariechen said quietly. Willy looked up at her, staring silently. It was the first time she had ever spoken directly to him. She picked Henry up, cradling him in her arms. "Louischen, come here," she said. Louischen came to her, and Mariechen put her arm around her little sister, as she examined the baby's face. Then she set Henry down on the floor next to Willy. She looked at him. "Has your Mama told you to never let your siblings out of your sight, like we –" She gazed after Willy, he having gotten up and wandered away to look out the window. She shook her head.

Vicky put her hand on Mariechen's shoulder. Mariechen jumped. "Oh, Aunt Vicky, you startled me. But why did Willy –?" She looked up at Vicky, a hurt expression replacing the previous look of alarm.

"Willy is only a little boy, and you have never spoken to him before."

"But I was asking him a question – and an important question. He – he just walked away!"

"I know, Mariechen. But he is such a little boy; give him time." She paused, thinking of the serious questions Mariechen had already asked when she was younger than Willy was now, when Vicky was first in Berlin. She sighed, wondering if she should tell Mariechen her thoughts.

"Mariechen," she began slowly, sitting on the floor and putting her arm around the little girl, "You often remind me of myself, in some ways, myself at your age."

Mariechen's face slowly broke into a smile "Thank you, Aunt Vicky. I would love to be like you."

Vicky smiled as Mariechen slipped her hand into hers. "You are – you are very intellectually precocious, as I was, and you are like a little mother to your siblings, as I was to mine. And yet, you are very different from me." She paused, unsure of what to say next. "Mariechen, would you consider it true to say that you have had no childhood?"

Mariechen's face changed, growing very serious. "Yes, Aunt Vicky. Mama relies on me so much to look after the little ones, and you can see what that is with how Papa is." Her cheeks flushed and the look in her eyes changed again.

Vicky nodded. "You are already your little sisters' protector and second mother, in a much greater sense than I was. My childhood home was so happy, my home here is, too. My Papa – you probably do not remember him, Mariechen. Do you remember the cake for his birthday? When my parents were here?"

Mariechen nodded, a slight smile returning to her face. "I remember being afraid of them, until that day. But, Aunty – I will ask you what I asked Willy. Have you told them to stay together, and Willy never to let the others out of his sight, like Mama has told me?"

Vicky shook her head. "We haven't felt that necessary. I keep my little ones close to me here, and they don't go about very much. Though I noticed myself – when I was in England – feeling anxious if Willy left the room without me, though I knew Uncle was in the next room, or my Mama was, or one of my siblings."

"So you feel it, too," Mariechen said. She sighed, looking down, and then glanced up at Vicky again. "I don't understand Louischen. You know the funny things she says, about colors and tastes and flowers and things?" Vicky nodded. "Mama always liked the funny pictures and things, vegetables with arms and legs, and so on, but Louischen really seems to see it. It is so odd."

Kronprinz Palais, Potsdam, December 22, 1862.

Fritz sat in the Council room, gazing up at the ceiling while he thought. Bismarck sat across the table. They had returned so rapidly to the usual Berlin life. That scene with Fritz Karl to begin with, and now, trying to reason with the unreasonable.

"Prussia's task is primarily Foreign," Bismarck went on. "I serve the King, and follow his orders in internal matters. The Minister-President must belong to no party, and I may take liberal measures upon request."

Fritz almost shook his head. Did Bismarck really believe all of this? Had he deluded himself as well as others? Or rather, had Onkel Karl led him to believe that he, Bismarck, belonged to no party, and was only the faithful servant of the King? It seemed impossible that anyone could say such things as Bismarck did, and then go on to do the things he did. Onkel Karl, at least, wasn't a hypocrite. He made no secret of his hostility.

"Liberal measures would, however, be of little use, as any concession would only be seen as weakness on the Government's part. We must be strong." His voice seemed as if it should ring with these words, but his voice was so high, so – sweet – was the word which always came to mind, it never seemed to match his words.

"The funds for the military reform are plentifully available now – and the budget shall go through in the new year as well," he went on. Fritz still didn't answer, but glowered inwardly. Bismarck had studied the constitution – but for the purpose of finding a way to gain control of the funds for what the King wished. There was nothing in the constitution directing what should take place when there was a stand-off between the King and the Landtag; therefore, Bismarck had advised the King to do as he saw fit, and use the funds as he saw best. "The Crown must be strong, and not give in," he had said.

Just after the first change of Government this year, during one of Fritz's conversations with his father, he had been accused of opposition to the King. He must be careful what he said. His father had then told him to be "more careful in his choice of acquaintances."

This had been so absurd. It was certainly the King who needed to be more careful about the company he kept. But he couldn't talk back to his father and King in that way.

"Money is very useful," Bismarck went on. "Especially when it is in the right hands."

Fritz flinched. It was torture to hear such things said and be unable to retort! The money was supposed to be used for the military reform, and as such, all well and good. But the means of obtaining it – and what it would really be used for, were an entirely different matter.

* * *

"Maroussy is engaged," Fritz said as Vicky joined him in the carriage for a drive. She was holding a letter.

"I was just going to tell you that," she said.

"I heard from Mary; here is her telegram," Fritz said, handing Vicky the message. Maroussy was the daughter of Fritz's cousin, Marie Nikolaevna.

"I am pleased at the news. I hoped she would marry some time. I know she was disappointed." Maroussy was also the first love of Alice's husband. "William of Baden is a pleasant fellow. And she will be a sister-in-law to Vivi, Marie Leiningen and Uncle Ernst – so your sister, my cousin and my uncle will be siblings," Vicky laughed. She glanced up at Fritz, and her eyes grew very wide. "Look out!" she screamed.

Smash! The cold wind blew through Fritz's hair as he leaned down, trying to shelter Vicky as the window of the carriage shattered over her. The lantern had also gone out.

"Oh, my finger!" Vicky cried, trying to staunch a stream of blood from her hand. Several people were running towards them.

"Is anyone hurt?" A man looked in. "I am so sorry," he said, holding up a cloth and bandaging Vicky's finger as he spoke. He was a farmer, his lanterns had gone out, and he had not made out their carriage until it was too late. His wagon full of hay stood on the road, the horses stamping.

"I must get back, my horses must not stand in the snow. Here is something," he said, slipping a coin into Vicky's muff. "It is all I can spare." He hurried away.

"He doesn't realize who he is speaking to," Vicky laughed, and tried to take Fritz's hand. "Oh, we must get out of this glass. I think there is something in my finger." They stood up carefully, shaking their arms to remove the glass. "I'm glad we hadn't gone very far;

it is too cold to walk any distance."

They were soon inside the palace again, and people were sent to take care of the carriage. Vicky's hand was in more pain, but they hurried to change before having it seen to, in case there were any more glass splinters on their clothing.

"Yes, here it is, it is quite large," Wegner said, removing the glass from her finger with tweezers.

"Ah! It feels as if you pulled my whole finger off," she cried.

Neues Palais, Potsdam, January 25, 1863

"Hold still, Ditta," Vicky encouraged. The photographs were finally taken. Willy ran to her.

"Was I good and still, Mama?"

"Yes, Willy, you were a very good boy."

"Ditta *not* still!" Charlotte cried, lying down on the floor and flailing her arms and legs. Vicky watched her hesitantly, but she rolled over and got up again. Vicky breathed a sigh of relief. She hadn't been sure if Charlotte was simply rebelling or if she was going to throw one of her tantrums.

It was Vicky and Fritz's fifth anniversary, but there had been an early ball, and then he was absent on inspection duty, and would not be back until night. Vicky had the children photographed for Grandmama. Both the children were dressed in sailor suits, Charlotte wearing Willy's clothes which he had worn at Osborne in '61. A few pictures had already been taken this way a few days before.

The New Year had seemed to be beginning peacefully, but Vicky felt an undercurrent of unrest. Fritz was unsettled every time he came back from the councils. Now, the old storm clouds of parliamentary trouble seemed to be rolling up again.

"Bismarck is interpreting the Constitution again," Fritz had said the previous night, before he fell asleep. He had been too tired to talk much lately.

"Mama?" Willy pulled at her dress as Mrs. Hobbs came in and took Charlotte. "Mama?"

"Yes, Willy?" Vicky knelt down, and put her hands on her little son's shoulders. She shouldn't be so absent minded while spending time with the children, especially when she had already been away for so long.

"You did say Uncle Arthur and Uncle Leo will wear their kilts at the wedding?"

"Yes. My brothers all wore the Scottish dress at my wedding."

"I wish I had been there. Why wasn't I?"

Vicky held back a burst of laughter. "Willy, you weren't born until a year after my wedding." She would leave further explanations for when he was older.

"Grandmama will let me come to Uncle's wedding?"

"Yes, Willy, you are certainly to be at the wedding." Vicky smiled to herself. She was so happy to bring Willy with her; it would be a great memory for his whole life.

Vicky sat on the bed, waiting for Fritz. He finally stumbled in, and collapsed on the bed.

"Fritz? Are you well?" Vicky asked. Many of the family had been ill that winter, though neither she nor Fritz had been confined to bed.

"*Ich bin so müde[17],*" he murmured. Then he sat up, went to his desk, and took something out of the locked drawer. He smiled up at her as he lay back down. He held a little statuette of Papa.

"It is so like!" she cried, taking it carefully. "It is wonderful." She took something from her drawer, fanning out a few photographs. "I had these taken for Mama."

It was the children. Fritz smiled. "Your brothers were never uncomfortable in their kilts, and I see you are insistent that our children won't be either," he said, looking at the one of Willy in Scottish dress.

He turned to the next card, and Vicky was surprised to see him frown. "I had more of these done today," she said, "isn't Ditta sweet? She is finally big enough to wear Willy's old shorts."

"I am glad to hear you praise her, but I do not like Charlotte to be in boy's clothes. It looks silly, to have him in a kilt, and her in trousers."

"But they were not so, they both wore their sailor suits in these."

"I do not like her to be in boy's clothes," Fritz said, laying the pictures down and turning his face away. "*Gute Nacht.*" He yawned enormously.

"They were only done for fun. I thought she looked so nice."

Fritz was already snoring. Vicky sighed. He had been rather short tempered, even with her, if anything upset him in any way. She didn't mind it. She knew he was worried and exhausted. "*Mein armer Schatz[18],*" she murmured, leaning over him and kissing his brow, before she snuggled down beside him.

---

17 "I am so tired,"
18 My poor darling

Neues Palais, two o'clock in the morning, February 13, 1863.

"Oh, are we really going to lose him?" Vicky's voice sounded tight and strained. She was obviously holding back her tears.

Fritz sat beside her, holding her hands. He shook his head, but he could not bring himself to say, "*Nein*[19]." It might not be true. Their poor baby lay in Mrs. Hobbs' lap, burning hot to the touch, breathing rapidly and shallowly; his lips were blue.

"Is the child any better?" Fritz felt a hand on his shoulder and heard his mother's voice.

"I – I don't know," Vicky sobbed. "I have had him so little – we were away for so long, and he was only two months old when we left, and now these balls and parties – it drives me frantic!" She looked at Fritz. He gazed back, trying to smile, but tears finally came to his eyes.

Baby had become terribly feverish yesterday. Wegner had given him an emetic, which Charlotte had also taken, she, too, having been ill. She had recovered rapidly, while Henry rapidly grew worse. He was terribly exhausted by the emetic, and his breathing and temperature worsened.

Then came the summons to the ball. The King would not hear of their not attending. Fritz's heart ached as he walked through the rooms and tried to smile a greeting to people. He saw the agony in Vicky's eyes.

Finally, they had come back, but only to find Baby in this state.

Fritz gazed at the child, but suddenly seemed to see a great black hand snatch him away. He shook himself, realizing he had dozed off for a moment. The child's breathing was stranger than ever. He gasped and sobbed rapidly, then, nothing for a stretch. Vicky fell into Fritz's arms, sobbing.

"I didn't know how much I loved him," she wailed. "I have had him so little. Oh, my baby, my baby!"

Fritz held her, speechless with pain. He could not comfort her

____

19 No

with words which might prove untrue. He felt her relax in his arms. She had fainted. He closed his eyes for a moment. They were both exhausted, having been up most of the previous night as well.

The door opened and Onkel Karl thrust his head in. Fritz watched, but he could not move. Onkel Karl picked up the baby and left the room.

"*Nein!* Come back here!" he cried, starting up. Henry still lay in Mrs. Hobbs' lap. It had been another dream.

"Vicky," he said, shaking her gently. "Vicky, Baby is breathing better."

Vicky woke, turning to look. She stood, taking Henry in her arms. He certainly did seem better.

"The fever's broke, I believe, yer 'Ighness," Mrs. Hobbs said. "Durin' that liddle doze. 'e is much better."

"Oh, thank God," Vicky murmured, pressing her lips to the baby's forehead.

Fritz tapped his mother's shoulder. She, too, had dozed off.

"What? Where? Oh."

"He is better. The fever has broken," Fritz said.

His mother nodded, lying down on the sofa. Vicky turned to the door to a little bedroom, next to where Wilhelm and Charlotte slept. "Let us spend the night here," she said to Fritz. "I don't wish to be far away if anything should happen. We will have to leave him again soon enough."

Windsor Castle, February, 1863

"Baby is much better. He took a definite turn for the better the next day," Vicky told Mama. "I couldn't have left him if it hadn't been so."

Mama smiled sadly. "He must not be taken from you; he is the comfort God sent you after Papa was taken," she said.

Vicky smiled, and took a letter out of her pocket. "Fritz writes that there are stories that the Kreuzzeitung people are trying to get him displaced, and attempting to make Fritz Karl the heir, or Prince Charles regent, if the King is ill. It is silly. Fritz is the Crown Prince. They can't change that! And there is such loyalty! When that was said at the military dinner, an old blind veteran jumped up and cried, 'We are here to prevent this!' Isn't it splendid?"

Mama sighed. "I wish I knew how to advise you as Papa did," she said. "Willy, come and kiss Grandmama." Vicky glanced around. A nurse was at the door with Willy. He ran to the bed, struggling to climb up. Vicky lifted him up.

"Grandmama, you won't send me back if I'm noisy, will you?"

"No, Willy, you are to be at Uncle Bertie's wedding."

"I hoped so. But they said they'd send me back if I was noisy."

Vicky laughed. "You were afraid you would have to go back at every station! I wouldn't send you back, Willy. I want you with me while Papa isn't here."

Fritz would arrive in a few days. The wedding guests were already arriving. In spite of the fact that the Royal family were still in mourning, it would be a grand wedding.

CHAPTER NINE

WARRIORS, DUCKS AND PICKLES

Windsor, March 10, 1863

Vicky stood watching the wedding guests gather. The drawing-room she had hosted in Mama's stead had gone very well. She had felt rather strange with Mama's pages and ladies waiting on her, as if she were the Queen. But nothing had gone amiss, and her nervousness had soon faded.

There was Fritz Hessen. He looked so handsome, and so much like his brother-in-law – who was also his cousin - except for the depressed expression, whereas Prince Christian always had a kind, jolly look about him.

"Vicky," came a voice from behind. "We haven't seen each other in *such* a long time, this is *such* a pleasure."

It was Anna.

Anna had addressed Vicky, but she was looking at Fritz. She looked at him sideways with her eyes half closed, her fan half covering her face. He nodded and turned away.

Vicky nodded, smiled, and held out her hand, not looking Anna in the eye. "It is very nice to see you," she said, and took Fritz's arm again.

"Fritz." Anna had stepped in front of them again, and locked her eyes on Fritz's. Vicky could see the intense gaze. She recognized it all too well, and knew how hard it was to tear one's eyes away from that sort of gaze. Fritz stood still. Anna stepped closer, and Vicky was about to pull Fritz away or step between them when he tore his gaze away and nodded.

"*Guten Tag[20]*, Anna," he said, and strode quickly away.

"Your Fritz is much handsomer than mine," Anna murmured in Vicky's ear as she turned and flounced out of the room.

Vicky stared after her, then looked up as Fritz took her arm again, the last words Anna had spoken repeating themselves in her head. *"Your Fritz is much handsomer than mine."* It was so odd that Anna should say that, just as Vicky had been thinking how handsome Fritz Hessen was – but it was in the same way she thought Prince Christian was handsome. They resembled Papa. She didn't admire them in the way she did Fritz. She thought of what Mama had told her shortly after her marriage. Aunt Cambridge had suggested that Fritz Hessen would make her a good husband. Vicky shivered, thinking what marriage would have been like with a dull, depressed husband who never seemed to wake up except to make strange remarks or to cry unexpectedly during formal events.

Fritz looked in the glass again. He felt himself blush, and blushed even more because he saw it. It was not like him to stand staring at himself in the glass. But this outfit felt so ridiculous. He told himself again that it was an honor, but he wished he didn't have to wear the jewels on his shoes.

He wore the robes of the Order of the Garter, England's highest honor; in a way, it was their equivalent to the Black Eagle. But he had to wear skin tight trousers and absurdly feminine looking shoes, with jewels on the buckle, as well as the jeweled garter round the knee. He glanced at himself in the mirror again and turned away. *This is an honor; I should not be complaining about*

---

20 Good day

it. His mind went back to the first time he had worn these robes, when he was invested with the Order at the time of his and Vicky's marriage. But he had worn his own uniform then, with the robe, garter and star. He didn't feel so ridiculous then, but still, there had been a moment of confusion when he and the other knights had to back away from the Queen's presence. He had nearly tripped on his robe, and he had heard Bertie laugh, or rather giggle.

He left the room without another glance at the mirror. He opened the door and found Bertie waiting outside, looking at him, a slight smile crossing his face. "I'm sorry I laughed at your investiture," he said, holding out his hand.

Fritz nodded. "Is everything ready?"

Bertie nodded. He wore his uniform with the robes and star of the Garter. He was ready to meet his bride.

In St George's Chapel, the procession had begun. Fritz took his place next to Onkel Ernst, standing on each side of Bertie. As they entered the choir, Fritz felt his throat tighten. Less than a year and a half ago, he had entered this room, in procession, walking with Bertie and Uncle Ernst. They had then been the chief mourners at Prince Albert's funeral. The sense of loss swept over Fritz overwhelmingly. Prince Albert had only lived to see Vicky married, of all his children. His grandchildren would never know him. He could not give Fritz the precious advice he felt he needed so badly.

Fritz raised his head, fighting back tears. The Queen stood in the gallery above, looking down on the ceremony. Fritz managed a little smile as she nodded.

He looked about as Bertie took his place at the altar. Vicky looked lovely. Wilhelm still held her hand, but Arthur and Leopold stood nearby. It had been arranged that they should look after him during the long ceremony, so that Vicky could stand with her sisters. Little Beatrice stood between Lenchen and Louise, looking sweet in her pink dress with her mass of golden red curls. Many knights of the Garter stood together, their robes making a splendid effect.

There was a blast of trumpets and the organ swelled. Fritz turned. The bride's procession had begun.

Alix held her father's arm as she walked down the aisle, her dress and veil a cloud of white. She did look very pretty, Fritz admitted.

At the same moment that Alix reached the altar, Vicky, Alice, and all the *Geschwichter* burst into tears. Fritz blinked back tears himself, glancing at Bertie.

The Archbishop stepped forward, and the ceremony began. As the words were pronounced, Fritz's thoughts went back to his own wedding. He saw Vicky in her wedding dress, her calm, gentle, softly smiling manner, the look in her eyes as she glanced up at him as she said, "I will".

The Archbishop was speaking the words, "keep thee only unto her, as long as you both shall live." Fritz looked at Bertie and Alix. Bertie bowed, saying nothing. When Alix's turn came, she blushed more deeply than Fritz imagined possible, and murmured something he couldn't understand.

The Archbishop was satisfied, and went on with the ceremony. Prince Christian gave his daughter away, and Bertie and Alix were surrounded by the *Geschwichter.* Princess Christian kissed her daughter, looking close to tears herself. Vicky and Alice threw their arms around Bertie at the same time, and they all turned to look up at the Queen. She smiled, though she had obviously been crying, and Alix blew a kiss to her, which she returned.

"May I kiss the bride?" Fritz said quietly, stepping up to Bertie and Alix.

"I wouldn't let any other Prussian do so," Alix said, smiling up at him as he kissed her cheek, "besides Vicky and your little darlings, of course. I love you all already," she said, kissing Vicky's cheek as she came up.

There were several more kisses and embraces, and then Bertie and Alix went to change their clothes for the dinner. They were to leave for Osborne afterwards.

"Was Willy a good boy?" Vicky asked Arthur when the family were alone together.

"No! He bit me," Arthur said.

"He didn't bite Leopold, did he?" Vicky asked anxiously.

"No, he understands your warning and was good with him, but he pried out and threw the pommel stone of his dirk, and when I told him to be quiet he bit me."

"He is as fierce a little warrior as Mama used to call you," Vicky smiled at Arthur.

Fritz sat on a sofa in the middle of an empty drawing room, reading through some of the papers his father had sent. He yawned, leaning back and closing his eyes. It was good to be away from the bustle finally. He should go to bed. He was quite tired, and Vicky would be expecting him.

He felt gentle arms go around him from behind, a kiss on his cheek, her hands lingering on his chest. He turned his head to meet and return her kiss, and sighed. He yawned and stretched, putting his hand up to touch her cheek or take her hand.

"Fritz," she whispered. She had come round in front of the sofa, and sat down softly by his side, leaning her head on his shoulder. "Fritz," she repeated aloud.

Fritz froze at the sound. He had turned his head to meet her kiss again when she spoke.

She – was not Vicky.

He started, trying to rise, but Anna's foot and dress were in front of his own feet, and she held his hand fast, so he fell back on the sofa again. She leaned over him, pressing herself against him, pressing her lips to his.

"Anna!" He pushed her away and started up, turning suddenly at a sound at the door. Wilhelm, Beatrice and Thyra stood there, Wilhelm and Beatrice staring at him with wide eyes.

Fritz felt sick. "Where is Vicky? Where Is Mama?" he said, kneeling down to be on a level with the little ones. He looked back. Anna was gone.

"Mama asked where Papa was," Wilhelm said.

Beatrice still stared at him, not speaking.

"Why did Papa kiss Aunt Anna?" Wilhelm asked.

Fritz felt himself blush. How to explain such things to little children? And yet, it was so important for Wilhelm to understand how things were, and at as early an age as possible. But he must discuss it with Vicky. He would let her decide what to tell Wilhelm.

Vicky, he thought. That was what he had been trying to identify about Anna the first few times he saw her here. She was dressing as Vicky did, even her expression seemed more like Vicky than like herself. At first he had thought it a relief that she was dressing more modestly than she normally did.

He shook his head. How had he allowed himself to think it was Vicky? But why would he not have thought so? He wouldn't expect any other woman to come up and begin caressing him. He hadn't even thought of Anna.

He covered his eyes. How much had the little ones seen of what had happened? He took Wilhelm and Beatrice's hands, and looked at Thyra. "Where do you sleep?" he asked.

"I am with Beatrice," she said, following them through the corridor.

"*Sie ist mit* Aunt Baby," Wilhelm said, twisting around to make a face at Beatrice.

"Wilhelm, be respectful to your Aunt," Fritz said, pulling his hand up a little so that Wilhelm had to stand straight. On Wilhelm's previous visit to England, Beatrice had wished him to call her Aunt, but he had refused. He had been only two and a half, and she four, and Fritz hadn't thought anything of it. But now he called her "Aunt Baby", and in a very snide way. Such an attitude must not be encouraged.

"Why did you kiss her like you do Mama?" Wilhelm said as they left the long corridor.

"I thought it was Mama; I had my eyes closed." Fritz thought it best that he should give Wilhelm the exact truth, and that he be present when he told Vicky. He did not want him to have any strange ideas, such as he knew could easily grow in a small child's head, about him keeping such secrets from her.

"I saw Uncle Arthur kiss you," Wilhelm said, looking at Thyra.

She glared at him, blushing bright red. "You said you wouldn't tell anyone!"

"But I didn't tell anyone; you already know, and I was only saying it to you!"

"But your Papa–" Thyra broke off as they reached the room she and Beatrice were sharing.

Fritz smiled at the little girls as they went into the room with their arms around each other. Beatrice usually slept in the Queen's room, and getting to sleep in a different room, and having another little girl – little Princess – close to her own age as a companion was a treat for her.

Fritz went on, finally reaching the suite he and Vicky shared. He led Wilhelm in, closed the door, and knelt down, looking Wilhelm in the eye.

"Wilhelm," he began, "please be respectful of ladies. Speak kindly to your Aunt, no matter how little your age difference, and do not tell secrets you promised someone you would not tell."

Wilhelm nodded. "*Ja,* Papa," he said, hanging his head.

Fritz lifted his chin so he looked him in the eye again. "What did you see happen with Aunt Anna when you came to find me? Tell me exactly what you saw."

"I – I saw her sit next to you, and you kissed her and you tried to get up and tripped and she kissed you," Wilhelm said in a rush.

Fritz nodded. "My eyes were closed until that moment when I tried to rise. I thought it was Mama. Did Auntie and Thyra see what you saw, or more or less?"

"They saw – the same," Wilhelm said slowly..

"Willy, here you are." Vicky entered the room and picked Wilhelm up. She looked at Fritz, her face full of laughter, but her expression changed as she saw Fritz's serious look.

"What is it, Fritz?" Concern sounded in her voice.

"Anna," Fritz said, looking her in the eye. "And Wilhelm, Beatrice and Thyra saw it."

"Saw what?"

"Aunt Anna kissed Papa, and he kissed her," Wilhelm said.

Vicky shook her head.

"I thought it was you," Fritz said, feeling his face flush. "I was sitting on the sofa in the middle of the room, reading the papers Papa had sent. I was tired. I felt you put your arms around me, as I thought. I never thought of Anna."

"So, you can't tell that it isn't me," Vicky glanced at him with a mischievous smile. "You know I am only joking, Fritz," she said, taking his hand. "Of course you thought it was me. Who else would it be?"

"She sat beside me and leaned her head on my shoulder as you often do when we are talking. I did not realize it was her until she spoke aloud." He sighed uneasily, glancing at Wilhelm. "If only the children had not –"

"Papa didn't mean to kiss Aunt Anna?" Wilhelm looked up at Fritz as Vicky set him down and embraced Fritz.

"Of course not. I never kiss any – hmm." Fritz looked at Vicky, and they both laughed. He had been about to say "I never kiss anyone except Mama," but how would a child understand that? But Wilhelm had specifically asked why he had kissed Anna "like you do Mama". "I never kiss anyone else as I do Mama on purpose." He rose and kissed Vicky as he finished speaking.

"Do you understand?" Vicky took Wilhelm again and sat down, looking him in the eye. Wilhelm nodded. "And you won't talk about it to anyone? It was only a little mistake." Wilhelm nodded. "Is Willy ready to go bye-bye?"

He nodded again, throwing his arm around Vicky and kissing her cheek. "I never kiss anyone like I do you, Mama!" Vicky laughed, and kissed him, and stood again, leading him to the door. A nurse waited outside.

"*Gute Nacht, Wilhelm,*" Fritz said, crouching down to kiss the boy's head. He turned to Vicky as he closed the door. "There is something else I need to tell you," he said. He looked at Vicky seriously. "I think it is time that you should know it."

"Time that I should know what?" Vicky crossed the room towards the bedroom door.

Fritz followed her. "Don't go," he said.

"I really am tired," Vicky yawned. "Can't we talk in bed as we often do?"

"I shall leave my lamp lit. I wish you to see my face. I do not wish to hide when I tell you this."

"Oh, is it so serious?" Vicky asked. "Is there bad news from your father?"

"No, it is something about Anna."

Vicky glanced away, then up at Fritz, and took his hand. "Come here, Fritz," she said, and sat down on the bed, pulling his arm around her. "Tell me everything," she said, leaning her head on his shoulder.

"When you were – not well, in February three years ago, before Charlotte was born. I –" He paused, biting his lip, leaning his face on his hand, his elbow on his knee, in the manner he had when he had first told her about Anna, and when he and Papa had first told her about Prince Charles. "Just before I went away for a week, before you began to feel better." He glanced at her, but didn't meet her eye.

"Tell me," she whispered.

"You were with Mama, I believe. I was – in our suite in the Schloss, and Anna came there."

Vicky felt herself blush, and she nodded, not speaking.

He spoke very low now. His face had turned redder than Vicky had ever seen it, but he looked her in the eye. "She said she knew what I was going through, that you were depriving me of my rights, that she was always – available to me," Fritz said, his voice growing stronger again, with a hint of disgust clear in his voice, as he lowered his head to his hand again.

"Why did you never tell me about this?" Vicky whispered, embracing him.

"I did not want you to be any more insecure than you already were then," Fritz said. "I thought of those words you spoke – 'You will have to find another wife,' and –"

"Fritz!"

"I *thought* of them," he went on, "but of course I knew you did not mean it. You were in the first shock when you said that."

"I don't even remember saying it," Vicky said. "I told you that before. What did you do?"

"I told her to go, and when she would not, I did. I waited until I knew she had – I saw her leave – and went to meet you. But that was part of why I went away then. It was not purely military duty. I did not wish to leave you alone, but I did not want to be around her. But I could not tell you then. You were insecure enough, without my telling you another woman was trying to seduce me." He met her eye again. "But how did she know – about – that we were – waiting – after Wilhelm's birth? She said something which made it clear she knew *that*, not only the time after – my birthday."

Vicky sighed. "I told – him – that we were waiting – when I was still trying to escape. He said – I had to tell him – what we would be doing that night – and I said – that I was still recovering from the birth – and that you wouldn't be so disrespectful." Vicky shuddered. Her voice had come out shaky and broken as she spoke. "Yes, it is his very words, that I was 'depriving you of your rights' – one of the things he said – when he was trying to play with – my mind and make me think *I* was doing wrong."

Fritz squeezed her hand. "Don't speak of it any more. I – I do not want you to upset yourself," he said gently.

Vicky nodded. "I can speak of it without crying," she whispered, hiding her face against his chest.

Vicky watched Willy running about with Beatrice. Mama called him.

"Grandmama, you're a duck," he said, as she gave him a biscuit. Vicky laughed. All of her family called him that, but it wasn't quite right for him to call the Queen a duck. He was such a little pickle, always getting into mischief.

Osborne, March 13, 1863

"Goodbye!" Vicky called tearfully, waving her hand to Bertie and Alix. They had already said goodbye to Mama and everyone else. She hurried down to the cabin, bursting into tears as she closed the door.

"We go back into the cage now," Fritz said with a frown as he opened the door. At the sound of Vicky's sobs, he hurried to her, taking her in his arms.

"Leaving – is always – so hard," she sobbed.

"I don't want to go back to nasty, dirty Berlin!" Willy cried, catching Fritz's hand as he struggled to climb onto the sofa.

Fritz shook his head. "We must not teach the children to hate their own country," Fritz whispered to Vicky. "Your Mama told me he said such things repeatedly to her. This cannot be."

"But Berlin is dirty," Vicky sobbed. "You know how nasty my dresses get when we go out walking. Even more so than in London."

"Yes, but it is not good for the children to think of that. I never minded it when I was small, though I remember Mama was always in a fuss when I came back from going outside. I rather liked it." He laughed. "Wilhelm, are you not glad to go home?"

"Can't I stay with Grandmama?" Willy asked. "She wanted to keep me longer."

"But Prussia is your home. You must love your own home," Vicky said gently. "I love mine," she whispered to Fritz. "Both of them. But I must say, with you away, there is so little for me in Berlin."

CHAPTER TEN

UGLY MONKEY!

March 15, 1863

"Out of my way, ugly monkey!" Willy cried in German, his little face reddening as he glared upwards.

A woman stood over him, her face equally red with anger.

"Aunt Adina, I must apologize," Fritz said, taking Willy's hand and pulling him away. "Our boy has been very ill-mannered." He picked Willy up and walked back across the room to where Vicky was sitting.

They were in the waiting room at the station in Hamm, on the way home. The Grand Duchess of Mecklenburg-Schwerin had happened to arrive at the same time.

"She thinks she owns the place, doesn't she?" Vicky whispered to Fritz.

"She comes through here much more often than we do. I would say she has more right to the comforts of this room than we have."

"But we came here an hour ago and she just arrived!"

"All the more reason we should let her have it. We have already enjoyed it so long."

Vicky looked up at Fritz. His face was serious. He rose, still holding Willy, and went up to his aunt. "Aunt, please, receive my apologies. You may have this room, if you wish. We can wait outside. Wilhelm, you should apologize too."

Willy scrunched his face unpleasantly, but Fritz held him so he couldn't look away. "*Eschudigun*," he said quickly, and squirmed so he hid his face against Fritz's shoulder.

Vicky laughed. It always sounded more like Willy said "I shoot a gun" than "*Entschuldigung*", the German word for "excuse me." People who didn't understand English didn't know what was so funny.

The Grand Duchess looked up at Fritz. Vicky thought she looked as if she was looking down her nose at him, although she literally had to look up.

"Hm," she sniffed. "I don't think I want this room, after *she's* been here, with her little insulting brat." She glared at Vicky, turning away. A moment later, Vicky saw her sitting on the partially covered porch, her umbrella dripping onto her elaborately embroidered black dress.

"Come, Vicky," Fritz said, picking Willy up again and going to the door. Vicky followed.

"Where are you going?"

"Out there. I want her to see I meant what I said." Vicky took his arm as they went out to sit in the rain.

The Grand Duchess glanced at them, but didn't move. Fritz nodded pleasantly, and sat down, setting Willy down so he stood between his knees. He held his feet up so Willy couldn't run away.

"Vicky," Fritz whispered, "I do not wish to train the children to be impolite to the relations."

"I know, Fritz, but she is so –" She sighed. She nodded, leaning her head on Fritz's shoulder. "I agree. But I never would have thought Willy would have repeated that!"

Shortly after Vicky and Fritz's return to Berlin from the Mediterranean, they had been at one of the family dinners at the Schloss. Willy had sat on the little children's sofa, as he usually did. Vicky had gone with Hedwig, her lady-in-waiting, to the far end of the room to look at some pictures on the wall. As she turned back, Willy had slipped off the sofa and begun to run towards her, never wanting to be far away from her since her return.

At the same moment, Fritz Karl entered the room, not having been at the dinner. He wasn't looking where he was going. Willy ran across his path, causing him to stumble and fall.

"*Aus meinem Weg*, you ugly little monkey!" he had cried as Vicky hurried to take Willy, who, thankfully, was uninjured.

Berlin Schloss, March 18, 1863

"Wilhelm, I'm glad to see you," Vicky said, shaking hands with William of Baden, a brother of Uncle Ernst's wife, Alexandrina and of Vivi's husband, Fritz. "Marie?" she said, turning to his wife.

"Please, call me Maroussy," she said, returning Vicky's smile.

Vicky studied her, and was about to speak, when someone touched her shoulder.

"Vicky." She looked up. It was her father-in-law. "I am glad to see you again," he said, bending to kiss her cheek. Vicky hadn't gone with Fritz when he went to see his parents on their return. He had told her that his father had been in a bad mood, so she had been glad she had not gone.

"I hope you are well, and that things are going well?" she smiled up at him, taking his arm.

He sighed deeply, shaking his head. "Things are not going well, and we shall probably have a revolution. I hardly know what to say about it." He shook his head again. Vicky thought of asking more questions, but she knew from Fritz that the King would probably only grow irritable. He was hardly telling Fritz any of the political news either.

"Your sister is happy?" Vicky curtseyed to the King, who

nodded and smiled, and she turned to see who had spoken.

It was Maroussy.

"Why, yes, Alice is very —" Vicky trailed off hesitantly. She knew Maroussy had been privately engaged to Louis, but the marriage had not been approved by the Grand Duke.

"I wish to know," Maroussy said, taking Vicky's arm. "Don't — you don't have to be uncomfortable for my sake. Is he happy? Of course he never writes to me now, so I don't know."

"Yes." Vicky didn't know what else to say.

Maroussy smiled. "I am glad," she said, blushing and looking down. "I hoped he would be, even if it couldn't be with me."

March 20, 1863

Fritz stepped out of his carriage, looking up at the Marmor Palais. It was a fine place on the river, with beautiful marble floors and columns.

He turned back to get the two large bundles. Carefully carrying these, he went to the door.

He was led in to the first dining room, where there was a table spread with presents, including several portraits, a glittering sword with turquoises in its hilt, and a not very identifiable purple knitted flower, which Fritz guessed was supposed to be a thistle.

He set down his presents, a candelabra made from deer antlers, and a saddle cloth. "Fritz?" he called. The footman had led him to that room when he asked for the Prince, but no one seemed to be in the room. He glanced at the glass door which led back into the courtyard. No one had been in the courtyard when he drove up.

He heard a door slam, and hurried footsteps.

"What are *you* doing here, Fritzch?" Fritz Karl stumbled over the doorstop as he closed the door. His face was red, his eyes bloodshot.

Fritz motioned to the things he had set on the table. "It is your birthday," he said, meeting Fritz Karl's eye for a moment. "I wish you well." He held out his hand.

Fritz Karl looked at the table, and Fritz saw a brief smile flit over his face, then he frowned again.

"Vicky made and embroidered the saddle cloth," Fritz said, "and the antlers are from Balmoral". Fritz Karl continued to frown, but nodded very briefly, and left the room, without shaking Fritz's hand.

Berlin Schloss, March 22, 1863

"Onkel Karl and Aunt Marie gave a dinner; Anna and Lolo were both there, and Marianne and the girls too." Fritz held Vicky's hand as they sat next to each other on the sofa. The dinner in honor of the King's birthday was over. Papa's speech had not been a bad one, though there was much praise of Bismarck.

"What did Fritz Karl think of your gifts? Did he say anything at the dinner?"

"No," Fritz said. "He wasn't even there. I drove past the Marmor Palais again, and saw him out walking alone, and then the carriages driving up – his usual company, the Duke of Brunswick, Wilmeck, Roon, etc."

"Wilmeck? Who is that?" Vicky laughed.

"Wilhelm Mecklenberg. That is what Fritz Karl calls him."

Vicky glanced up as someone came towards them. "Fritz Karl," she called, and rose, smiling and holding her hand out. He stopped, looking back and forth between her and Fritz. He seemed about to come nearer when Vicky said "How did you like your birthday presents?"

He turned away sharply, his face flushing.

Berlin Schloss, March 23, 1863

Vicky yawned, rubbing her eyes and hurrying down the stairs to the big sitting-room where the ladies-in-waiting sometimes gathered when unoccupied. She had thought of stepping outside, as she longed for fresh air, but something seemed to call her to the room. She glanced through the doorway. No one was there. She sighed and turned away, when she heard a groan from the other end of the room.

"What happened?" She hurried forward. Someone lay on the floor next to an overturned armchair, groaning.

"I – I caught my foot on the chair, and my knee aches! Oh, I don't know how to get up."

It was Maroussy.

"I will send for someone." Vicky turned to the door.

"Oh, don't leave me!" Maroussy cried.

"No, I will only step out the door. You know the bells are right there." She rung for one of the ladies to come, hurrying back and kneeling at Maroussy's side.

"Maroussy," she whispered, "did you – were you – being – pursued?" She hardly knew what to ask, but she felt sure she knew what had happened.

Maroussy nodded, her face reddening. She looked away, and then up at Vicky. "You know – what it is, don't you?"

"Yes," Vicky murmured. "I pulled a chair down on myself too, trying to run away. He does this to all the women and girls who come here, except those who are his sisters or his descendents."

"I know. This isn't the first time," Maroussy said. There was no smile on her face. "Back home, it was just as bad when he came. But Großmama never listened to me if I spoke of it. When he was there, he was perfect, her *darling* little brother. After he was gone, – then she was indignant enough."

"Großmama – you mean the Empress Alexandra Feodorovna? My Fritz's aunt Charlotte?"

Maroussy nodded. "I just didn't speak often enough about it, or she wouldn't have invited him so much. But I hardly remember." Her voice trailed off, the look in her eyes changing.

"You mean – you have – you are –" Vicky began.

Maroussy took her hand. "Yes. I know all about him. And you notice I wouldn't give you your fan when you asked me for it? I understand it all, though I did unfortunately take presents from him when I was small."

Vicky nodded, opening her mouth to speak when Maroussy's lady-in-waiting entered, as well as two of the pages. They stopped at the door, seeming to take in the scene at once, and leaving again to return in a few minutes with a sort of stretcher. Maroussy was carried to her suite, and laid on the sofa.

"Maroussy," Vicky whispered, as the others left the room. "These are beautiful! I've never seen any so splendid!" She picked up a ruby necklace. Nearby sat a large ruby tiara, and a bracelet with the biggest ruby Vicky had ever seen.

Maroussy smiled. "You saw Großmama's, didn't you? When she was here?"

Vicky nodded. "Yes, but the ones I saw were so poorly cut. None of her jewels impressed me. These are beautiful."

✷ ✷ ✷

Kronprinz Palais, Berlin, March 24, 1863

"Another here – now that is quite like!" Vicky told Professor Hagen. "Mama will be quite pleased with it, I hope." She gazed at their work. "Dear Papa," she whispered, smiling as the door opened. "Fritz, do you think–"

It was not Fritz, but his mother, who entered the room.

"How are you, Aunt?" Vicky crossed the room and kissed her mother-in-law's hand. "Would you like to see our work? Do you think it like?"

"Why do you call me Aunt? I told you to call me Mama long ago, and you never do." Vicky gazed at her. She always wished to call her Mama, but she never had told her to, and Vicky didn't wish to presume. "What are you doing to make such a mess?"

Vicky looked down at the floor. Sculpting was a rather messy business. "Aunt – Mama, Professor Hagen is helping me with a bust of my dear Papa. Do you think it like? He is no judge, as he never saw Papa, but he has based it from Theed's and Marochetti's busts. The latter is a better work of art but the former so much more like. And he does everything by my guidance."

"And you know so much about sculpting as to be able to guide a sculpter," the Queen said. "You are rather full of yourself. I think you would be better employed in taking lessons, than trying to guide your superiors in the art."

"No." Vicky struggled not to let her indignation show. "I meant I guide him in making it as like Papa as possible, not that I know more about–"

"Never mind what you mean; you only wish to brag about your own talents. You really ought to take more lessons, Vicky, and not in sculpting but in French. You have such a bad English accent, the Ambassador was appalled." She glanced at the bust, and at

Professor Hagen, who Vicky knew was a good friend of hers. He held out his hand.

The Queen drew herself up and glared at him. "*Guten Tag, mein Herr*[21]." She turned back to Vicky. "Your friends are far too familiar with strangers, particularly at court. Such company is dangerous. You and Fritz both must be more careful in your choice of acquaintanceship." She nodded, briskly cutting off Vicky's attempts at speech. "I must go now, I have so much to do. You really should try to occupy yourself more usefully."

Vicky stared after her, and turned to the Professor. "I am very sorry my Queen and mother-in-law has been so rude to you."

"Never mind, your Highness. I know her well, and all her oddities, too."

Vicky nodded. "I hoped you would not be offended. And you know not to take any notice of it if she is your best friend the next time you see her?"

He nodded again. Vicky heard a door close downstairs, but ignored it, turning back to the bust.

April 4, 1863

Vicky sighed and rolled her eyes. "They are up to it again," she said, handing Fritz a newspaper.

"I wish–" Fritz began, but shook his head. "I was going to say I wish we had left the theater at the same time as Papa, but I really do not wish that. I am glad the audience understood our staying to see the whole play as a statement, because it was one."

"Yes, Fritz, people must see what you intend to do."

---

21 Good day, sir

A few days before, they had gone to the theater to see a play called *The Secret Agent*. There had been tremendous applause, obviously directed towards Vicky and Fritz even more than to the actors, after a scene with the words "the Duchess should dismiss her Ministers so that her husband can appoint younger men, who understand the times, because he promotes the welfare of his country."

Just after this scene, the King had left, but Vicky and Fritz had remained. Vicky had thought Fritz seemed uncomfortable at remaining when his father left, when they were both sitting in the same box, but he hadn't moved.

"But what did you mean?" Fritz asked, glancing over the paper. "What are they up to?"

Vicky pointed to another article further down.

" 'We are very sorry to see that our Princess Royal is among the breakers of the Sabbath. As Queen Victoria's child, she might be expected to know better.' "

It was written as if it was quoting an English paper, although the English papers had praised Vicky's attending the play.

"If only we had chosen a different day, that would not have given them something to grab a hold of," Vicky said. Fritz shook his head.

"They would have thought of something. But enough of this." He put the papers down, put his arm around Vicky and pulled her towards him. "Have you heard any news from England?"

"Alice is still keeping us waiting," Vicky said. "I can't believe she will be a mother when I see her next. It still seems so strange to think of her being married. Oh, has your Mama spoken to you of wishing to go to England?"

Fritz nodded. "I told her you would write to your mother."

"I have. But Mama said she didn't know how to invite her and not the King. But with how matters are going here, your Papa is not popular there, so that to invite him would be nearly equivalent to an insult." Vicky shrugged. "She will have to go to England on her own, and visit Mama privately, I suppose."

"Alice and Baby are going on very well. I haven't heard from Mama yet, but I hear regularly from Sir Charles Locock and Sir James."

Fritz smiled at Vicky as they spread a plaid from Balmoral on the ground and unpacked bread and fruit. It was a beautiful day, which they had taken advantage of to take a long ride on horseback, stopping in the Grunewald.

"Alice was such a little thing at the exhibition, when I first saw her."

"I still can't really imagine her as a wife, much less a mother." Vicky smiled, looking up as a squirrel dashed by. "The nurse they have for the baby is born on the same day as me, and has a child born the same day as Willy. What an odd coincidence!"

Kronprinz Palais, April 28, 1863

Vicky struggled to hold back her tears as she watched the straps go around Willy's head. An iron bar ran down from the base which held the straps – looking very like a horse's bridle – to a belt round the waist.

"It makes no difference if people see this; the man who made it will speak of it in town."

"But – oh!" Vicky covered his face. To see her little son treated as one deformed tore at her heart.

"He ought to wear this for an hour a day, and see if his head is straighter. We shall then decide whether to operate."

Vicky flinched at the word "operate". Willy's head, shoulders and posture were becoming more and more crooked as he grew; his arm still hung quite limp, though he could use it a little. The doctors had decided to do "a small operation" which would help him be able to hold his head straight, but she had insisted that something else be tried first.

"It can also be used as a support after the operation," Wegner went on.

Vicky nodded. "*Danke*, I understand. You may go now." She waited until Wegner had left the room, and then knelt down on the floor next to Willy.

"Does it hurt you, Willy?" She asked, clasping him to her and kissing him.

"No, Mama," he said. "I'm a horse!" He broke away from her embrace, trying to trot about the room in the way he did when the children played horses, but he couldn't do it with the bar running down his back.

A little horse with a bridle on, which can't move the way it wishes to, but has to be led and directed, Vicky thought sadly. Willy walked so awkwardly with the brace on, but also so awkwardly with it off. It seemed such a shame to torment him, but she must try her best to help him. It would be no kindness to delay the treatments till he was older.

Babelsberg, May 9, 1863

Fritz rose, about to leave the council-room, where he had been sitting with his father, Roon, Bismarck, Onkel Karl, Wrangel, and several others. "I will hold fast to my beliefs," he said somewhat sharply as he went towards the door, pausing next to Wrangel's chair. "None of this can lead to anything good. We must uphold the spirit of the Constitution, and not dig our way through it, searching for every hole we can find." He met his father's gaze very briefly, both looking away at the same moment.

"You will hold to your foolish ideas that will run us into being a Republic!" Wrangel said, shaking his head. He rose and came towards Fritz. "You think your little Crown Princess is an angel, but she is leading you astray. Only yesterday she –"

"How dare you!" Fritz turned sharply, his hand flying out and catching a blow on Wrangel's face. "Oh! I'm so sorry!" He stood frozen, glancing from one face to another. No one said anything.

"It is nothing, I have received far heavier blows," Wrangel said. Fritz breathed a sigh of relief and turned again to the door, closing it before Wrangel or any of the others could begin again. He shook his head. Wrangel had always been friendly to him and to Vicky before this. He had always called her an angel, and been rather absurdly fond of her. But this year, he, too, had joined the other camp.

May 18, 1863

Vicky saw the familiar green-papered walls, the Rafael prints on the wall, and pink vases with white roses on the mantel. Out the window were the wild hills and forest which she knew reminded Papa of home, *his* home, in Coburg. The skirl of bagpipes drifted in the distance. She looked towards the desk. There sat Papa, writing. He looked up with his usual kindly smile, patting the seat beside him.

"*Kommst du, meine Liebling*[22]. You are ready for your lesson, I see. What shall we read today?"

She could almost feel his arm go around her, but she knew it was only a dream. She squeezed her eyes shut, gazing at the picture in her mind's eye, not wishing to leave it.

"Papa, I will try to do as you wish," she whispered.

"Vicky? Are you awake?" It was Fritz's voice which awakened her, and it had been his arm around her. He kissed her cheek as she opened her eyes, stroking her cheek. She realized her face was wet with tears.

"I was dreaming of Papa, and his nice little room at Balmoral. Mama had invited us in her last letter." She rolled over and threw her arms around Fritz. "How I wish we could go there, to our memories," she whispered.

"The beginning of our happiness," he whispered, stroking her cheek. "But I do not think it possible for us to go. Tell Mama so. She shouldn't expect us."

Vicky nodded, snuggling in his arms. "It was so good to feel you were by my side again, Fritz," she whispered. He had been away so much since their return from Bertie's wedding, and he had often left in the evening. This was the first time he spent a whole night at home in a month.

"You cannot imagine what a comfort it is," he said, drawing her into his embrace.

---

22 Come, darling

CHAPTER ELEVEN

TO HURT MY FATHER'S HEART

Neues Palais, Potsdam, June 3, 1863

"Oh, no! It cannot be!" Vicky looked up from her painting as Valerie Hohenthal read to her from the English papers. "It cannot be!" The last words Valerie had read repeated in her mind:

"Prince Carl, the brother of the King, has been appointed *Statthalter*, the King being absent for the sake of his health. The Crown Prince has declined the position."

Valerie gazed at her, but didn't speak. "Valerie, go on." Vicky felt her voice catch in her throat. "No, give me the paper. Let me see it." She leaned forward and snatched the paper, ignoring the colorful stains her fingers left behind.

The papers also said that the Crown Prince was not true to the Liberal party as he had claimed to be, but part of the Kreuzzeitung, hand-in-glove with Bismarck. Vicky felt her blood boil as she read these declarations. Then, a sudden shiver of fear went down her spine.

She rose, hurrying to her dressing-room, where she sank down, covering her face. Could it be true that Fritz had refused the position? Surely not. Surely it was only a ruse, a lie in the papers. If the Regency had really been appointed, Fritz must be unaware. He would never agree to let Prince Charles become Regent. Fritz was Crown Prince, the natural Regent in case of the King's illness.

"Oh, keep him safe!" she prayed aloud. Surely it was true that Fritz had simply been overlooked. But the horror of the other possibility stared her in the face.

There was always a deep fear in the back of her mind, and in Fritz's too, she knew, that one of them would be caught off their guard and drawn into the web of the Kreuzzeitung party.

On May 24, Mama's birthday, Vicky and Fritz had left on a tour on the Elbe river. Before they left, Fritz had written his father that he was not trying to give advice or criticize the Government, but that he would not be party to any unconstitutional act which might be committed.

Before their departure, Fritz Hessen and Anna had paid a visit to Berlin.

Vicky was agreeably surprised when she saw Anna greet Fritz with no sign of flirtation in her manner.

"Fritz, it is so kind of you to come," she had said, and nodded to Vicky. "I'm glad to meet you at last." Her eyes remained on Vicky's face, as if studying her. "Will you come and see my baby?"

Vicky and Fritz had gone to the nursery. Anna's little boy was a strong, vigorous child, but sadly afflicted with blindness – one of the eyes being completely blue with no white, the other all white with just one blue spot.

"My poor baby," Vicky heard Anna croon as she laid her baby back in the cradle. Vicky watched Anna. It was indeed as if she was meeting a different person, just as Anna had said "it was pleasant to meet… at last." She had none of her usual affectation, she was dressed prettily, but neither in a flamboyant manner, nor in the way she had been the last time Fritz had seen her, when her dress had been disturbingly similar to how Vicky herself dressed. Even her facial expression, he had said, had seemed like Vicky on that occasion.

Anna still held the little baby in her arms, and Vicky realized she looked – old. Her face was haggard and drawn. Vicky's heart went out to her.

"So, you have met Anna, the real Anna, now," Fritz had whispered as they left.

Vicky nodded. "She is not happy, I can see that."

Fritz shook his head, his face very serious. "You understand, do you not, about the baby?"

Vicky looked at him, perplexed.

"You know Mama says she knows Anna is not Onkel Karl's child. You remember what I told you when I first told you about him. 'He does have the scruple not to attack his own daughters or granddaughters – or those he believes are such – but if he thinks someone is and finds out they are not.'" Fritz looked away, out the window of the carriage as they drove away.

"You think this baby is his?" Vicky asked. Fritz nodded, not meeting her eye. "Poor Anna. I knew something about her – discomfort – seemed familiar, but I couldn't tell what."

Fritz nodded again, putting his arm around her. "The baby is blind. You know what that means. We were so fortunate not to have that happen."

Berlin, May 30, 1863

"Fritz, we are free of these deputies, who think they know everything. What the next step is to be I do not know."

Fritz stood before his father, unsure of what to say. Parliament had been dissolved, but the King did not seem to think the situation at all serious. He barely mentioned politics, and took Fritz to see some new hats and helmets for the uniforms of different regiments.

The next day, Fritz went to the family dinner at Glienicke. Again, his father said little of politics, seeming in good humor and unconcerned. That evening, Fritz left again on a military inspection tour.

Neues Palais, Potsdam, June 3, 1863

Vicky hurriedly changed into her travelling dress, and hurried out to her carriage. She was leaving at once. She must join Fritz, and be there to support him in whatever came. She felt sure he was ignorant of the Regency, or at least had been. She stepped into the train and sat down, wishing she could be on horseback, to use some of her nervous energy. She knew she wouldn't be able to concentrate her thoughts on reading.

Graudenz, June 3, 1863

Fritz yawned as he looked out the window. The entire regiments he was to review were drawn up in the square outside.

After the review, there was a dinner given by Oberpräsident Eichmann, to receive him and the other authorities of the town. Fritz walked to his place across from the Oberpräsident, nodding and saluting as he passed the others.

Everyone was sitting down when a man appeared in the doorway. He stepped quickly to the Oberpräsident's side, handing him a telegram and other correspondence. There was a hurried, whispered conversation, and the Oberpräsident rose.

"*Es tut mir leid, meine Herren*[23]," he began. "I must excuse myself from your gracious company. *Guten Tag.*"

Fritz gazed after him, as did everyone else, as he followed the other man from the room.

"*Eure Hoheit*[24]? The Oberpräsident wishes to speak to you," a young man – or rather a boy – murmured nervously.

Fritz nodded, rising. "Take me to him."

Fritz followed the boy through the long passages of the mansion, finally coming to a large, ornate door. The boy clicked his heels, and the door opened.

"Ah, *Eure Hoheit*, there is not good news," the Oberpräsident said. "We have received notice that a strict censorship has been proclaimed on the press, on the first. It took two days to get to us. I had not heard of this before."

Fritz met his gaze. "I shall write to my father the King, and to Bismarck," he said gravely.

"I am afraid writing to the King will do little good. You know Prince Karl is Regent."

Fritz stared at the man, hardly able to take in his words. He opened his mouth to speak, but his mind was blank.

Warlubia, June 4, 1863

---

23 Excuse me, gentlemen – literally "It does me sorrow, my Lords,"
24 Your Highness

"Fritz! Are you well? Is everything –" Vicky broke off with the thought, *I cannot ask if everything is going well, when I know it is not!* "Is – are you – did you – decline?" She couldn't put the thought more wholly into words, it was too awful.

Fritz shook his head, taking her in his arms, and guiding her to his carriage. "We should not discuss this in public," he said. She had just gotten off the train, and he had been waiting to meet her. He met her gaze. "Vicky, I am as well as I can be. I have written another letter to Papa, but I did not know –" he paused, looking down, then back up at her again. "I did not know that Onkel Karl is *Statthalter*, Viceroy, Regent, call it what you will."

Vicky sighed deeply, relief flooding over her, feeling sure now that Fritz had not been drawn in to the other camp.

"They are impertinent enough to say that you refused the position, when really you were only absent when he was appointed!" Vicky sighed deeply, leaning her head on his shoulder. "What will this mean for our future?"

"It will probably mean demonstrations, perhaps a revolution."

"And you will protest?"

Fritz turned uneasily away from her. "I only hope Papa understands what I mean, that I am not against him, personally."

Vicky squeezed his hand. "I will be there for you, whatever comes. You said you had written to him again; have you already sent it?"

"No. I have it here. But I have sent my protest to Bismarck." Fritz took the letter out of his pocket.

"I have your Papa's answer to your last letter with me. He sent it to me, to bring to you."

"*Mein lieber Papa,*

"As your son and first subject I must tell you when I disagree with the views of your government. I do not believe that this rescript of the press law follows the spirit of the article of the Constitution; indeed, it really does not follow the letter.

"I shall continue to keep my reserve, doing nothing which is not strictly demanded by my position as heir. Certainly opposition towards <u>you</u> is not in my mind. I will ever strive to retain your love and confidence, but I must speak my mind and warn you when you are treading in dangerous waters."

Danzig, June 5, 1863

Vicky drew the curtain aside to look out at the square. It was as empty as it had been on their arrival the evening before. There was no reception prepared; the station was empty; no flags or decorations hung from the houses.

"There is no one out still," she said, turning back to Fritz, who sat writing to his father.

He nodded shortly. "Did you finish the papers?"

Vicky took her seat again at his side. "Yes, and they are all clamoring for you to come forward and state which side you are on," she murmured, putting her arm around him. "When is Winter's speech?"

"Soon. I must finish this and send it first," Fritz answered. Winter was the *Oberbürgermeister*[25] of Danzig, and a good friend of Fritz's. He had told Fritz that he would speak at the *Rathaus*[26] and wished Fritz to answer him.

---

25 Mayor
26 Town Hall

"Are you going to speak about the Press Law?"

"*Ach*!" Fritz covered his eyes. "How can I – Papa will never understand this!"

"Fritz, you must declare yourself. This will not do! Our people must not believe these things of you!"

Fritz looked at her and then away. "I do not know what to do. I certainly would not have left Berlin now if I had known a Regent was to be appointed. I knew Papa was ill; he was before we went to the Elbe, but I believed it nothing serious, and you know he seemed better before I left. But I cannot publish my letter to Papa. You know I had promised Papa not to speak."

"But your year of silence is over! You said so." Vicky gazed up at him. "You must do something, or everyone will lose faith in you – the people I mean," she added hurriedly, as a look of pain flickered over his face. "But you see the things said in the papers, and you see the letters you receive. Everyone is clamoring for you to come forward, and says either you do not have the courage or you are on the other side!"

Fritz joined Vicky in the carriage after the parade and review of the Grenadier regiment quartered in Danzig. They drove towards the *Rathaus*. Vicky felt his hand tremble, but his face was calm.

"I must apologize to your Highnesses for the meager reception greeting you. But, if your Highnesses will pardon the expression, you can imagine that the Berlin Government and its associates are not much welcomed here after the enforcement of the Press rescript. We have all felt shocked and depressed since the news, which is a feeling I feel certain is shared by most of the nation. Your Highness," Winter paused, bowing to Fritz, "is the most welcome of all of the Princes who could have appeared, and we hope you will live up to our expectations."

Winter paused, bowing again to Fritz and then to Vicky, and stepped towards them. Fritz rose, shaking his pro-offered hand. There was a small amount of applause from the fifty or sixty people present.

Vicky watched, clenching her hands as Fritz stepped onto the dais. He glanced towards her, and she gave him a small smile. He nodded, took an obvious deep breath, looking out at the crowd. She had never seen him so nervous before making a speech. Usually, he was such a calm, poised speaker, whom she wondered at and admired, but felt she could never emulate.

"*Meine Herren*," he began, his voice shaking slightly, "Winter, I thank you for welcoming me and my wife here." He paused, taking another deep breath, his voice growing steadier as he went on. "I, too, was deeply astonished and grieved at the news of the Press rescript. It occurred after my departure from Berlin, as did the appointment of my Royal uncle, Prince Karl, as *Statthalter*. I certainly have had nothing to do with the Press rescript, and would never have left Berlin if I knew a Regency was in question. I have not refused the position; I did not know that these particular actions were in contemplation."

He paused, gazing out at the crowd. There had been moments of applause, but he hadn't paused for them. Vicky sensed that he felt he needed to speak his mind fully, before pausing and possibly losing his nerve.

"This is all the doing of Prince Karl, and of Bismarck!" he called. The crowd hissed, and cheered as he went on, "I will do what I can to uphold the people's rights, and to bring Germany together through *moral* conquests."

Vicky saw that he went on; his mouth moved in speech, but the cheers were deafening this time.

"I deplore this conflict within my country, but I must urge everyone to trust the generous intentions of our King, my Royal father, for he, too, truly intends to foster the right and the good for the country, though he often accepts false advice."

Fritz nodded, shaking Winter's hand again, and returned to his seat at Vicky's side.

Winter returned to the dais, smiling and bowing to them again. "I must thank your Royal Highnesses for gracing our hall with your presence. Three cheers for the Crown Prince!"

The crowd rose, cheering loudly.

"And three for the Crown Princess!"

The cheers were repeated.

"And three for our King!"

The cheers were repeated again, but half-heartedly, with several hisses as well.

"And three for the well-being of our country!"

The crowd rose again, cheering wildly. Vicky heard cries of "*Hoch lebe der Kronprinz!*"[27], "King Friedrich!" and "Down with Bismarck!"

"So the die is cast," Vicky said, squeezing Fritz's hand as the carriage door closed.

"Hmm." Fritz didn't answer, but continued staring out the window.

---

27 Long Live the Crown Prince!

"Fritz, I am proud of you! You have stood up for your people as you should, and let them know what you think of these actions. They will know which side you belong to, and will love you the bet–"

"*Ach!*" Fritz struck his hand against his forehead. "It is this 'taking sides' which torments me so. I know Papa will never understand it!"

Vicky caught his hand again, rubbing his fingers. "Hush," she murmured, "he must understand. I know when he is – 'on the other side' as you say, he will not, but HE truly will, and he too will love you for it."

"But I have never given him a moment's trouble. Now I have taken this line, and nothing will ever be the same! Vicky, how would you feel if your father, your dear Papa, was in my father's place, and you in mine, and you had to disobey him and hurt his heart?"

"But he would never –" Vicky broke off. She had been going to say that Papa would never make her do something like that, but she paused, trying to really put herself into Fritz's position. Tears sprang to her eyes, and she threw her arms around him. "I know how you feel, Fritz. But I am here for you, and will do anything I can for you, in the face of any persecution which may come!"

Danzig, June 7, 1863

"A letter from your Papa," Vicky said, holding up a letter as Fritz took his great coat. She had already been ready for some time.

"You open it. I cannot," Fritz answered, looking at the seal and then handing it back to her. His hands had suddenly begun to shake with nervousness.

Vicky tore the letter open and glanced over it, her face growing very grave. Fritz took it, sitting down to read. It was the rebuke he had expected.

"You said you would never speak out against my Government. You said you intended to offer NO opposition. Your speech has made it to my ears. You must keep yourself aloof from people who encourage such disloyalty, and turn towards the party of the Kreuzzeitung. You must retract every trace of what you have said. The Press law is in accordance with the Constitution, I cannot believe that you and Vicky are so ill-informed as to think it is not. It would have been fully approved by Prince Hohenzollern, and that is the only reason I sanctioned it."

Fritz looked up, meeting Vicky's eye. "We must go," he said, in a choked voice. They were to visit Marienburg, a beautiful old castle which he wished to show Vicky. But his heart would not be in it now, he knew.

Vicky yawned. "It is nearly one o'clock now," she whispered, struggling to keep her eyes open.

Fritz nodded. "I shall send this letter. It is nearly finished now. But you must make the copies. We must send the papers to someone for advice, as we have no secretary."

Ernst Stockmar, Vicky's private secretary, was away. His father, the old Baron, was dying. "It is like losing Papa over again," Vicky had cried when she heard that Stockmar was in such a state. "Where will we ever turn for advice?"

Vicky yawned again, taking the last page Fritz had written and starting on a copy, and another, and another. They were to send the papers to Mama, to Fritz of Baden, and to Prince Hohenzollern. Fritz's mother was in England. Vicky was glad she was not in

Berlin during this time.

"My speech is not the impulse of the moment; it is a long, drawn out answer to the questions which have plagued my mind and my conscience. I must profess before the whole world the truth which I see daily, that your Government has done much harm, and led you to believe that truth is false and falsity truth.

"I know that with these words, I am most likely forfeiting my place in the Army and Ministry. I mean no longer to remain a member of the council, as you will not hear my advice when I dare to speak. Your Ministry has completely ignored me. I cannot take back my words. I beg you to allow me to choose a place of residence withdrawn from politics, as, if I am not allowed to speak my mind, I must wish never to be involved.

"I mean for the Government, and all the more so the <u>Regency</u> to feel itself rebuked, but to <u>you</u>, my dearest father and King, I mean to show no opposition. I am your most loyal subject and son, and shall ever remain so, and it is with the deepest pain that I give you pain. My actions are out of love to you and to our country, and I cannot stand by and watch you make mistakes which will tear my children's inheritance to pieces."

June 7, 1863

"Dearest Mama,

"We are in the most difficult situation imaginable, and Fritz is perfectly miserable at having to directly oppose his father's actions for the first time in his life."

Vicky yawned, laying her pen down for a moment. She was still so tired, as neither she nor Fritz had slept well that night. But she must write to Mama again. She had written twice since Fritz's speech, but new – and dreadful – possibilities continued to appear every moment.

"Mama, I will be very happy to see you, as it is very likely that we must leave the country soon. I am prepared for any catastrophe, and I should not be astonished if Fritz be put under arrest!"

CHAPTER TWELVE

THE OTHER CAMP

Gastein, June 1863

“ “Something must be done with the Crown Princess,” Karl said. “If she were not here he would be obedient to your wishes. She must be –”

“Remember who you are speaking of,” Wilhelm said, glaring at him across the table.

“*Ja, der lieber Engel* must not be harmed,” Wrangel said.

“I was not speaking of harming *the dear angel*,” Karl went on. “I only meant, something must be done to keep her at bay, Helmkin.”

“I have told you again and again not to call me that in front of the Ministers! And I will *not* agree to that. She is my daughter-in-law, and our Crown Princess; don’t forget who you are speaking of.”

“I do *not* forget who I am speaking of; I never could. If Fritzch is in the fortress, what does it matter if she disappears for the time?” Helmkin had been so furious at first over Fritzch’s protest that he had eagerly agreed that he be imprisoned. Wrangel had also agreed. Now, it didn’t look like things would go so smoothly. Helmkin was resisting him again, as he had two years ago, over the attempt to convince Helmkin to legally separate from Augusta. He would leave Bismarck here. The Minister-President’s presence was far more necessary for the King than for the Regent, even if the

King was absent for the sake of his health.

If Fritzch is in the fortress, and she is sent home, the Prussian prerogative can be invoked, and the marriage put an end to, Karl thought. In Germany, each sovereign held the power to pass a law applicable to their family. As the marriage had taken place in England, it would still hold good there, but what did that matter if he was in prison? "And I only mean that she go home, by 'disappearing', *Wimpy.*" Karl continued in a whisper, "I will call you that, since you dislike the other, and you cannot object in the same way. No one here will understand it."

Wilhelm sighed, turning away. "Your Majesty!" he snapped.

"Thank you, I didn't know you were letting me take your place permanently," Karl retorted.

"I was telling you what to call me," Wilhelm hissed between clenched teeth.

"The Crown Prince must not be locked up." Karl turned, surprised. Yes, it was Bismarck who had spoken.

"Bismarck, how can you say such a thing? It must be! He has committed insubordination to his King!"

"The liberals will make a martyr of him, if you imprison him. Think. And none of their people will believe the stories about her. They know it is a fabrication." Bismarck looked into the King's eyes. "Let your Majesty decide nothing in anger. 'Deal gently with the young man, Absalom.' Remember the days of Friedrich Wilhelm the first. Do not bring them back." That King had imprisoned his son, who was regarded as a martyr.

"Thank you, Bismarck," Wilhelm said. "I knew you would not wish imprisonment for my son. I, for myself, have already gotten past my anger."

Karl stared at Bismarck for a moment, and then nodded. "Settle it with him. Let him know what he must do to be kept in touch with the affairs of the Crown, as he wishes." He turned to his brother. "Farewell, *your Majesty.*" He spat the words out. "I must get back to Berlin. One can't stay away too long from the capital when one has charge of the country. One never knows what might happen." He left the room, laughing to himself.

Karl stepped into his carriage, and the door was shut. He vaguely heard the coachman speak to the horses, but he was far away in thought.

If Fritzch was freed, and the marriage had been put an end to in Prussia, what would he do? Would he stay at his post like a true Hohenzollern soldier? Would he attempt to keep the image he obviously treasured so highly as the Liberal Crown Prince, the people's darling?

If he would, he might actually be worth something. If he could stand his ground in this matter, he could be convinced to do so about other things, especially without *her* there to meddle. He would be heartbroken, of course, to be separated from his precious "Frauchen". At least he would be at first. *But what is heartbreak?* Karl thought. The end of love and happiness, that was what heartbreak was. However, love, when it came to an end, turned to hatred very quickly. He knew that all too well.

But all of these musings were probably useless. None of this would happen, Karl suspected. Fritzch was far too weak a character to stand on his own two feet. He had already written that he would, if he was pressed to join the Kreutzzeitungpartei, resign his military and government positions, and retire to the country. He would crawl back to England and tie himself again to his wife's apron-strings.

Of course, that meant Germany would be free of their meddling, but did it really? He shook his head. He couldn't leave them together to plot behind his back from the safety of England, as her father had done for so many years.

Viktoria. It was such a good German name; it was a shame that it should have been turned into an English name by popular association.

Viktoria. He remembered the first sight he had caught of her, running up the stairs outside the Schloss, her manner and voice so free and childlike. He had been curious to see what she was like, this *Lieblingstochter*[28] of Louise's son. So this was the "stupid, useless girl", as he had called her when he first heard of her birth. She was not stupid – she was clever, and she was attractive – far too clever and attractive for her own good – and Fritzch was clearly under her spell. She thought herself intelligent – well, so had her mother-in-law, and what good had that done *her*? Intelligent women never learned their lessons. Helmkin himself had admitted that.

Viktoria. He whispered the word, and saw the V trace itself in the air, then the other letters following. It was the ornate V, as on her dagger, but he saw it in the deep, burnt-ocher orange of anger instead of the brilliant blue of the sapphires on the little knife. At the sight of the color, a flavor like that of a bitter orange flooded his mouth, and he heard the sound of a bird's wings flapping heavily over his head.

Viktoria. He remembered the look of terror in her eyes as he had traced the same shape across her chest with the point of the dagger. He would not harm her with the point of the dagger – he knew *that* would be going too far, but it was good for her to feel that fear.

She had felt the fear intensely enough to give up her charade and tell the truth. Normally, the letters of each word wrote themselves across his vision in broad strokes. When someone was lying, the words became small and thin, the color also fading, as if they were trying to hide themselves from him.

When she spoke and thought of Fritzch – her voice became so unbearably white it had forced him to close his eyes. Was that – love? he wondered. He had never experienced that blinding whiteness in his own voice. He remembered as a child, his feelings for his parents and siblings were a creamy haze. It was the same now for those he was truly fond of.

---

28 Favorite daughter

What overwhelmed him about the whiteness was the contrast with the black cloud which wrapped round him like a cloak. That cloud was a comfort to him. It had been there for so long, he could hardly remember what it was not to have it. It was like a shield, and never left him except when he was desperately ill. He wondered if anyone else could see it. But that bright whiteness could not be obnubilated even by the cloud cloak; it was too obnoxiously pure.

The moments afterwards, when the orange turned to red, and the sweetness of cherries replaced the bitter tang.

At the sight of the actual sapphires, he tasted dull metal, as if he had taken an empty spoon, and heard the sound of loud footsteps, but the sound came from directly above his head, so he always knew it wasn't real.

Viktoria. She and Augusta were the root of all the current trouble. Things would be so easy if they could be gotten rid of in some way.

If anyone could see the cloud cloak, it would be Marianne's youngest girl. She often made remarks which made him believe that she saw, heard, and smelled things similarly to how he did. She definitely saw the colors for feelings, personalities, and so on, even if they were different colors than he saw. Little Louise might be useful someday, as the Crown Prince and Crown Princess were so fond of her. Louischen – why did they have to call her that? Of course, she was called Louise after his mother, but – *Louischen, Louischen.* The name repeated itself tauntingly in his mind.

"He emphasizes that I have no vote in the cabinet, as the former usage given to the heir is now unconstitutional," Fritz said to Vicky, reading from Bismarck's notes on a memorandum his father had sent. "He uses our claims against us, as usual, saying that what I wish is unconstitutional."

Vicky nodded. "What else does he say?"

"He says my freedom to be at the councils or not is not restricted. I may come and keep myself up with everything, or not, as I wish." Fritz rolled his eyes. "He also says I am encouraging a revolution, by giving an example of a disobedient son not being punished, in the highest position.

"He says I have committed a criminal offense in allowing state secrets to be published. I have not allowed it! He also calls me vain in always thinking of 'what the country at large' will think of my conduct. I only wish the people to know where I stand and that I support them!" He turned to look at Vicky before he read the next part.

"He says that if I wish to be regularly informed about government affairs, I must let my place of residence be always known and always within reach, so that I may be more accessible to the ministers. My advisors must be of the government, not the opposition," Fritz went on, glancing at Vicky. "I do not mean it to be opposition to Papa!"

"They only wish to force you to join the other camp," Vicky said. "Go on."

Fritz leaned his head on his hand as he read the next note to himself. "I must tell you nothing, as long as you acknowledge your own family," he muttered, just loud enough for her to hear. She could tell he didn't want to say it.

"That is too much!" Vicky cried, looking at the paper. "The nearest of kin must not be aliens, but allies! There ought not to be a frontier line between Mama and me, or Bertie and me, when he is King!" She paused, reading over the passage again. "Always accessible, and within reach," she muttered, shuddering. "No thank you."

"The messenger told me about part of Papa's conversation with Bismarck. 'Deal gently with the young man, Absalom,' Bismarck said – as if he reads the Bible." Fritz frowned.

"They may not be intent on learning God's laws and obeying them, but they do read the Bible. Bismarck often quotes verses. Prince Charles does too. Indeed, he may as well have quoted the Bible – at the laundry." Vicky shivered, clinging to Fritz's arm. "I offer thee three things; choose thee one and I shall do it unto thee." She shuddered, but laughed briefly. "That is more or less what he said to me."

CHAPTER THIRTEEN

OUT OF THE CAGE

Königsberg, June 11, 1863

"Papa has written again," Fritz told Vicky. "He writes in a kind, fatherly way, as he rarely does, but commands me not to speak again in the way I did."

Vicky took his hand. "There is no need for you to speak again, for some time, at least."

Fritz nodded, picking up more letters. "Mama and Schleinitz defend my stance valiantly. But –"

"What is it?" Vicky asked, clutching his arm. Fritz felt that his face showed his concern.

"Onkel Karl and Manteuffel and others support my being court martialed and imprisoned in a fortress. Even old Wrangel does, who has often been our friend!"

Rastenburg, Lithuania, June 14, 1863

"Look, Fritz," Vicky called back, wincing at the pain in her throat as she pointed instead of speaking further. She and Fritz both were not feeling well with the stress of the situation, and she had a blister on her thumb from writing so much.

But today, they had a welcome distraction from politics. They had crossed the Baltic sea to Memel, seeing a troop of men and women, who escorted their carriage. All the women rode astride. The garments of both men and women were brightly colored and covered with beads and embroidery. They called as they went along – Vicky supposed it was singing, though it seemed like wailing and screaming to her.

The day before, they had taken a walk in the wild forest of Ibenforst, filled with hundreds of unknown wildflowers. Just before them on the road, an enormous herd of two hundred elk crossed, Vicky catching a glimpse of the little ones – which were quite large – in the middle.

They had returned to their carriage through a violent thunderstorm, Vicky sinking nearly to her knees in the marsh, where Fritz had to help her out.

They had also visited places where his grandparents, Friedrich Wilhelm the third and Queen Louise had lived in exile. Königsberg was where the King and his siblings had grown up, not Berlin, and was where his coronation had taken place nearly two years ago.

Potsdam, June 27, 1863

Vicky looked about nervously as her carriage drove across the Glienicke bridge. She wished she could have come a different way, but this was the fastest route into Potsdam. Prince Charles owned the bridge which was the major connection. There were many carriages visible in the distance, heading towards Schloss Glienicke, and many decorations were obvious. Prince Charles's birthday was the 29th, and there was obviously to be a large celebration.

Vicky had returned to Potsdam to gather the children. She and Fritz were not yet to return to Berlin or even Potsdam. Mama and many others had encouraged them to remain away for as long as possible, but Vicky did not wish to leave the children behind any longer than necessary. Also, if it was essential that they leave the country, she did not wish it to be possible for the Prussians to "hold the children hostage".

It was half past eleven. Vicky went into the garden, sitting in one of her favorite seats overlooking her garden. The roses smelled beautifully, and the moon shone down on her. Why could everything not be so beautiful and peaceful as it seemed? *How Papa would have loved this garden we have created*, she thought, and suddenly, her eyes were full of tears. She wiped them away, and hurried inside, and to the nursery.

"Come, Willy, quietly, and don't wake the others. Mrs. Hobbs? Good, you're awake. Don't speak. I'll take Baby; you bring Charlotte."

Emma Hobbs, the nurse, nodded, going into the next room. A few minutes later, she reappeared, carrying Charlotte, who still slept peacefully. Emma's sister, Georgiana, followed, as well as two footmen carrying trunks.

"Good bye, yer 'ighness," they both whispered, kissing the children softly.

"Thank you," Vicky whispered. "I will send to let you know what happens, Georgiana. Emma, come."

Everything was loaded into the carriage, Emma joined the children, and Vicky climbed carefully in, cradling Henry in her lap. He still slept, his fingers in his mouth, his foot twitching.

"Mama?" Willy whispered. "Where we going?"

"Hush, Willy. I will tell you when the others wake."

Stettin, July 1, 1863

Fritz watched the parade, listening carefully to the orders called. He glanced at the sun, guessing the time. It would be time to meet Vicky soon. The parade was drawing to a close. He rode down the line of men, nodding and returning their salute.

By the time he returned to the castle, a carriage was driving up. It was Vicky.

"Papa!" Wilhelm leapt out, throwing his arm around Fritz's leg.

"Fritz!" Vicky called. "Is everything prepared?"

"*Ja*, we are to cross to Putbus this evening." Fritz picked up Charlotte, kissing her, and then bent down to kiss little Heinrich in Mrs. Hobbs' arms. "There is one more inspection before we go."

"Abbat and Addy are in England. I hear often from Mama."

Vicky looked up at Fritz. He nodded. "Abbat writes to me. Your Mama suspects he is there to meet Lenchen."

Vicky gazed out to sea, watching the gulls wheel about. "Mama did not wish that, as she wishes Lenchen to remain in England. I wrote to her that so many other young Princes had been to England of late, he did not see why he should not go. Alix's brothers, Louis' brothers, and others, too, though Freddy did wish to propose to Lenchen." Vicky took Fritz's hand. "I am glad Addy is away from Berlin. I wish she had a good home."

Fritz nodded. "I wish this could be one of our homes," he said, nodding towards a distant castle on an island they were fast approaching.

Putbus, July 2, 1863

"No, no, Fritz, you must stay here! Even if the Regency is over, I do not wish you to go! It will do no good. Carlsbad is certainly not a place where your Papa ought to be!"

Vicky watched Fritz as he paced up and down the room, clutching a letter in his hand. He had received many letters since their arrival here, trying to persuade him to go to Carlsbad to meet his father, and apologize for all the pain he had given him.

"But I must do as Papa wishes," he said, still pacing.

Vicky shook her head, then nodded. "You will be of more service to your father if you stay here, where it is calm and peaceful, and do not try your health with this anxiety. It will do you no good to go there, or your father either. You know they only wish to entangle you!

July 3, 1863

Fritz had left Putbus, but not to go to Carlsbad. He had seen that it was only a ruse, to try to make him disown his own convictions and take up with the Kreuzzeitung party. Vicky sighed. Just now, when she was so much missing her own dear Papa, she wished it was possible to become closer to Fritz's father. He had often been so kind to her in the past, but now this seemed impossible.

Today would end Fritz's inspection tour, but they would remain at Putbus for some time. It was a very pretty place, which reminded her of Osborne, with its terraces and flowers, and the deep blue sea. Vicky picked up the *Times*. She had been reading through all the English papers Mama had sent her. She glanced over the foreign news, when a word attracted her attention.

"The Crown Prince's speech..." The paper detailed Fritz's correspondence with his father quite accurately. She sighed. This would give them a new reason to be incensed with her in Berlin. Everyone, she knew, would say that she had allowed the papers to be leaked when she sent them to Mama. They said that she lived "to receive the praise of the English press", that this was one of her highest aspirations. She must write to Mama at once.

Putbus, July 4, 1863

"No, Ditta can't find me!"

Fritz smiled as he opened the door of the room adjoining the bedroom. He heard the children's happy voices, and Vicky's laughter. He sighed deeply. It was so pleasant to come in to happiness, laughter and love. *His* childhood had contained so little. He paused, thinking of how empty his life had been, up to the time he met Vicky and her family. Even though he knew his parents loved him deeply, they showed it so little.

He tiptoed forward, pausing at the bedroom door. Vicky lay in bed, a book tossed aside on Fritz's pillow, and Wilhelm and Charlotte ran about the room, obviously thinking they were playing hide and seek, but never giving the other time to search before bursting out into laughter. Fritz struggled to hold back a laugh as he saw the blankets hanging off the edges of the bed bunch together and wriggle strangely as Wilhelm walked along the edge of the bed beneath it. He poked his head out.

"Papa!" he cried, running to Fritz.

"Fritz! I didn't see you," Vicky called, laughing.

Fritz came to the bedside, Wilhelm and Charlotte clinging to his hands.

Wilhelm let go, struggling to clamber up onto the bed. "Mama, I want to kiss you!" he called. Fritz sat down to take off his boots, and lifted the children up onto the bed before leaning down to kiss Vicky.

Wilhelm wriggled between them, pushing his hand over Fritz's face and trying to kiss Vicky's cheek. Vicky grabbed his hand and sat up. "No, Willy, Papa gets the first kiss," she said, leaning into Fritz's embrace. Wihelm sat, staring at them for a moment, and then slid off the bed to hide under the edge of the blanket again, wrapping his arm around Fritz's leg.

Vicky lay down again, turning her head. "Willy, where did you go?" she laughed.

"I get second kiss!" Charlotte cried, throwing her arms around her mother's neck and kissing her cheek.

Fritz saw a shudder cross Vicky's face as Charlotte met her eye, and he quickly picked Charlotte up as Vicky pushed her away. Fritz hugged and kissed her, and set her down. He took Vicky in his arms.

"Children, go to Mrs. Hobbs," he said. Wilhelm ran to the door, Charlotte following slowly.

"Wait – Willy didn't get a kiss," Vicky said shakily. Fritz looked at her. She didn't meet his eye, but nodded, and he went to the door, picking Wilhelm up and bringing him back. Vicky took him, hugging him tightly, pressing him to her even after he tried to wriggle away.

"Wilhelm, stay with Mama a moment," Fritz said. He went to the door, where Charlotte was standing uncertainly. He picked her up, cuddling her in his arms as he went into the next room. Her little hand touched his cheek. He felt a little tremor pass over her.

"Why Mama aways push me way?" she asked, her voice small and shaky.

"Hush, Ditta, Papa loves you," he said, kissing her face. He put her in Mrs. Hobbs' arms. "Wilhelm is coming also; come to our door, but not in," he said in English to Mrs. Hobbs. "And take them to *Bett*."

"Yes, yer 'Ighness." Mrs. Hobbs followed him to the bedroom door.

Fritz went to Vicky, gently picking up Wilhelm and setting him down. "Go to Mrs. Hobbs," he said, ruffling his hair and bending down to kiss his cheek. "Close the doors," he called, and turned to Vicky as the door closed. She lay in bed, tears on her cheeks, but trying not to cry.

"Fritz, I thought I was better; this hadn't happened in so long," she said, pulling his arm around her.

"You have not had her with you so much, except for when I am reading to you."

"I know," she said, shuddering again. "But things had been so easy then, that I thought I might be able to –" She sighed, "to have her there. And not see – him." Her voice choked and she pulled the blanket up around her, shivering away from Fritz's touch on her shoulder.

Fritz nodded, watching her. Her eyes stared toward him, but she was not seeing him. "Your Mama has written to me," he said, speaking softly, "and Alice writes about her little one. She is so well and strong. What a delight it will be to see them. Think of Alice as a mother! And little Beatrice is an Aunty again, and sees her little niece regularly."

He went on, speaking in a gentle voice of Vicky's family, until Vicky's eyes met his again.

"*Danke*," she whispered, and seemed to relax when he kissed her forehead.

Fritz lay awake, watching Vicky sleep. She trembled often in his arms, and occasionally tried to struggle away or strike out at him. His thoughts went back to the first times she had slept after his return the day after his birthday in '59. She had obviously started awake from nightmares, struggling and trying to strike out at him. Before that time, her sleep had always been so still and peaceful. Mostly, that peace had seemed to have returned. Vicky often slept solidly, and when Fritz woke in the night she was still and peaceful. But occasionally, she had a return of the nightmares of Prince Charles – she had never told him what the nightmares were exactly, but from her broken speech when he woke her it was clear enough – and then everything became very difficult again for a few days. She slept badly, started at every noise, and couldn't bear to let Fritz see her undressed, sleeping in her dressing-gown as well as her nightgown.

These episodes often came after she spent any time alone with Charlotte, even if Mrs. Hobbs was present and talking, which she usually was. She said she usually felt well if Wilhelm was there too, and completely comfortable if Fritz read aloud to her while she played with Charlotte, as long as she didn't look her in the eye. *That* was what brought on the burst of panic and uncontrollable revulsion.

"I see *him* again when she looks me in the eye," Vicky said the next day. "And it is worse than actually being in the same room with him. When I am, I know what is going on, and I don't have to sit next to him anymore, so that doesn't make me feel sick. But to look her in the eye –" She broke off, shuddering and clinging to Fritz's arm. "The whole situation returns, as if I am reliving it, all in one moment."

July 9, 1863

Baron Stockmar had died. Vicky felt as if she couldn't cry. It was too great a loss, this man who had been Papa's mentor.

Vicky sat at her desk, listlessly reading letters. She still was not feeling well, but she knew she must not lag behind in her correspondence.

Mama had answered her about Fritz's correspondence with the King appearing in the English press, saying that the King had better look closer to home for who had leaked the information. She had never let it leave her hands, except to be translated by Mr. Ruland, who had been one of Papa's German librarians, as well as art tutor to Bertie and Affie. He was trustworthy, she felt, and no one else had seen it. The Queen had read the letters herself aloud to Lord Clarendon and others Vicky had wished.

July 20, 1863

Bang! Fritz broke the surface of the water, looking about, startled. He had gone out for a swim daily since their arrival at Putbus. He had been under water, when he was sure he had heard the firing of a gun.

There it was again. *Bang! Bang!* He scrambled ashore, water streaming over his face as he ran his hand over his hair, and hurried up the beach towards the castle, forgetting his state of undress. He must know what this was about. He crouched down, stepping carefully through the underbrush, not wishing to be seen.

Bang! "Yes! I hit the top one!" he heard Vicky cry. "Can you?"

He paused, watching the scene. Vicky had said she would teach Princess Putbus to shoot. He had forgotten about it. *Bang! Bang!* He watched, feeling a burst of pride as Vicky hit nearly impossible targets.

He was about to call out to her, when he became suddenly very aware of the twigs and brambles scratching at his legs and his bare chest as he crouched in the undergrowth. Water pooled at his feet, dripping heavily from his *Schwimmhosen*[29].

"Vicky?" he called softly. She looked around, obviously puzzled where his voice came from. "Vicky!" he called a little louder. She turned in the direction of the path to the beach, obviously expecting his voice to be coming from that direction. "Over here," he called again.

"Fritz?" she called, hurrying towards him.

"Vicky, tell Princess Putbus not to come," he said. Vicky paused, returning to her friend who was just starting towards them. She whispered something in her ear, and the Princess returned to the castle.

"Fritz, where are you?" Vicky cried, running back towards the thicket.

"Here." He waved his arm, making the bush he knelt behind wave about. "I heard your shooting, and had forgotten what you said you would be doing, and wondered what was going on. And – ach! I think I need help getting up. These are digging into my legs. You have a sword with you, too, I see. Will you lend it to me?"

The sword hilt protruded through the bush, and he took it carefully, quickly cutting away some of the sharp branches. He rose, stepping out from behind the bush, but not fully. "I must go back to the beach."

Vicky doubled over with laughter. "Fritz, it is not like you to forget your clothes," she giggled. "I wondered why you did not wish Wanda to come. Now I see."

---

29 Swimming trunks

He met her eyes, feeling his face flush. Vicky was looking better today than she had since their stay in Danzig. "Vicky," he whispered, taking her hand as they walked down to the beach, "you are feeling well again?" he asked, seriously.

"Yes. I felt well enough to have Charlotte with me again this morning, during the lessons. I had hardly seen her since –" She didn't finish her sentence. Fritz nodded, picking up his shirt and coat and dressing hurriedly. "You will have to change again when we go in; you're soaked!"

"I hope Charlotte's birthday will pass pleasantly," Fritz said, wiping water out of his hair again.

"Mama wants you," a little voice said as they drew nearer to the castle. It was Marie, the eldest of the little Putbus girls. She ran to Vicky, reaching up to take her hand. Vicky smiled down at her, and looked up towards the castle. Willy stood outside. Vicky was surprised that he, too, had not run to her.

"Willy? Won't you come and join us?" she called. He looked towards them, and blew a kiss, in exactly the same manner Fritz often did to her. Vicky watched him, realizing he was looking at little Marie. He had been acting strangely of late, and she hadn't realized what it meant.

Later that evening, Vicky went to see the children at their dinner. Willy sat between the two elder girls, hardly looking up, his face quite rosy, as the little girls asked him questions and put their fingers through his curls. He had barely touched his food.

On the train, July 30, 1863

"Prince Alexander mourns his father deeply, and very noticeably. Prince George, on the other hand, is very formal, speaks to everyone as if nothing had happened, and meets all the visitors. He is always so formal, the opposite of his brother."

Vicky sat at Fritz's side, listening to General von Roeder speak. Prince Frederick of Prussia, "Uncle Fritz Louis" as Fritz called him, had died. He was the son of Prince Ludwig Karl, a younger brother of Fritz's grandfather, who Fritz had said was who trained Prince Charles. He, however, had always been friendly to Vicky and Fritz, as had his elder son. The younger, as Roeder had said, never abandoned his formal demeanor for a moment. Vicky felt as if he never acknowledged having met her, even though he went through the motions of it.

The funeral had called them back to Berlin. Fritz was to stand with Alexander and George, who were really his father's cousins, but were a sort of in-between generation, close to Mama's age.

The month at Putbus had been very peaceful. They had traveled around the Isle of Rügen, taking long walks or rides through the forest.

August 1863

"Fritz."

Fritz looked up from the book he was reading. Vicky had just come out of her dressing-room, and spoke nervously. She took his hand, playing with his fingers.

"What is it, Vicky? Are you feeling well?"

"I – I have to go to the laundry, Fritz."

He stared at her. "Vicky." He rose, taking her in his arms,

"Why? Why would you do that to yourself? Why would you wish to –"

"I must, Fritz. I – I don't want to be paralysed by that fear anymore, and I am still, about certain things. I need to see it, to face it. Please, Fritz, come with me."

Fritz held Vicky's hand tightly as she turned the key in the door of the laundry. The mistress had given her the key. Fritz opened the large, heavy door, and held it open, watching Vicky's face as she walked forward with a determined expression.

He looked away for a moment, a wave of overwhelming, indescribable emotion sweeping over him.

"Oh," Vicky gave a long, shuddering moan, and slumped against him. At first he thought she had fainted, but she began to try to speak. He couldn't make out her words, as he gently wrapped his long cloak around her and guided her back out the door, speaking softly as he did so.

"Vicky, why? Why did you do this to yourself?" He stroked her cheek as she lay across the seat of the closed carriage, staring blankly upwards towards him.

"I – I'm not doing it to myself; I'm undoing it. I must – I must go again – no, I don't mean just now. But I must conquer this." She spoke sharply, the determined look coming back to her face.

August 8, 1863

"Vicky, I must go to Gastein. I have an order to go and report about my inspection trip."

"But, Fritz, this is only a way to get you to go to them, and let them try to manipulate you." Vicky set her book down, rising and taking his hand. "Surely you will not go," she said, anxiously.

He shrugged. "I would rather report directly to Papa, but I do not know." He put his hand to his head, sighing deeply. "I wish all of this was over, and we could be at peace." He turned, leaving the room.

Vicky tried to settle down again to read, but her thoughts were busy. As soon as the words began to clear on the page, Fritz came in again. "Here is another telegram. Papa wishes to see me again, after all that has happened, and before we meet again in Berlin."

Vicky looked up at him, nodding. "So it is *he* who wishes to see you."

"I hope so." Fritz paused, sitting down, and putting his arm around her. "This will lead to nothing but a disagreement, I am afraid. Papa will never understand what I did."

"Don't always expect the worst, Fritz. Try to look forward to something. You will see your Papa again."

"But you must stay here. You understand that, don't you, Vicky?"

She frowned. "I wish I could go to support you. I know it will not be your Papa alone. You must be careful."

Vicky watched Fritz as he went in and out, preparing for the trip. Every time he entered the room, he looked more and more anxious. He had looked well again, while they were at Putbus, but now, with this meeting hanging over him, he looked ill and worn out with worry as he had in Danzig, after his speech.

Vicky knew Bismarck and others were determined to put a stop to Fritz's efforts, and that the King had written that he counted on Fritz's "repenting" of his "disobedience". She knew that violent scenes with his father were one of the things Fritz dreaded most. She sat down, beginning to write a letter for him to take with him, to read that night.

"I know they will try to intimidate you, to manipulate you with your feelings for your father, and so on, and squeeze as many promises out of you as they like. But you won't comply with their wishes. I know well that they take silence as consent – in all matters – so you must openly express your disapproval. Only stay calm; don't let them upset you. My love goes with you always,

"*Deine Frauchen*, who will love you, 'till death do us part'."

The Rosenau, Coburg, August 19, 1863

"Mama!" Vicky threw her arms around her mother, laughing and crying at the same time. It was so good to see Mama again after all that had passed. "Fritz will be here in a few days. His meeting with his father was more peaceful than he expected. I was so glad, for both their sakes."

"If only the King had come to Frankfurt. Everyone thinks his absence very strange, and not a good sign for Germany."

Vicky nodded. There was a meeting in Frankfurt of all the German sovereign Princes, including the Emperor of Austria, and excepting the King of Prussia.

"You say the King was kind to Fritz?" Mama asked, sitting down. They were in the room where Papa had been born.

Vicky nodded. "He repeated his usual point of view on politics, but he was personally kind to Fritz, and glad to see him again. He said very little about Fritz's protest."

Potsdam, August 20, 1863

Fritz sat in the saddle, watching the maneuvers. Fritz Karl and Fritz Schwerin were leading the opposing regiments this time. With a thunder of hooves, the cavalry charged, raising a heavy cloud of dust. Fritz couldn't see clearly, but he heard a shout, and the usual noise of the maneuvers suddenly ceased. When the dust cleared, he could see Fritz Karl kneeling on the ground. He hurried over. Others, too, crowded around.

"Someone is injured, I believe. Make way; don't crowd around," Fritz called. Two men hurried forward with a stretcher at the same time as Fritz reached the fallen man's side.

It was Abbat.

He lay still with closed eyes, and there was blood on his lips. Fritz knelt by his side, lifting his wrist. "His pulse is strong," he said quietly to Fritz Karl.

Fritz Karl didn't move. He sat perfectly still, staring at Abbat's still face, a shocked – indeed, horrified – look on his face. When the men carefully lifted Abbat onto the stretcher, Fritz Karl rose, turning dumbly, following them. He still didn't speak.

"What happened? How did it happen?" Fritz asked the others who still crowded around him.

"I don't know. The charge raised the cloud of dust, and it was so much no one could see. He was on the ground when the dust cleared."

Coburg, August 23, 1863

"Abbat was conscious again the next day. But I have never seen Fritz Karl look so conscience-stricken! That is how it appeared. He still wouldn't speak, except to ask about him, and he goes about in a daze. I have never seen him act so about anyone."

Berlin, September 1863

Fritz held Vicky's hand as she walked through the passageways in the laundry. This was the fifth time they had gone. Each time, she had been able to stay a little longer, to look about more, though the second time she had actually fainted. This time, her hand was steady, she even let go of his hand once or twice.

They stood in front of a door. Vicky looked up at him. "Fritz," she whispered, "I – I need to –" She clutched his hand again, as she opened the door. Her hand trembled slightly, but was steady again as they went in.

"Here," she said, stopping at a sofa. Fritz looked down at the sofa, and then into her eyes. She gazed up at him, without the blank stare he feared his gaze would meet. His eyes were drawn to a mark on the sofa. He bent down to look closer. It was a bloodstain.

"That was where my feet were." Vicky knelt down. "Feel how rough the floor is. Imagine running about on it for a quarter of an hour with bare feet." She took his hand, sitting down. He sat beside her, leaning down to feel the floor. When he sat up again, she was looking at him, a pleading look in her eyes. "Please."

He looked at her questioningly, and glanced round the room. She had closed the door behind them. "Vicky," he spoke slowly, thinking he might know what she meant. "Surely you do not mean –"

"I do," she said, leaning forward to kiss him. "Fritz, I need that memory to be swept away – no, to be swept clean. I can't remain a prisoner. I have to get out of this cage of fear which still holds me. Please." She took his hand, pressing it to her heart.

September 1863

"Vicky?" Vicky heard Fritz's voice and a tap at her dressing-room door.

"Fritz? You don't have to knock. You know that." She came to the door, putting her arms around him and kissing him. "You remember what I said about that."

"I did not wish to startle you, as you had – sometimes not been well these last two months – oh!" He stared at what she had been doing, and then looked back at her. "You *are* feeling well again."

Vicky smiled, turning to follow his gaze. She had put up the dressing screens in the bedroom and dressing-rooms. They had taken them down nearly four years earlier, as she had been extremely uncomfortable around them. It had been a dressing screen that Prince Charles had hidden behind and watched her undress before she became aware of his presence in the laundry.

Fritz put his arm around her. "I am so thankful," he murmured against her hair.

"Going to the laundry – and everything – was what had to be done," she whispered, taking his hand. "It wasn't pleasant, but it has unlocked the cage, I think. I don't wish to attempt to look Charlotte in the eye, but – I feel more at peace when I think of it all than I ever have," she said, taking Fritz's hand and putting it on her shoulder. "You touched my shoulder here yesterday, and I didn't flinch. Neither of us even thought about it at the time."

Fritz bent down, pressing his lips to the place where she had placed his hand, drawing her to him. She smiled, leaning her head against his chest. "I feel well – in a way I haven't in so long – since before – I can't describe it."

Oktober 3, 1863.

Fritz gazed up at Balmoral. He shook his head. He could not control the smile which spread over his face. There was the doorway where Vicky had stood eight years ago. He could see her in his mind's eye – in the simple white dress with red bows and a tartan sash, holding her hand out for him to kiss, gazing at him with obvious emotion.

That stay at Balmoral had been magical to Fritz, the foundation of his life's happiness. He squeezed Vicky's hand. She glanced up at him with tears in her eyes.

Oktober 5, 1863.

"Mama, Papa, the Princess Royal's come! She's really come!" Fritz heard the girl shout as she ran back towards a tiny house which stood ahead of them. Several heads appeared in the doorway, and a crowd of children ran towards Vicky.

"Welcome! Welcome! Oh, ye must come in and see Mama!"

"And don't forget Grandmama! She's prayed she'd live long enough to see ye again!"

"Come in!"

Vicky was enveloped and pulled towards the house. One of the boys turned back, beckoning to Fritz, who lingered where he had stood with Vicky

"Come, sir, they'll wish to see ye, too."

Fritz looked about curiously as he stepped into the little house. The family stood in the little kitchen, still gathered around Vicky. An old woman lay in a bed by the window, knitting. A curtain hung across the room, drawn to one side. On the other side was a large bed, with another, smaller bed at its side, which could easily slide under the large one. Across the small room, a cradle stood. There was a rough staircase leading upwards, which could only lead into the loft, there being no second story.

"Ma'am, you have long wished my wife to see?" Fritz spoke slowly in English as he knelt on the floor by the old woman's bedside. She squinted up at him.

"Yer the Prince of Prussia we're all so proud of? Yes, sir, yer wife, our Princess Royal, was a little thing when I first saw her. I couldn't bear the thought of deein' without seein' her again. Ye must be very happy." She smiled, resting her hand on his arm.

Vicky broke away from the crowd, and knelt by the woman's side. "Mrs. Smith, I am so glad to see you all again," she said, smiling and resting her head against the woman's shoulder. "You have met my husband, I see. You were not well when he was here eight years ago. Is it really eight years?" She murmured the last words to herself, turning to Fritz. "You remember this place, don't you? From the outside I mean."

Fritz shook his head. Vicky nodded towards the door. He rose, stepping outside. He looked about. It did seem very familiar. He glanced towards the door. Vicky had appeared in the doorway, and joined him. She led him forward a little bit, and sat down. "Don't you remember this place?"

Fritz looked about, then nodded, smiling. "This is where we had luncheon, and had to share the spoon," he whispered, putting his arm around her.

She laughed. "Go inside again and ask young Mrs. Smith to show you her spoons."

Fritz went in, feeling Vicky's eyes on him as he went up to the farmer's wife. "Ma'am, may I see your spoons?" he said, in English. He felt himself blush. It was such a strange request to make. But to his surprise, the woman's face lit up.

"Come with me, sir," she said, leading him through the bedroom to a small door. She knelt down, unlocking it, and taking out a small case. There were several sets of spoons. He saw ten perfectly polished silver spoons, and ten intricately carved wooden ones. "My husband made these all afore we was married," she said, taking the wooden spoons. "Would ye like to take one, sir? I'd like to think yer wife had one of my husband's spoons."

Fritz knelt beside her. "These are beautiful," he said slowly, attempting to speak without too strong an accent. "But I know something – woodwork, and how long it takes, though I have not – artist trained. Do you wish me certainly to take one? You then will not have your set."

She blushed. "My man can make me another. And he isn't any trained artist, as ye say. He's learned from his father afore him. And here's another set ye should see. It's my best," she said, taking another case from the cabinet. This case itself was silver, and had a crown on the lid. She unlocked it, revealing ten sparkling golden spoons, which looked familiar. "Yer dear wife's mum – beg pardon, sir, her Majesty, I should say – gave me these," she whispered.

"May I ask – in what year you were married?" Fritz took the wooden spoon, looking at it closely. It was beautiful work, with an intricate floral design.

"Oh, just about eight years ago, just afore ye were here then," she said, smiling.

Fritz nodded. "And – my mother-in-law gave you these as a wedding gift?" He motioned towards the gold spoons.

"Hmm – well, a late one, ye could say," she said, not looking up as she put the spoons away and locked the little door.

Fritz nodded. "*Danke* – I thank you. This will be a special remembrance," he said, bowing and putting the spoon in his pocket.

Vicky sat on the bed in her and Alice's old room, hurrying to finish her sewing before the candle went out. It had begun to flicker, but she was on the last seam. She hurried, but was careful not to make untidy stitches which would simply have to be pulled out again. She was on the last stitch when everything went dark.

She sighed, lying back on the bed. It was so pleasant to be here at Balmoral, where she hadn't been in six years, since a few months before her wedding. She smiled, thinking of the joy on the faces of the old women who had said goodbye to her then, some of them having feared that they would never see her again.

She sat up quickly as she heard a noise outside the door; someone was opening the door. She shook herself. She didn't need to be nervous here as she was in Berlin. Everyone here loved her. But who was it? Fritz had stayed with Mama, deep in discussion about the Schleswig-Holstein question, so they hadn't returned to Abergeldie before nightfall. She didn't know where Alice and Louis were.

"Vicky?" It was Alice.

"Alice? I thought you had gone to bed early."

"No, – well, I had, but I am feeling better. I thought I might find you here, since you were not in the library and Fritz was still talking with Mama." She sat down next to Vicky, then rose, lit a candle, and took two hairbrushes from the table. "I thought you would like to talk as we used to – and yet, not as we used to. You know what I mean, don't you, Vicky?"

Vicky put her arm around her sister, and took one of the hairbrushes. They both let their hair down and began to brush as they talked.

"Yes, we are not the little girls we were when we used to sit here. And it is different even than when we sat like this in Coburg, three years ago. Was I right then?"

Alice smiled. "Yes. Louis is a wonderful husband, and I love him with all my heart. And his family – his family are *so* nice. And I am taking my place in the world as Papa would have wished me to. Oh! How I miss him!" Alice became silent, averting her face.

"Yes, Alice, I know. But you were with him. I never said good-bye." Vicky stopped, feeling her throat tighten. "And I feel the want of his love and of his advice more than ever." She paused, looking at Alice. "But your hopes and dreams have come true, as you say. Louis is the wonderful husband I said he would be, and marriage is a beautiful thing to you?"

Alice wiped a tear away and nodded. "But I can hardly say it fulfilled the hopes and dreams I had when we talked in Coburg. You remember, I said I had a horror of the whole thing, because of – what happened to you." She paused. "What about you? Your hopes and dreams?"

Vicky sighed. "Personally, yes. But politically – you remember my saying if Fritz and I become Emperor and Empress we would make Frankfurt the Capital, and it would be in your domain."

Alice nodded.

"But it all seems further away," Vicky said, "Papa's hopes – *our* hopes and dreams – seem so far away now."

"Further still than they were then?"

"Yes. Even though Fritz is the Crown Prince now, they seem so much further away. And with the Schleswig-Holstein question everyone is off their heads about in Germany, I hope our family won't be torn further apart. It may be very hard for Alix if we go to war."

Alice nodded. "Mama is much concerned about that, and you know the Ministers in England mostly take the Danish side. But let us speak of something else. I said I would like to talk as we used to do – and I know that is different, since we are both married, but I meant – a little chat, about the little joys of life. I know you and Fritz need relief from your political existences." She smiled and kissed Vicky's cheek. "What were you doing in here?"

"Making something for Fritz. No, it isn't a birthday present. Perhaps I might tell you, but not quite yet." She squeezed Alice's hand. "Your Baby is so splendid! I was so glad to make her acquaintance. I am pleased she is the first Victoria in the next generation; she deserves it!"

Alice glanced at her, seemingly about to speak, but went silent again. Then she began, "Louis was talking to the ghillies when I came to find you. They get on very well together, though they have some trouble understanding each other, they with their brogues and he with his broken English – but he goes out hunting every day and enjoys himself thoroughly! It makes me think of Papa, and how he loved it here." Her smile quivered a little, but she went on. "He even wears the kilt! You have not seen him in the little skirt yet, have you?"

"No," Vicky said, laughing, "but please, don't call it a skirt. I am trying to convince Fritz to wear it, at least for the pictures, and he is very sensitive about that."

"Why?"

"Because Fritz Karl –" Vicky sighed heavily. How could she tell Alice what it was like? "Alice," she whispered, taking her hand again, "you cannot understand what our life is – and I am glad you cannot."

Alice looked at her seriously. "Papa told me about what – what happened to you, and many other things in Prussia."

"I know, but still – Fritz told me how things were there, but still – one cannot really understand such things without experiencing them. You mentioned just a moment ago the 'little joys of life'.

You do not know the '*little* annoyances of life'. You know how the boys tease each other a little about wearing skirts when they wear their kilts, but they don't mean it meanly. It is a joke. Things in Prussia aren't so lighthearted." She sighed heavily again. "But, to tell you the story – I don't know if you remember when my Mama-in-law sent the Bavarian costumes for me and Bertie when we were small. You were so little."

"The lederhosen and dirndl you and Bertie used to wear? I didn't know where it came from, but I remember them. I thought you looked very nice in it and was sorry when you outgrew it."

Vicky nodded. "My Mama-in-law sent them when they were traveling in Bavaria. Mama, in return, sent a Scottish outfit for Fritz. But he was fifteen – and it is very different at that age, than for a little child, to be dressed up in that way. Mama was not thinking of that. Anyway, Fritz's Mama required him to wear it to a dinner party. Fritz Karl teased him about being a girl. And I know there was something more to the 'joke'. Fritz always seems uneasy when he does speak about it, and I think he hasn't told me everything."

Alice met Vicky's eye, nodding. "I can see why he would not like it. Vicky," she whispered, leaning her head on Vicky's shoulder, "I wish you had so happy a family to be with as I do. Prince Charles is such a kind, pure-minded, *sweet* man."

Prince Charles. Of course Alice had meant Louis' father, Prince Charles of Hesse, but Vicky couldn't help shivering at the name being spoken. "My Papa-in-law is very kind when he can be," she said, looking Alice in the eye again. "You know what I mean by that, don't you?"

"Yes, Papa told me all about the – hypnotism, as we call it."

Vicky nodded. "I am glad. I wouldn't like to think of your being in Germany without knowing. I have met your Grand Duke, your Mama-in-law – and your Prince Charles," Vicky broke off with a nervous laugh. "Your Prince Charles is a true gentleman. May you never have to meet ours." Vicky shuddered at claiming

Prince Charles as part of her family.

"Please, don't speak of that. Don't upset yourself," Alice said uncomfortably, taking Vicky's hand. "What were you making for Fritz?"

"Something to help convince him to wear the kilt."

"How can something you make do that?" Alice laughed.

"You know how Fritz shrinks from anything which smacks of indelicacy," she said, holding up her handiwork. It was a pair of short underwear, like what the men wore to swim in.

Alice laughed. "Louis wears it as the Scotsmen do," she said, blushing and glancing away.

Balmoral, October 16, 1863

Fritz watched Vicky's face as they climbed the hill side by side. They were nearly to the top of Craig-na-Ban.

"What a beautiful sunrise there was this morning." Vicky glanced up at him. "I wished we could watch it together, but I didn't wish to wake you so early."

"Here is the spot," Fritz said, catching her in his arms. It was the very spot where he had proposed. "It was the sunrise of our life together." He looked down at her, stroking her cheek gently, as he had then, brushing his thumb over her lips.

She smiled and blushed as he bent down to kiss her. "That was the first time you touched my face – that you touched me at all, besides my hand." She hid her face against his chest. "What a thrill that little touch gave me in those days. I'm not saying it doesn't still," she said, blushing again as she looked up to meet his eye. "I remember telling Mama then I had never been so happy as when you kissed me."

"She wrote about that to me," Fritz said, smiling, as he bent down to kiss her again. "You look so irresistibly happy, even more than you did then."

"I was so happy and glad and embarrassed and scared and – afraid I was doing something we didn't have permission to do. You remember how aware I was that Mama thought me too young."

Fritz bent down to kiss her again, but suddenly looked away. Something had caught his eye. He turned from her, kneeling down.

"Fritz?" Vicky turned around, startled.

"*Meine* Vicky," he murmured, pressing a bunch of white heather into her hands.

"Please, hold it a moment," Vicky said, burying her face in the heather but then handing it back. She took the plaid off her shoulder and spread it on the ground. She sat, taking the flowers again.

Fritz sat down, putting his arms around her as she leaned back against him, holding her face up for a kiss before she buried her face in the sweet-smelling heather-bells.

"Fritz," she whispered. The flowers fell to the ground as she took his hands, pressing them to her heart.

PART THREE:
WAR AND PEACE

CHAPTER FOURTEEN

A NEW KING

Sandringham, November 6, 1863

"Vicky?"

"Yes?" Vicky looked up at Fritz, but he had picked up another letter, and covered his face. "Oh, Fritz, what is it?" she asked, alarmed.

He shook his head. "Nothing fearful. Only that they have decided to open the Chambers early, and Papa says I must be present, if there are no storms brewing on the channel. The papers say it is perfectly calm."

Vicky shook her head. "Must they recall you? It is so rude. And just before Bertie's birthday, too!"

Fritz shrugged. "I must go."

"Why can't you say you didn't receive the message?"

He looked at her, meeting her eye. "I cannot do that."

"But you told Bertie to do it!"

"What do you mean?"

"About Princess Christian's letter while we were on our tour! Don't you remember? You told him to ignore it and act as if he had never received it!"

Fritz looked away, out the window. He turned to meet Vicky's eye again. "Vicky," he said, taking her hands, "I cannot lie to my father and King. I have received his own message. I will not do

190

that."

"But it is so rude!"

"If your Mama asked you to come for an event, before my birthday, would you not go?"

"She wouldn't do that to us!"

Fritz shrugged and nodded.

"But Bertie is expecting–" Vicky began.

"Bertie will enjoy his birthday just fine without me, as he usually does. And he will have company."

"What do you mean? If we must go, what company will he have? He said he isn't inviting anyone else."

"He will have you."

"Oh. But, Fritz, shouldn't I accompany you?"

He shook his head. "I am unsure of what is going on at home just now, and would rather you stay here, with the children. But do not expect me to be able to return again."

Vicky smiled. "I *do* hope you will be able to. Oh, Fritz, I hope things are not going too badly."

"From what I hear, it is not any worse than it has been, but you know I do not hear much."

Fritz's birthday had passed peacefully at Balmoral, though it was a dark, stormy day – "a reflection of the state of things in Berlin," as Fritz had said. Vicky tried to distract him from his gloomy political musings, and they had taken a long walk with Alice and Louis and Lenchen.

Towards the end of October, Vicky and Fritz had said goodbye to Balmoral, and to Alice and Louis. They had gone about in the Highlands – sightseeing, Vicky had said, but it had rained so heavily they had seen very little of the scenery the first few days. They visited many of Mama and Papa's old friends, at Gordon Castle, Blair Atholl, and Inveraray. Finally, the storm clouds cleared, and they were able to enjoy the beautiful old castles and romantic scenery.

In Edinburgh, they visited Louis' brother William and Affie, who were both at college there.

Mama had taken the children with her when she left for Windsor, and Vicky and Fritz went on to Bertie's estate in Norfolk, Sandringham, to spend Bertie's birthday there.

Sandringham, November 9, 1863

Bertie had been indignant that Fritz had to leave the day before his birthday.

"Last year when he was recalled before our tour you said he must go if his King needed him," Vicky had told him. "Don't make the separation any harder for him. You can imagine he is disappointed."

"You will only have your bossy old sister," Vicky said to Bertie as they sat down at a little table in her sitting-room.

"Vicky, you know I don't think of you that way anymore." He smiled and took her hand. "You remember how I felt when I was in Berlin, and that Papa told me about – Prince Charles. I understand your difficulties. I often wish I could do something to help you."

"You can do something for us – two things, actually. One is – please, remain as neutral as you can if difficulties come with Denmark, and help Alix to be too."

Bertie scowled comically. "I don't know how successful *that* will be. You know how passionately fond of her country she is, and how passionately against the Prussians."

Vicky nodded. "But she says she loves me and Fritz. She must see that he does not mean anything against her family personally."

Bertie shook his head. "I don't think she will be reasonable in that matter, at least while the war goes on. But are those the two things? Or is that one?"

"One. The other is to sign some papers on our farm."

"Your farm?" Bertie laughed. "How will that help you?"

"We have taken a little farm property, and we were trying to make it so I own it, so that if anything – you know what I mean, but to have you sign it is the closest way, I believe."

Bertie nodded. "Very well."

November 16, 1863

Fritz sat on the train. He had been able to return, after all, and would be at Windsor before Vicky's birthday. The crossing had been a good one, one, he thought, which would not have made Vicky sick. He dozed on the train, which stopped at Calais.

"For you, sir," someone said in French, dropping something on his lap. He shook his head, trying to wake up, and tore open the letter.

The King of Denmark had died yesterday. Fritz shook his head. He knew this would probably mean war for Prussia, with the way things had been going in Denmark.

It also meant that Fritz Holstein – or rather, Fritz Augustenburg – was, in his eyes, reigning Duke of Schleswig-Holstein. Papa, he knew, would support this claim as well, as would most of the German Princes.

He lay back, thinking, and soon drifted off to sleep.

"Vicky!"

Fritz stepped off the train, not expecting to see Vicky waiting for him at the London Bridge Station.

"You have heard the news about Denmark?" Vicky looked up at him anxiously as they got into the carriage.

"I know about the King's death."

Soon, they reached Windsor. "The children are asleep, at least they were when I left," Vicky whispered.

He nodded. "I am tired. I wish to go to bed, to think."

Windsor Castle, November 17, 1863

"What will you do now?" Lenchen asked Fritz as they sat at breakfast. He looked down, unsure of what to say. He had to think more of exactly what line he would take politically.

"I do not know if we may not have war, so it is difficult to say," he said, looking back and forth between Lenchen and Louise. "You have talked with them about this, haven't you?" he asked Vicky.

She nodded. "They wanted to hear more from your own lips, but I told them you probably would not be ready to speak of it." She rose, coming behind Fritz. He felt her hand on his shoulder and she bent down to kiss him. "Won't you come and see the children?" she whispered. "They miss their Papa."

Fritz nodded, and excused himself to Lenchen and Louise. "I am not hungry, anyway." He had hardly taken any breakfast.

"Papa! Papa!" Heinrich called as soon as Fritz entered the room. Fritz hurried forward to pick up the little boy. He tottered forward, beginning to fall just as Fritz reached him.

"Papa!" Wilhelm and Ditta ran to him as well. Fritz knelt down on the floor, letting the children surround him. He looked up at Vicky, but found his eyes were dimmed with tears. Would he have to leave them in a few months – possibly only a few weeks – and go to war?

"Prince Christian – His Majesty Christian the ninth, we must call him now – is the rightful King of Denmark," Bernstorff, the Prussian Ambassador, said. "He and his wife are entitled to the inheritance as his wife's mother is the closest living relative of the late Friedrich the seventh, and her brother has renounced his claim. But you are right in saying he is not the lawful King of the Elbe Duchies. Denmark has no right to spread its constitution over Schleswig. Schleswig and Holstein are not to be parted."

Fritz nodded. "Fritz – Prince Friedrich Augustenburg – is the rightful heir to the Duchies. His father has renounced the claim, so he is the Duke, in all but proclamation."

Windsor, November 24, 1863

"You must see that England has done Prussia wrong through the London Protocol. In '48 it was a revolutionary war, Schleswig against the Danes, and we supported the Duchies. England forced us to withdraw. And we were not –"

"Fritz, I will not have any more of these discussions!" The Queen rose, sweeping the papers off the desk. "I cannot change the political views of my government. You know I support you, personally, and have many reasons to have sympathy with Germany, but I cannot change things! And I cannot have my family torn apart by these discussions!"

Fritz sat still, meeting his mother-in-law's gaze. "We must have England's guarantee whether she will be involved in the war. That is all I am trying to say. Are you for–"

"I cannot give you this promise!" she cried. The door opened, a babble of voices suddenly audible.

"But the Duchies belong to Papa!" Alix cried, glaring at Aunt Feodora. "They have been Denmark's property for so long, they must not be snatched away!"

"No! No more of this!" the Queen cried. "There will be no more political discussions on this matter here," she said firmly, looking around the room. Fritz stood now. Vicky, Bertie, Alix and Aunt Feodora had all entered the room.

The Queen nodded to all of them, and left the room. Fritz sank back down in his chair, covering his face. He sighed deeply. He could understand what she meant. Bertie supported Alix, as he should, who in turn supported her parents' claims. Aunt Feodora was Fritz Augustenburg's mother-in-law. Fritz supported the Augustenburgs, and felt obliged as well to sound England's feelings towards the possibility of a war between Denmark and Prussia. Lord Palmerston, the Prime Minister, was pro-Danish. But surely England would not go on the side of a war against their Princess Royal. The Queen would not allow war against her daughter's country, he felt sure.

He felt unsure. Alix, as the new Princess of Wales, was madly popular in England, and this turned the tide of public opinion in Denmark's favor.

"Fritz?" Vicky opened the door to her and Fritz's suite, the same suite they had had after their wedding. She looked around. No one was there. She went into the bedroom. She had expected to find him discussing the political questions still with Mama, or Bertie, or someone, but he didn't seem to be anywhere. He hadn't gone out.

She heard a muffled sound. "Fritz?" She felt her way towards the bed. She wished she had lighted a lamp. She pulled the curtain aside, letting in the faint moonlight, and turned back to the bed. She heard the same muffled sound again.

"Fritz? What is it?" He lay in bed, his head under the pillow. She lifted it, sitting and bending down to kiss the back of his head.

Fritz turned on his side. He wiped his eyes, but seemed unable to speak at first. "*Ach*! Why – why must this happen?" he whispered, and his voice was choked with emotion. He tried to pull the pillow back over his face, but Vicky took it, stroking his hair.

"Fritz, please, calm down. I will be back in a moment." She hurried to her dressing-room to change out of her dress, and returned in her night-gown, and lay down. She took Fritz's hand, making him face her, and pulled his arm around her. "Tell me everything," she whispered.

"I – I, I must go," he muttered. "I have lost your Mama's good opinion, I am sure," he said, meeting her eye, and struggling to control his emotion.

"I am sure you have not done that; you couldn't. But what has happened? Tell me."

"I went to her to talk things over more, and the conversation – became –" He broke off again, covering his eyes. "Vicky, I promised myself long ago that I would never shout at a woman for no reason."

"So, you and Mama have quarreled?" Vicky squeezed his hand. She shook her head. "She will not hold it against you, Fritz. She wishes you to stand up for yourself."

"But I wasn't standing up for myself. I let my temper get the better of me, and – and – I said something I shouldn't have."

"You think Mama cannot tolerate raised voices? She is not so weak as that. She is not a delicate little creature. She will forgive you, I know. You must forgive yourself. I do."

Fritz shook his head. "You would not if you knew what I had said. I – it is such a dreadful thing to say."

"Fritz, of course I forgive you. Don't upset yourself like this."

"It is – not only that – I –" Fritz tried to hide his face again, but Vicky made him look at her. "I do not only mean I said something rude," he went on in a whisper, covering his eyes with his hand, "but – I said a word I shouldn't have – a word I should never say."

Vicky looked at him. "Oh, do you mean, you –?"

Fritz sighed, covering his face again. "*Ja*. That – you know in what company I grew up, and I – when I am in the midst of an argument, those words slip out."

Vicky shook her head. "I can't imagine *you* – saying something like – that!"

"You have never heard me argue at length. And I never think those words are there in my mind to begin with, so it is hard to guard against it. But I have broken these two promises to myself."

Vicky kissed him. "I know you don't mean it, and Mama does too. I still forgive you. Forgive yourself."

December 15, 1863

"Goodbye!"

"*Auf wiedersehen!*"

Vicky turned and hid her face against Fritz's shoulder as they got on the train. They had said goodbye to her siblings, to Mama, and, in the evening, would say goodbye to England.

Peace had been made again in the family, though Vicky could tell Alix was boiling over internally with indignation over the possibility of a war. Mama had had several more discussions with Fritz on the question, alone, without the others knowing.

Now, they were going back to Berlin. Back "into the cage," as Fritz had said. On the way, they would stop to visit Alice and Louis, and Louis' sister, who was engaged to Fritz of Mecklenburg Schwerin. They would also stop in Baden, to discuss the situation with Vivi and her husband.

Berlin Schloss, January 1864

"How did your dinner party go?" Marianne took Vicky's arm as they walked through the sitting-room.

Vicky sighed. She had been trying to speak about the war, but Marianne kept changing the subject. "Very well. Bismarck and Manteuffel can be very charming when they want to. Roon was as he always is."

Marianne nodded. "I know what that means, all too well."

Vicky squeezed her hand. She and Fritz had given a dinner

party on Christmas eve, and invited all their enemies. Roon, the Minister of War, had formerly been Fritz Karl's military governor, and was very like him.

"Your father-in-law did not come. I hoped he would not, but we invited him all the same," Vicky said. "But if this war does take place –"

"Can you please explain the reasoning behind this war? I don't have the head to understand politics as you do, you know," Marianne said.

"Marianne, don't denigrate yourself! I have heard your explanations of political matters to others, and you understand things perfectly well! Don't let Fritz Karl cow you into believing you are not clever!"

Marianne sighed. "Well, I may say that this particular matter does puzzle me, and I can't keep it straight in my head."

"But I heard you talking about it the other night, and you seemed to understand it quite well."

"If you don't wish to explain it to me, tell Mariechen. She keeps asking about it, and I don't feel adequate for the task." Marianne rose, taking Vicky's hand. The girls sat at the other end of the room. Mariechen sat at a little desk, writing, Ebi worked away at some handiwork, and Louischen lay on the floor, holding a large orchid from one of the vases in her hand, turning it this way and that, occasionally pressing it to her cheek.

Vicky sat down in an armchair next to the desk. "Mariechen, did you wish to know about the war?"

"Oh, yes, Aunt Vicky. I have tried to ask Mama, and she said she didn't think she knew it well enough, and I tried to ask Papa, and he said that girls had no business asking about such things." Mariechen grimaced, and then smiled as she looked up at Vicky again. "Will you explain it, please, Aunty?"

Vicky sat down. "You know the old King of Denmark has just died," she began.

"Yes. Frederik the seventh. He died while you and Uncle were away."

Vicky nodded. "And you know there was a war between us before?"

"Yes, of course. Papa was in it, so we hear of it plenty."

Vicky nodded again. "I won't try to go into all the details of the history of Schleswig-Holstein right now. But at the end of that war, there was a treaty made, which stated that the two states must not be parted. England and other countries guaranteed the treaty.

"Fritz Augustenburg – who was Uncle's best friend at college, and is married to my cousin – is of a family which claim to be the rightful sovereigns of Schleswig-Holstein. We believe in him, and uphold him, as much of Germany does – and support Schleswig-Holstein becoming a state in its own right.

"But Schleswig-Holstein was – is – a personal possession of the King of Denmark, while Holstein was also a member of the German confederation. But the old King has gone against this treaty. He has written a joint Constitution for Denmark and Schleswig, thus parting Schleswig and Holstein, and potentially absorbing Schleswig into Denmark. He also ruled that German would no longer be taught in the schools, in spite of the large German population.

"The old King died, and left papers which had already been confirmed by the government, but which he had not yet signed. They had to be signed by the new King, Christian the ninth, my brother's father-in-law. If he signed it so that he did not attempt to take possession of Schleswig, there were complications in what had already been done which would have made it equivalent to signing his abdication.

"But in signing the papers to take possession of Schleswig, he breaks the treaty of '52, and the Germans are indignant about this oppression of their countrymen. We – Uncle and I – support the cause of Fritz Augustenburg, and Prussia fights for his sake, to free the states from Denmark."

"But – Uncle will have to fight your brother's wife's father?" Mariechen looked horrified.

"His people," Vicky sighed. "Yes, that makes this war much harder for us. Already, there is the dread of Fritz – Uncle – having to go at all. But it is fighting the injustice done to Schleswig, and supporting our friend, and he may go. But if he does, he will not be overly exposed to danger – he would be at headquarters, not in the fighting. He will come back to us safely." Vicky felt as if she was trying to reassure herself as much as she was trying to reassure Mariechen or Marianne. Fritz would not be in the fighting. But he would most likely be in the war, and that fact was terrible.

"You dread the idea of his not coming back." Vicky met Mariechen's eye. It was as if she had read her mind. Mariechen took her hand. "I wish –" she looked up towards Vicky, leaning her head on her hands, her gaze wandering to Marianne's face. "I wish we could have what you have, Aunty." She took Vicky's hand. "Papa – I – of course I don't mean I want him – to die, but we would be happier if Papa never came back." She shrugged. "I can't deny that."

Vicky leaned forward to embrace her, wiping tears from her eyes. She didn't know which was sadder, to see Marianne's often resigned expression or to hear the words plainly from the children's lips.

"Aunty? Would you like to have this?" Ebi had come up to Vicky, holding out her handiwork.

"What is it, Ebi? Come here and show me." Vicky didn't take the creation from Ebi's hands, but patted the arm of the chair. Ebi ran to her, climbing up and sitting in her lap.

"It is beautiful," Vicky said, as Ebi showed her the knitted flowers she had made. There was a rosebud and a white lily. "You do it so wonderfully."

"Would you like to have it, Aunty?" Ebi looked up, smiling a little.

Vicky looked away, wondering what to do. She couldn't take them from Ebi, but she must not hurt the little girl's feelings. She nodded. "Please, put them with my things. On the table at the door." She hugged her. "Thank you, Ebi. They are beautiful."

Ebi's face seemed to glow; Vicky had never seen her look so happy as she did at that moment. She ran to the door, placing the flowers next to Vicky's gloves and muff.

Vicky turned to Mariechen again. "Did you have any other questions?"

"Oh, no, Aunty, your explanation was so plain, I could follow it perfectly. And I wrote down things, here." She held up her notebook, letting Vicky see her notes.

Vicky glanced over them. "You understood it all so well." She glanced away, wondering if she should say what was on her mind. She glanced at Marianne, who was watching Ebi.

"Mariechen," Vicky began, "has your Mama told you about – taking gifts?" She wasn't sure if Marianne wished her to speak to the girls about this, and she wished to begin in a way which wouldn't seem too mysterious if she didn't continue.

Marianne's expression changed; she did not smile and nod, or shake her head. She sat silently for a few minutes, as did Vicky. Finally, she nodded.

"Vicky, your explanation of the war was very good. I could follow it very well too. Thank you. But –" She sighed. She rose, taking Vicky's hand, and walking back towards the door.

"Have you not spoken to the girls about the – hypnotism? Surely you have noticed Ebi – and does Mariechen know? I noticed she doesn't take things from her, but I wasn't sure if she really understood it."

Marianne nodded. "I have a little, but have not explained everything. But I don't want you to speak of it in Ebi's presence. She – she tells things."

Vicky nodded, realizing what she meant. "Would you like me

to speak to Mariechen? Or would you rather I not?"

Marianne nodded, turning back towards the girls. "Ebi, come with me. We must –"

Vicky sat down next to Mariechen again. "Mariechen, you must listen very carefully." She took the little girl's hands.

"Mama has told me not to take gifts from Großpapa and Papa, and Ebi," Mariechen said quietly.

"Has she told you not to take anything from them? Or from the Emperor and Empress, too?"

Mariechen nodded, her face growing more serious as she met Vicky's eye. "What – what is it, Aunty? Mama always seems so uneasy when she tries to speak of it."

"She should be uneasy. Mariechen, you have heard of hypnotism, have you not?"

"Yes, Aunty. It is when someone takes control of someone else's mind, is it not?"

Vicky nodded. "There is much more to it, but that is enough for now. Your Großpapa is the Grandmaster of this sort of hypnotism or mesmerism. You must be more careful than you can even imagine. Anyone can be a spy."

Mariechen nodded. "Ebi's strange behavior sometimes is because of this, is it not?" Vicky nodded. "I have never taken anything. I am careful, and take things after they leave the room. And putting something into someone's hand doesn't have the same effect, as if they actually take it."

Vicky nodded. "You understand it all much more thoroughly than I thought. I am very glad."

"Aunty? Who is it like?" Louischen held up the orchid, gazing at it intensely. "I don't a-member."

Vicky knelt down on the floor, kissing Louischen's forehead. "I haven't met anyone who made me think of an orchid, but you are like a little rosebud." Louischen always said things like this about people and flowers, and she liked to play along.

"Rosebud? You saw it?" Louischen sounded surprised and delighted, as she looked up at her, her big eyes even wider than usual. Vicky picked Louischen up, hugging her.

"I saw Ebi's work. It was beautiful, wasn't it?"

"Cherry trees," Louischen whispered as she laid her back down.

Vicky turned to Mariechen again. "I must go now."

Mariechen nodded. "Thank you, Aunty. I understand things much more now."

Berlin, January 9, 1864

Vicky opened a telegram from Bertie. She hoped it would not be in the same tone his last letters had been in. She didn't want to argue with him.

She stared, not believing what it said.

"Fritz?" She hurried into the next room, but then remembered Fritz was at the council today. "Valerie?" She must tell someone the news.

"Yes?"

"Alix has a son! Yesterday. It must be premature, as I only heard of her hopes five months ago. But Mama has her first English grandson! I only hope Alix has not brought it on early with her worries."

Berlin, January 11, 1864

Fritz knocked at the door of his father's study. He had received a message to return several government dispatches, which he had already returned. He knew the King – or rather Bismarck – had not wished to send them to him, but it had become absolutely necessary in preparation for war.

"Fritz. Why have you not returned the dispatches? I told you to several times," the King said, not looking up.

"I returned them to Bismarck, who sent them to me, two days ago." Fritz sat down at the other side of the desk.

The King shook his head. "He should never have sent them to you. England will know everything already."

Fritz looked up. "If you mean to insinuate that Vicky or I are spies, you –" He trailed off, unsure of what to say. He couldn't speak to the King in that way. "I assure you, I returned the dispatches to Bismarck two days ago. You can trust my word."

The King looked up at him, glaring, and then back down at the papers he was signing. "This is a warning to you. If this happens again, I will know that you are not trustworthy, and you will certainly not receive any more government dispatches! I had better not find our affairs in the papers from English sources."

Berlin Schloss, January 18, 1864

"So, these stupid Danes have refused to withdraw their stupid Constitution? Why would they bring war on themselves like this? It is so obvious they cannot win a war against us. But the new King is not very clever, is he? He is about as clever as his brothers are polite to us."

"Fritz, how can you say that? The Danish family are always extremely kind to me!"

"So, you will take the part of the new little *English* Princess, too, I suppose. Although I hear she takes a position violently against your *dear* Fritzch."

"Alix – the Princess of Wales – supports her own country and family, as one might expect," Fritz said. "No one would expect her to be completely happy with me, when I represent her family's prospective enemy, though she was as kind as ever, personally." He nodded to Fritz Karl. "Any more than one would expect her father's brothers to be friendly, when they must feel nearly as if they are prisoners."

Fritz sat between his mother and Anna, listening to the conversation during the dinner. Everyone was upset by the possibility of war. Fritz Karl sat on Anna's other side; they had been arguing through most of the dinner. Jules and Jean, King Christian's brothers, had been in the Prussian army for some time, though they had been pardoned from service by the King in the prospect of a war. They, and their brother, Fritz admitted to himself, were not particularly clever, but they were not stupid, and he would not think of remarking on their mental development in company.

Prussia had sent a message – for the third time – to Denmark, telling her if she didn't withdraw her new Constitution, Schleswig would be occupied by Prussian and Austrian troops. This time, they had given Denmark twenty-four hours to comply. Denmark had replied that she was prepared to meet any occupation attempts violently. The war was to take place. The troops were mobilized, and Fritz Karl and Abbat were to leave in two days. Fritz Karl seemed to enjoy the prospect.

Anna's eyes seemed to blaze as she spoke to Fritz Karl; her cheeks were flushed and there was an angry and also a hurt look in her eyes as she spoke. She turned to Fritz.

"Fritz, I am so glad you spoke up for your sister-in-law. It was so kind of you." She leaned towards him, raising her fan and half hiding her still deeper flushed cheeks as she spoke.

When Anna was little, it had sometimes been puzzling to tell who she was speaking to when he and Fritz Karl were together, as she had always called them both "Fritz". She, like Aunt Marie, never called him "Fritzch" as Onkel Karl and Fritz Karl and Lolo did.

But now, as it had been ever since she was about 11 years old, it was always easy to tell which of the two she was speaking to. Her manner was sometimes brusque and challenging when she spoke to Fritz Karl, sometimes timid and submissive, but it was completely different when she spoke to Fritz. Her manner immediately changed. Sometimes she was coy, sometimes very bold, but almost always flirtatious in some way. The occasional times Fritz saw her when she was not, she was kind and friendly, but more sisterly to him than she ever was to Fritz Karl.

"Denmark herself has broken the agreements of the London Protocol, which was created to protect her, so we should not be blamed for doing so. It is already made void."

Fritz sat at the council table with his father, Bismarck, Wrangel, and several others. Onkel Karl was not present at the Council; he was in bed, very ill, and had been for some time. Bismarck insisted that they should not break the Protocol treaty, as it might draw the hostility of England, Russia and Austria against them. Others argued for other methods of keeping the rest of Europe neutral.

"Prussia and Austria fought for the Elbe Duchies in the first Schleswig war. The rest of Germany should not involve themselves," Bismarck said.

"Baden, Meiningen and Weimar have all acknowledged Fritz

Augustenburg's proclamation, declaring him the reigning Duke," Fritz said. "We ought to, too. The people all over Germany seem indignant at Denmark's presumption. Austria as well."

"Wrangel shall be our commander-in-chief," the King said. He turned to Wrangel. "You have led us honorably in many battles, and shall do so again."

Fritz winced at the thought. Wrangel was an old man now. He was nearly eighty. He had been a young commander in the Napoleonic wars, and had still been in command in the wars of '48. But now, he was only an eccentric, perhaps partially senile old man, hardly fit to be the commander-in-chief of an army.

"Fritz Karl shall command the troops, and Gablenz is Austria's commander," Papa continued. Fritz smiled. He was glad Fritz Karl would be the commander. He laughed to himself. He would never have thought that fact would be gladdening to him, but it was.

"Your Highness?" Fritz heard the words, but didn't look up. He was still absorbed in his own thoughts. "Your Highness, would you like to be part of my entourage? To be an observer, in a relatively safe position?" It was Wrangel. Fritz realized there was no one else Wrangel could be speaking to. He was the only Prince present.

Fritz looked at Wrangel, and then at the King, who nodded.

"Yes, Fritz. I think it would be a good experience for you. You will not be unnecessarily exposed, and yet will gain your first campaign experience."

Fritz nodded slowly at first, and then rose to shake hands with Wrangel. He couldn't speak.

January 20, 1864

"How can everyone be so cheerful? I don't understand it!" Vicky cried.

Fritz caught her hands and swept her around in a circle around him. This was to be the last ice-skating party before his departure.

Fritz sighed, pulling her close to him. "I know how you feel. But you know what so many men's conception of war is – glory, honor and becoming a hero. They have no idea of the carnage. Come here." He caught her hand again, and led her towards a large building near the end of the Tiergarten.

"Here," he said, pointing. "That is the window which was shot out in the revolution in '48. You remember I told you, I fainted at that moment." He led her across the ground in front of the building. "Here," he said, his face very serious. "This is where I first saw the slain from a battle – for that was a battle of sorts. I know what it is." He shuddered.

Vicky looked up at him, and he bent down to kiss her. They had hardly spoken of his going to the war. He could see her feelings all too plainly in her eyes.

They walked carefully back towards the ice, stopping under a birch tree at the shore of the river. Vicky paused, looking up at Fritz, but her gaze went past him. Her eye was caught by a mark in the bark above her.

She stretched up to look closer. "Lotte FW PvP 48"[30]. It was cut plainly into the bark. She turned to meet his eye.

"What is this?" she asked, reaching up. She couldn't quite reach the spot. Fritz laughed.

"This tree has grown well since then, but that is as legible as ever."

"You carved Lotte's name in the tree? I thought you said she was only like a sister to you." Vicky looked up at him. He met her eye.

"She was." Fritz looked from her to the name carved in the

---

30 FW PvP 48 – Friedrich Wilhelm Prince von Preussen 1848

bark. "I thought so. Other boys might have thought – indeed, did think – that I was in love with her, and said so. I never thought so. She – she was always so kind to me, as no one else in the family was, when Vivi and Abbat were so young. I loved her, indeed, as I loved no one else at the time, but it was a brotherly love, as far as I knew." Fritz stepped closer to the tree, and took something out of his pocket. Vicky watched as he unfolded it. It was a little knife.

"This is the same knife I used then," he said. He reached up, and carved away at the bark, just under where he had written Lotte's name. "Vicky FW KPvP 64"[31]. He put the knife back away, and took Vicky in his arms. "You aren't jealous of my long dead cousin, are you?" he whispered.

"No, Fritz. It was only a little surprise. I believe in you."

January 30, 1864

"Oh, Fritz, I can't – I can't believe it. It must not be. You can't go!" Vicky sobbed as she lay her head on his shoulder, burying her face against his neck.

She felt him stroke her hair, and began to cry a little more quietly.

"Vicky," he said softly, "you have said it was my duty to go, when we spoke of it before."

Vicky nodded. "I know – I know it is, but I can't bear the thought of you – going," she sobbed. "I am so – glad – you didn't have to – go – a few days ago."

Their anniversary had passed peacefully, as had Willy's birthday. Willy was already five years old. That seemed so hard to believe. All of the family who were still in Berlin, except for

---

31 FW KPvP 64 – Friedrich Wilhelm Kronprinz von Preussen 1864

Prince Charles, had been at the informal dinner, and all had been kind. Fritz Karl and Abbat had already left for the front.

"Vicky," Fritz murmured, "I – you know many have always considered me something of a coward."

"How can you say so! Is that really true? Your father does not – and Fritz Karl's opinion does not count!"

Fritz sighed. "I – I cannot say that I have not considered myself so. I wish to prove that I am not – to prove it to myself as well as to the world. Even if I am not to have a position in the fighting, I must go to the war. I cannot sit here in safety while our troops expose themselves."

"Do not speak of your not being in safety!" Vicky sobbed. She couldn't bear the thought. "Fritz, I know what you mean. Don't let me hold you back. I only –" She threw her arms around him, kissing him passionately. "Come back safely to me."

"Don't expose yourself needlessly. You will be in a safe enough position." Fritz nodded and embraced his father.

"Mama," Fritz murmured, bending to kiss his mother's cheek. She still sat motionless, her face unmoving. He knew she felt his going quite as deeply as Vicky did, but she would never show it. Finally she rose, embracing him.

"Make us proud of you," she whispered.

Vicky clutched at Fritz's hand as they went upstairs to the nursery. Henry was asleep. Fritz lifted him carefully from Mrs. Hobbs'

arms, kissing his head, and gazing into the peaceful little face. Vicky saw Fritz shut his eyes and mouth tight for a moment, and he swallowed, turning to the next door. He entered.

"Papa?" Willy called as they entered.

"Papa must go," Fritz said, lifting him up and hugging him tightly. "Take care of Mama," he whispered.

Willy nodded. Fritz turned to Charlotte's little bed. He knelt down, kissing her cheek. She opened her eyes, blinking and yawning, and settled back down. Vicky couldn't hear what he whispered to her.

Fritz turned back to Willy, lifting him out of bed, and carrying him with him as they returned downstairs. Fritz's parents were gone. She and Fritz went on to their suite, and into the bedroom. Vicky took Willy, went into her dressing-room, and set him down. "Willy, stay here. I must say goodbye to Papa, alone. But I think he wishes you to be with me afterwards. Stay here until you hear the door close." Willy nodded silently.

Vicky came out, and threw her arms around Fritz's neck. She couldn't speak, and she couldn't cry any more. He was really going.

She felt his arms tight around her. Finally, he let her go. His hands rested on her shoulders; he gazed tenderly into her eyes. She saw his eyes fill with tears, and the sight moved her unbearably. She burst into tears, embracing him again. Then, he turned, and went out, closing the door.

She sank down on her knees. Her head felt strange, and her legs wouldn't hold her properly. She could hardly tell if she was still crying.

Suddenly, there was an arm around her, and a kiss pressed on her cheek. "Mama, Mama, don't cry! I'll take care of you, Mama!" were the words which he half cried, half whispered into her ear.

CHAPTER FIFTEEN

"OUR SIX YEARS HONEYMOON"

Berlin Schloss, February 1864

Vicky stared at Fritz's letter which Mama had sent to her, trying to read it through her tears. She shook her head again. *How many men would call that year four years ago part of their honeymoon?* Fritz had cared for her so touchingly. "In spite of everything we have gone through, nothing has actually come between us, and we can speak gratefully of our six years honeymoon," Fritz had written to Mama. They *had* gone through so much together, with Willy's birth, and – Charlotte – and, of course, all of Prince Charles' persecutions. The rumors that Fritz mistreated her and was unfaithful, all that had come since Bismarck became the head of the Government, the threat to put Fritz in prison after his speech, and now – the war which had come.

It was perhaps Fritz's greatest fear – his greatest fear for himself – and he must face it now. Vicky knew he would face it as he had all his fears for her which had come true – the horrible pain of Willy's birth, and the fear which had come with it of losing his wife and child, what she had gone through at Prince Charles' hands, the fear of what might happen to her if they had put him in prison – but now, he must face the war. He had said so often he was always sick at the sight of blood as a child, and he was always so gentle, so pained at others' pain. How would he bear the horrors of a battlefield?

Vicky's heart went out to him. She was so glad he had not had to leave before their anniversary. Her thoughts wandered to Bertie and Alix. How awful this war was for Alix, placing her family at odds with her new family's in-laws. Bertie supported Alix quite vehemently; Vicky did not resent this; she was glad he should stand up for Alix. She was sure things would come right again after the war. Fritz was Crown Prince, he supported the Augustenburg family, but it did not mean he had anything against the Danish Royal family.

Fritz yawned as he sat on the train. He may as well get some rest now.

Abbat and Fritz Karl had already joined the army before him, but Onkel Karl, he knew, was still in Berlin. Dread sat on his heart when he thought of that fact. Onkel Karl was in bed, very ill, but was he really? Was he using it as a reason to stay in Berlin after the other men had left? *Gott keep them safe*, he prayed. His thoughts were with Vicky, his mother, Addy, Maroussy, and many others.

It was still the social season in Berlin, and the balls went on, in spite of the war. Vicky had written that Marianne danced all night every night and seemed much more contented than she had ever seen her before. Fritz sighed. He was glad Marianne could have some joy in her life, but it was so sad to see such marriages, where the happiest time the couple spent was the time spent apart. He had dreaded, in his youth, the possibility of being pushed into such a marriage.

He thought of Vicky. Her face seemed to float before him as he began to doze, but it was a tearstained face which looked at him, the last vision of her he took with him as they said goodbye. He lifted his hands to cradle her face, but it was only a dream. He shook his head, took her note out of his pocket, kissed it, and settled down to sleep.

"*February 3*

"*Meine* Vicky,

"I have arrived in Jevenstedt, and write from the kitchen of a small farmhouse. The town here is decorated with the Schleswig independence flags and our German colors. Lieutenant Wrangel greeted me, telling me his uncle waited to meet me. Wrangel himself is far too confident of his position. He can say anything to anyone, it seems, as everyone regards him as such a hero. You know he had joined the other camp, but just now he has anti-Bismarckian views. He supports Fritz Augustenburg whole-heartedly.

"Fritz Karl is in the battle at Missunde. I shall be nowhere near, so you must not be anxious on my account."

"*Mein Schatz*,

"How I wish I could give you interesting news as you send me. But the life is the same here as ever; your Mama goes about every night to the balls, and requires me to go with her. I am not at all well, with a bad cold and sickness, but this makes it more likely for me to be allowed to remain at home.

"I feel to unwell too write on serious matters. Willy is very well. He takes great care of his Mama. He is such a sweet little boy. He lives in our rooms; I have the eldest chick in the nest as the cock is away.

"How I miss you already I cannot say. My heart and prayers are with you,

"Your little hen,

"Vicky."

"*March 5*

"*Meine* Vicky,

"The battle at Missunde is lost. Fritz Karl has been greatly shaken by this, but things still go well for us in the war. I shall soon see the works at the Dannewerke, the famous 'Thyra's fortress'. I cannot imagine what it is like, a 100 mile long earth wall with great fortresses behind it. It is a legend for the Danish, being named for their first Queen.

"But the Danes do not take into account its great weakness: It is winter, so a border wall is no wall. We can simply walk around it on the ice when the freeze is slightly deeper.

"There is a plan to cross the Schlei in two days. This is still open water, and Fritz Karl and his men are very uncomfortable at the idea of crossing the open water in row-boats, within firing range of the Danes. Who would not be?

"Wrangel sends his regards. I gave him your medallion, for which he kissed my hand, calling you *Engel* as he always does. The old man is absurdly fond of you, and keeps your picture on his desk, and in his breast-pocket."

Fritz lay on the floor in the farmhouse, trying to sleep. This, at the moment, was Wrangel's headquarters. There were three rooms, ordinarily a kitchen, bedroom, and small sitting-room. The man who owned the house allowed one of the soldiers to sleep in his bed. This had been offered to Fritz, but he had declined in favor of one of the men who had a bad cold. The farmer, his wife, and three small children slept in the loft. There was a cradle at the foot of the bed. In the evening, when everyone was coming in, Fritz watched the baby for some time before the family retired. He sighed as the farmer's wife took her little son in her arms, and climbed the ladder.

The sight made Fritz long for home, Vicky and the children. He had only been gone a week, but he was already more homesick than he ever had been. He had been away for longer periods, but this was very different. He closed his eyes. Everyone had put out the lamps. He yawned, and soon began to doze.

He jumped awake. At his side was a low window. Something moved outside, rattling the shutters. Was someone trying to break in? He sat up, trying to clear his head. There was no sound. *Did I dream it?* He lay back down, trying to get comfortable on the wood floor.

Something moved again. He opened his eyes, leaping up as something slammed itself against the window.

Fritz shook hands with the farmer. "Someone tried to get in the window last night, I believe. I was awakened several times. I hoped the bandits would not already be following the army."

The man laughed. "That is our dog. He always sleeps just where you did, but we put him outside for the night. He doesn't like so many strangers in his room."

"*February 6*

"*Meine* Vicky,

"I have never seen Fritz Karl look so deflated as he did when he and the troops returned today. But he was not alone. When we should have been thanking God for sparing many lives; we were all embarrassed, indeed, humiliated.

"You will have heard the news already before this reaches you, but I must tell you: Just as they were launching the row-boats, a man ran up to Fritz Karl, calling that the Danes had retreated. We were all prepared to surround them, and we did not even have a chance to look them in the face. They had vanished when the messengers went to beg for a truce to collect the wounded, which was a ruse to put them off their guard as Fritz Karl's men crossed the Schlei."

Later.

"We arrived in the town of Schleswig. The people told us about the Danish retreat. They had passed through, but were not welcomed in the town. By contrast, we were, very enthusiastically. Every house was hung with flags, German flags, as Bismarck has now forbidden the Schleswig-independence colors among our troops. This makes my blood boil, as you can imagine. No one should forbid a country to fly its own flag.

"We stopped at an inn where Wrangel lived in the campaign fifteen years ago, where he met the old landlady with a kiss. The King of Denmark was here only yesterday.

"Gablenz took breakfast with us. I had not seen much of him or the other Austrian commanders before today. The tablecloth bore the stains from the Danish King and Crown Prince's breakfast of yesterday.

"At the Dannewerke, we have taken possession of the cannons left behind; also, a heavy stock of good woolen blankets. These are very useful indeed, as the men's uniforms are not fitted for this Russian weather. Your Scottish woolen-wear keeps me very comfortable; even lying on the ground I feel the cold very little."

"*Flensburg, February 7*

"We have arrived here, where our headquarters is to be. Fritz Karl's is at the castle of Gravenstein, or Grasten as the Danes call it. This is much nicer, clean, warm and comfortable, where Gravenstein is an older building with thin walls, and only large rooms. Here we have a chamber per two men; at Gravenstein the large rooms are divided by curtains. Wherever the Danes have evacuated, the Schleswig colors fly, though the German colors are hung out when we pass through.

"Today, I saw the dead from the battle for the first time. My stomach has behaved itself, and I did not make a fool of myself before everyone. But I saw none of the worst; the men I saw were shot in the back, and were laid out on their back, as if they slept. This is an example of how cold it is: the dead freeze so quickly they do not bleed out, so that when not obviously wounded, as in these cases, they don't look dead – their faces have fresh color as if still excited in the height of the battle."

Flensburg, February 8

"Your Highness, I am to report to you." Fritz turned at the sound of a voice at the door.

"Karl?"

It was Karl Sigmaringen, who had applied before Fritz's departure to be his aide-de-camp. Fritz had refused, not wishing to encourage what he saw: many young Princes were joining the army in this way, from a sense of adventure. They had no battle training, and it would not do to have the headquarters overcrowded with the Princes who would expect to be given room inside. Fritz shuddered at the thought of the thousands of men who had to bivouac, sleeping on the ground in such fiercely cold weather.

"Karl, I told you –"

Karl saluted again, clicking his heels. "I have applied to the King to allow me to come here. I wish for the training."

Fritz shook his head. "I have not been to war before; I can give you none." Karl shrugged, and turned to the door. Another man soon came, bringing a few of Karl's possessions. He was obviously taking up residence here.

That night, Fritz couldn't sleep. He felt overly aware of Karl's presence. For the most part, the men had to share beds, or sleep crammed together on the floor. Here in Denmark, everyone normally did so for warmth, but Fritz had been glad to have a bed to himself.

"*Meine* Vicky,

"Wrangel gives the craziest orders. He is really quite mad by spells; his former energy has turned to obstinacy. He insists on the strangest things, such as not allowing the men to write anything down. When we meet for orders for the day, he declares that we write with our swords, not our pens, and – verbally – tears apart anyone who dares to make notes. Everyone turns away or wanders off to write things down while he isn't looking. They are like schoolboys, afraid of being caught cheating.

"My presence at Headquarters is very necessary. Papa had told me my accompanying Wrangel was his wish, though he let Wrangel invite me himself. I did not know why Papa wished it exactly, but I take the responsibility to countermand Wrangel's mad orders. The other day, he attempted to ride towards the front, with no troops accompanying him!

"He takes it into his mind that he must protect me, so that if I go anywhere, he runs after me. This draws attention to my presence, rather than the opposite.

"But he is an old hero, and his reputation must be kept intact. I cannot hide that I look forward to the day when Papa recalls him, 'to give him the honors he deserves', as my position is a very delicate one. I do this on my own responsibility, but it means that I am, in fact, the acting commander-in-chief of the whole operations!"

"*February 9*

"Falckenstein, our Chief of Staff, complains to me of his impossible position between Wrangel as Commander-in-Chief and Fritz Karl as Commander of the army. Both – entirely unintentionally – make his life quite unbearable. Wrangel himself appointed Falckenstein, but he cannot agree with him. In the morning Falckenstein submits a plan to Wrangel, who immediately says 'Oh, no, my dear fellow, that will not do. We must do…' Falckenstein goes to discuss the new plan with Fritz Karl, returns with the finished alterations, to which Wrangel says 'you did not understand me. This is what I wish…' and proceeds to give the original plan again. Fritz Karl is immensely frustrated to be torn back and forth in this way, and you know he is not pleasant to deal with when frustrated.

"I was encouraging Falckenstein when Fritz Karl came up and began to berate him in his usual manner, also complaining about Wrangel's interference. I, as always, must be the voice of reason in the midst of chaos.

"I have written to Papa about these things. We must preserve old Wrangel's reputation and let him retire in honor, not recall him in disgrace. Perhaps someday my part will be acknowledged; perhaps not."

February 13

"*Meine* Vicky,

"You have never seen such volumes of snow," Fritz wrote. He sat by the fire in the kitchen of a little farmhouse. "I felt many times that we would not make it. I write in a farmer's little house, having slept comfortably on a bed of straw on the floor, and wearing wooden shoes while my boots dry."

He paused, thinking of what had happened the night before. He wanted Vicky to know the truth, but not to be badly frightened at the thought of the ordeal he had gone through.

"I was once thrown into a drift up to my armpits, but we are safe now, and I feel well. Your clothes keep me very warm.

"We were on the way back to Flensburg, when a blizzard caught us. I will tell you of it when I am home again, as it is difficult to describe such an experience in writing."

He leaned his head on his hand, the scene of the night before vividly in his mind's eye.

The conductor came hurrying towards Fritz as the train ground to a halt. "Your Highness, it is necessary for everyone to leave the train, if we do not wish to be buried alive! The snow is too much. The station is still more than a mile distant, but one can see the telegraph poles. Make your way in that direction. May *Gott* bless you!"

Fritz nodded, picked up his small satchel which could be strapped over his shoulders, and went to the door of the train.

The door was opened with great difficulty, and the snow whirled in. The temperature immediately dropped; the atmosphere filled with tiny particles. Many men followed him, several lingered behind, and the door was closed. Just before he left, someone handed him a saddle-blanket.

Fritz started forward through the snow with the other men. The train track was not visible. Indeed, nothing was visible but whirling, blinding, thrashing snow. He closed his eyes. It was no good trying to look at anything in this storm; the whirling snow made one feel blind, and as if thousands of tiny daggers tore into one's eyes. He turned back, the snow for the moment blowing in one certain direction, bending over double and cupping his hands over his mouth to breathe. He opened his eyes, holding the blanket around his face. He could make out the other men doing the same thing. They turned to move blindly on again.

"Help!" He could barely hear the cry, but instantly turned back, running into another man. "Someone is lost!" he shouted. The wind whipped his voice away, but he could hear just enough to tell someone had heard, and the shout went down the line of men. They turned back. One of the older officers had been blown off his feet and was quickly being buried in snow.

They gathered together as he was lifted up, their faces turned inward, all bent forward, creating a protected space in the middle so they could breathe and speak. "We must rope together," Fritz Schwerin shouted over the wind.

Karl Sigmaringen shook his head. "It would only work to cling onto the rope; if we wrap it round ourselves, it could strangle someone, if one of us is blown away, the wind is so strong."

A rope was taken out of Fritz Schwerin's bag, and they made sure everyone had a good grip.

Several times, Fritz nearly lost his grip. The rope was then woven back and forth between the men so that if anyone fell there would be an obvious jerk on the rope, without it being so tight as to strangle anyone. They went on, marching as steadily as they could. Sometimes they came to drifts where the snow was up to the chests of the shortest men. They bunched together, plowing their way through.

Thump. Fritz staggered, wondering for a moment what had happened. He continued on, and ran into the man in front of him. They had run into a building.

"Hadersleben, February 18

"Meine Vicky,

"I passed the marketplace, and saw Wrangel standing on the small dais where the Bürgermeister addresses the people. 'How do you receive us?' he called.

'As liberators from Danish oppression!'

" 'Yes, and we come as such! If God is willing, you shall be Germans soon!' He waved his arms, rousing great cheers. The crowds in the towns always greet us enthusiastically so far, and are far from being offended by our occupation.

"I hear from Berlin that Bismarck praises my conduct loudly. This, as you can imagine, makes me very suspicious. I do not know what they are up to, but he does nothing uncalculated, as you well know."

"February 20

"Wrangel is as odd as ever. Yesterday I had to speak to him

very seriously about some orders he gave which put many men in grave, unnecessary danger. He was ready to cry, knelt and kissed my hand, then asserted that he had given different orders which had not been followed, that he was not to be blamed, and so on. He is a very odd character, especially when he has not had enough sleep, which no one ever has here. Whenever you are mentioned he flies into the heights of ecstasy.

"To speak of serious matters: You will well remember that we have gone into this war with the pretext of forcing Denmark to comply with the London Protocol of '52. This also means we must not cross the border of Schleswig into Denmark proper.

"The Austrians have been particularly anxious about this, not wishing England to enter the war against them. I – and you – are, of course, quite certain that England will never fight against *us*.

"However, the news today is that our troops crossed the border on the 18th by mistake, never guessing it, in pursuit of the enemy. Bismarck is very nervous about this fact, and has reprimanded the responsible officers severely, but Denmark seems to take little notice of the fact. She is too occupied with punishing de Meza – their ex-commander-in-chief – for commanding the Danish retreat. Copenhagen is said to be mad about the retreat, not understanding that he took the responsibility of saving their army.

"The Danes have surrendered Kolding without a fight, so the war has now moved into Denmark proper, with no international objection. So this war goes on, without an end in sight.

"I may not have actually seen any battle, but I still go through the school of war, and it is a good one for me. Many make rude comments about my staying at headquarters, and continue to call me a coward, in great contrast with Fritz Karl, who, in the papers, is called '*Prinz Voran*' – 'the Prince who is always in front' – though of late he has not been so. But my position with Wrangel teaches me many important lessons, which cannot be learned in either the battlefield or the diplomat's office."

Berlin, February 25

Vicky sat on one of the sofas along the edge of the ballroom, just outside of an alcove. What time was it now? She looked about for her mother-in-law, but she was still involved in a long conversation with several ladies. Vicky yawned, and wiped perspiration from her forehead. These rooms were so hot, it was difficult not to become drowsy soon after entering them, even before the hours had dragged on late into the night. It was half past one.

I wish Marianne was here, she thought. She wished she had someone to talk with. But Marianne had been dancing till two in the morning at every ball she attended, so that she wouldn't be so much company after all.

Vicky would *not* dance while Fritz was away, and besides, she couldn't think of dancing when she felt so sick. She smiled. It would be wonderful to have a new little one to love, but it was so hard to keep her spirits up with the worry about Fritz. At least he wasn't in the active part of the fighting. He had promised not to expose himself more than necessary. And surely he would be home long before it was time for the baby to come. This war wouldn't last that long.

She shook her head, trying to stay alert. Prince Charles had still not left Berlin, although the doctors had declared him well again. It wouldn't do to fall asleep in an out of view corner. She rose, slowly walking up and down the length of the room.

The second time she returned to her former seat, a man and woman hurried past her, nearly bumping into her as they hurried into the alcove. She didn't see the woman's face, as she wore a heavy cloak and a thick veil. The man turned back and motioned her away.

"Count Hanstein?" Vicky called involuntarily. She winced as

she saw him shake his head and motion her to leave again. She hadn't meant to speak aloud. She turned away, beginning again to pace the room. The curtain was pulled across the entrance to the alcove when she turned back.

The man had looked very like Count Hanstein, Grandmama Louise's second husband. But, Vicky realized, he was much younger. Count Hanstein was sixty this year, and looked considerably older. This man was no more than forty or so. Vicky pondered the question of who he was for a moment, before sinking onto another sofa, a wave of nausea overtaking her.

There was another dance beginning. Vicky was glad no one seemed to be taking notice of her. She was so tired and sick. *I hope Fritz's letters arrive safely.* She rested her head against the back of the sofa, praying for his own safety.

She shook her head, and stood up again, realizing she had dozed off again. She began to walk up and down the room again, and noticed the curtain was no longer pulled across the entrance of the alcove.

"Vicky!" Someone seized her arm.

"Marianne!" Vicky threw her arms around her. "I was wishing you were here; I longed for someone to talk with." She looked at Marianne. There was something different about her. Her face was glowing, and she looked happy – truly happy. Vicky realized she had never seen her look really happy before, even when she first met her, before Fritz Karl had begun to persecute her for refusing to accept one of his father's sons in the place of one of her daughters.

"I was here, the whole time, but I was sitting in the dining room, waiting – waiting for *him*." Marianne's voice was as joyful as her face; she beamed such intense happiness it seemed almost strange, it was so uncharacteristic. "Didn't you see me when we passed you?"

"That was you?" Vicky stared at her a moment, and then took her arm again. "Marianne, please, come and sit down. I can't stand about so long," she said, putting her hand on her stomach. Marianne nodded sympathetically, and they returned to the seat Vicky had occupied outside of the alcove.

"Oh, yes, I am glad you couldn't recognize me," Marianne said, as she settled down by Vicky's side. Before sitting down, she had looked to see that no one was standing nearby, and no one was in the alcove.

Vicky nodded. "Your veil was so thick, I couldn't even guess. And you wore that cloak, so I couldn't even guess by your figure."

Marianne nodded, her face flushing. "*He* only arrived yesterday, hearing that Prince Charles was leaving soon."

"Is he? Fritz will be glad to hear that – for our sake, though I know it will make his life more difficult. He has been very concerned about Prince Charles's remaining in Berlin while he and Abbat are away."

Marianne nodded, giving Vicky's hand a little squeeze. "He couldn't come while Prince Charles was at home. You know, I told you before."

"Who is he? You never did tell me." Vicky studied Marianne. She still could hardly recognize the radiant, smiling, blushing face.

"Hubert. Count Wangenheim. I did tell you, didn't I? When you were first here?"

"You only told me part of the story, and you thought you had told me more, when you were injured. And it is his resemblance to my step-grandfather that you were referring to, was It not?"

Marianne nodded. "I heard you call him Count Hanstein. I thought I had told you everything all these years, and you were simply keeping the secret, as I told you to." She laughed. Vicky smiled and sighed. Her laugh was so free and joyful Vicky could not continue to feel sad and lonely.

"But why does Prince Charles hate –"

"*He* is here, and Fritz Karl is away, and everything is wonderful," Marianne murmured, her face flushing again. Then she blushed more deeply, but her expression changed. She looked at Vicky. "I didn't mean to say that to you. I know how you are feeling, with your Fritz away at the war. I'm so sorry." Tears started to her eyes as she spoke.

Vicky met her gaze, tears flooding her eyes, too. "Marianne," she whispered, "I have been cheered by seeing you *so* happy. I have already noticed you seemed so different. It – it is a – something which has cheered me a great deal during Fritz's absence. I don't want you to – to suppress yourself in an effort not to hurt me."

Marianne smiled through her tears, turning her head on one side and looking down, not meeting Vicky's gaze. "I – I have often resented your happiness. It is – so perfect – and still so perfect, in spite of what happened to you. I – I don't mean I want you to not be happy, but I have so little it is hard to bear sometimes."

Vicky took her hand again. "I know what you mean, Marianne. There have been many times I began to speak of – us – and then felt badly because I could see it made you feel so lonely, and worse than lonely, I know. But please, speak of your happiness and love all you wish. It does not hurt me in the way it hurts you. Yes, Fritz is away, and in the war, and that same war is going on, with many people being killed or hurt every day, every minute, but we still must live. Fritz writes to me every day. I am always secure in his love. You – you poor thing, you have had so little."

Marianne smiled again, wiping her tears away. "I had not seen him in so long, since before Louischen was born. Four years, Vicky! We have seen each other so little, when he is here, we are still on our honeymoon. I have endured these four years waiting, waiting, but there was never an opportunity for him to visit, since they know about us."

"But why does Prince Charles hate him? You said it was because he looked like my – my step-grandfather, you were going to say, but why does that make him hate him?"

"Vicky, come here!"

It was the Queen. Vicky sighed, embracing Marianne as they parted. It was time to go at last. The clock was striking three now. Vicky couldn't believe that the last hour and a half had passed so rapidly. She had been there since ten. The first four hours had seemed endless, but from the moment that Marianne and Count Wangenheim had passed her, it seemed as if only a few minutes had passed.

Vicky hurried to join her mother-in-law, nodding at Count Wangenheim as she passed him. She looked about the room again. Prince Charles had not been at the ball. Perhaps he had left this evening after all, though it seemed unlikely for him to miss the party.

CHAPTER SIXTEEN

NIGHTMARES AND BATTLEFIELDS

Hadersleben, February 28, 1864

Fritz sat in his room, reading. He thought he heard the sound of another train coming. Who was it this time? He opened the door and hurried out.

The train was drawing up. When it finally stopped, many soldiers stepped out. Several men with a Royal household uniform joined them. Fritz stepped closer, ready to receive the Prince.

"Onkel Karl. I am glad to see you here." Fritz held out his hand. Onkel Karl glared at his outstretched hand, and turned away with a brief nod. Fritz smiled to himself. He meant what he had said. He was glad to see Onkel Karl *here*, that is, glad to see that he was not in Berlin.

Fritz felt a shiver run down his back. The whole atmosphere of the place seemed to have changed since Onkel Karl's arrival, and he often felt uncomfortably as if someone was watching him.

"And I am glad to see you, *here*." Fritz jumped at a touch on his shoulder and the sound of Onkel Karl's voice at his side, and froze as he realized what had just happened. Onkel Karl had fastened the chain of the Order of the Red Eagle around his neck; now he was fastening the pendant on. Fritz raised his hand in salute, standing at attention. That way he had a reason for holding perfectly still and not meeting anyone's eye. Onkel Karl pinned something on to his uniform, and pressed something into his hand. Fritz held his hand perfectly still; he would *not* take it from him.

The wind blew coldly, pressing the paper into his hand as Onkel Karl stood directly in front of him, straightening the decoration. He tried to meet Fritz's eye, but Fritz tilted his head slightly back, so he looked up and over his head.

Onkel Karl turned away. Fritz let the paper drop from his hand, but stepped on it before it could blow away. He raised his boot. Yes, it was stuck on the bottom of his boot. He walked, careful not to dislodge it, back inside. He reached his quarters, and sat down to change his boots. He closed and locked the door, looking about to make sure that no one was present. Finally, he tore open the filthy envelope, and took out a letter.

It was from Papa. Fritz read it carefully, his eyes filling with tears. He knew everyone praised him at the front, but he had ignored that. Most of these people were not those who he wished for praise from. But it had made an impression on the King, who had written that he was greatly moved to be able to give him the Order of the Red Eagle with Swords, an Order given for bravery. Wrangel had told him that Fritz had passed the test with "true Hohenzollern" fearlessness. Fritz rolled his eyes. He had done nothing to deserve a decoration for bravery. The shells had been far in the distance.

But Papa had also written that he felt that Fritz had redeemed himself politically, by his actions at Headquarters.

Fritz sat, leaning his head on his hand. All of this praise was gratifying, but he deserved so little of it. To see the shells and bullets from afar was no reason to be decorated for bravery. What decorations would be left for the truly heroic if those who sat at Headquarters were given this? And what did Papa mean by his having redeemed himself politically? He did his best to keep Wrangel reasonable, but that did not mean he wished to have the flattery and attention of the other camp, who claimed Wrangel as their own.

When he came out again, others had also been decorated. Abbat, Fritz Karl, Onkel Albrecht, Wrangel and Gablenz had all been highly decorated, when none except Fritz Karl had been anywhere near the action.

"Prince Karl is certainly not in a good mood. It is because all the other Princes are decorated, and he had to bring the medals, and gets none himself!"

Fritz heard Wrangel talking with Gablenz after a dinner given by Onkel Albrecht. It was true that Onkel Karl was not in a good mood. He had been very silent, with none of his usual jokes. Fritz was glad. He didn't need his mind filled with off-color humor at a time like this.

"He will not leave until he has a chance to win them himself!" Fritz went back to his room before he could hear any more. He had no use for such gossip. He sat down to write to Vicky about what had happened.

Berlin, Kronprinz Palace, March 3, 1864

Vicky paced up and down her dressing-room. *When will Fritz write?* she thought. *When will I receive his letters? He writes every day, I know, unless...* She shivered at the thought. The only reason he wouldn't write would be that something had happened to him. But surely she would have heard that news? Surely the letters were only held up. But when would they come?

"We are very well. I hope the Crown Princess is, as well?" Vicky flew to the door, and then froze. She couldn't move. That was Fritz's voice in the next room.

A strange feeling swept over her as she heard the voice again, talking and laughing with Valerie and Hedwig. She came to the bedroom door which led to her sitting-room, but felt she couldn't open it. Who could be there? Not Fritz. He would have come straight to her, she felt sure, if he had come home. It wasn't Abbat, either. As like Fritz as he sounded, his voice was recognizably – though very slightly – higher. She heard steps and the door opened.

Valerie had opened the door, but behind her stood a young man. Vicky looked up at him. He looked like – he looked as if it *could* be Fritz, but younger; he looked like Fritz, but around the age Fritz had been when they were engaged. She stared up at him, unable to find her words. She studied his face. He had red hair, not blond which darkened to brown as Fritz did. He was not so tall as Fritz was, nor so handsome.

She looked up at the young man, who looked as awkward as she felt, and there was a faint blush on his cheeks as well. She met his eyes – kindly eyes, with a similar expression to Fritz's. There was something else in them, too, which seemed familiar, but she couldn't decide what it was.

He knelt, taking her hand and kissing it. "*Ihre Hoheit*[32]," he began, and then went on in English, "Your Highness, I have only just been able to get through; the trains have been blocked since the storm. Your hus – the Crown Prince wished me to stay here rather than joining him on this campaign. I am to be in your household, but you know that." He trailed off nervously as he stood, finally released her hand and clicked his heels.

Vicky felt a shiver run down her back when he spoke the first

---

32 Your Highness

words in German. His voice and accent were so exactly like Fritz's. She looked up at him, nodding. "You must be Count Seckendorff. You are to be our new gentleman in our household, only it wasn't to be until after the war," she said, as she realized who he must be. She remembered the shy, silent boy who had attended her during the festivities for her and Fritz's wedding. Of course, he had been her page, which meant he wasn't allowed to speak on duty, but he had rarely spoken to her at any time. His voice had been changing, and he had been at a very awkward age. But she remembered how much he had reminded her of a picture of Fritz at about the same age.

She looked up again, meeting his eyes again. "Welcome, Count Seckendorff. I shall be glad to have someone else who speaks English so well here."

He nodded, clicked his heels, and bowed, again kissing her hand before he turned to leave. Valerie hurried forward. "He brought this for you. They were held up by the blizzard. The army hasn't been able to send any letters for these nine days." She pressed a bundle of letters into Vicky's hands.

Vicky shook her head, taking her eyes from the spot where Count Seckendorff had stood. In her mind, she was in Scotland, as a girl of fourteen, riding by the waterfall at Balmoral at Fritz's side. She looked up at Valerie, smiling. A burst of joy flooded her, and she threw her arms around her. "Thank you, and please, thank him! I have been so worried about not hearing from Fritz." She stopped to look at the letters. Here were nine days of letters – nine days of precious letters from Fritz, which she had been longing for so much. She would read the most recent one first, and then go back to February twenty-first, the next after the last she had received.

"March 1 – Onkel Karl has arrived here," she read. She laid the letter down, breathing a sigh of relief. Ever since she knew Prince Charles had been declared well, she had been having nightmares about him. She thought he had gone to the war, and had written to Mama that he had on the 27th, but she couldn't be sure. She didn't want Mama to worry about her. But no one in Berlin would answer her when she tried to ask. Even Marianne didn't seem to know for sure. She had not seen his departure announced in the papers, either.

"His presence here is a nightmare to me," she continued reading, and laid down her letter, a rush of conflicting emotions sweeping over her. She had felt so relieved to know he was gone, but she hadn't thought of what that might mean for Fritz.

"His very atmosphere is so creepy. I seem to feel it more than I ever have before. He has come to *einmischen* – or as you would say in English – meddle – or should I say, medal or *Medaille* – here. By this I hope you will gather what has happened, when I say he has brought the Red Eagle many times over. I am well, and I think have had no ill effect, being more cautious than ever.

"I must say, in spite of the now constantly contradictory reports, and endless gossip – he tries to turn Wrangel against you, which is quite impossible. The old man, as I have said before, has an absurd fondness for you which nothing can conquer it seems. That day I slapped him was the only time he has breathed a word against you, and he was under the spell at the time. But as I was saying, I must say that I am glad to see Onkel Karl here – glad for your sake, and for the sake of many others. I can feel more at peace in one way, knowing he is here and not in Berlin, though ill at case for myself."

"*Hadersleben, February 21*

"Bismarck says things go very well in Berlin since I am absent. This attitude is, of course, not unexpected. But I am satisfied, as my presence here is very necessary. But after the campaign is over, where shall we be? After what has passed last year, I cannot see my being given an important post in Berlin.

"There is a standstill in action and orders, and I sit about with nothing to do. I feel so desperately homesick, and it is only made worse when I often fall asleep and dream I am in your arms, only to wake up to a cold room and only the company of Karl Hohenzollern, though he is not an unpleasant companion.

"Wrangel has suddenly taken notice of the fact that I am in fact leading things here. I hope he will not take offence. So far, he does not, but one cannot know what to expect from him.

"I received a message from Fritz Karl, asking me to come to Gravenstein. From what he says, there will probably be a battle tomorrow. Falckenstein does not think I should go, but I must."

"*February 22*

"I mentioned my journey to Wrangel, who responded that he was entrusted with the responsibility of keeping me safe, and that he must attend me at all times. It is comical, to think we each think we have the responsibility of looking after the other, and this counteracts the other at times. So he, too, drove seven miles at one in the morning, through another great snowstorm. In the carriage, all was cozy.

"Fritz Karl, Wrangel and I rode up a mountain near Broaker, passing the bridges. We took a view of the Düppel positions. The snowstorm continued, however, and prevented a proper reconnaissance, but there was, and not too far distant, a battle.

"Of course I did not take part in the gunfire, and did not expose myself to danger, but I was considered within battle range for the first time. I certainly heard the guns and the cannon of the sea monster, as the men call the Rolf Krake, the Danish ironclad which haunts the shore. The snow prevented us from seeing what went on, but the others knew well where the battle was. However, I was congratulated as having had my 'baptism of fire', and hardly taking any notice of it. They praised my bravery absurdly, when there was nothing to be brave about. I am not certain if they were in earnest or not, but they make 'much ado about nothing'.

"The sight of the battlefield is a terrible thing, the earth torn up by shells, nothing left but mud and filth where the ground is not re-covered with snow. The cold and snow is a terrible thing for the wounded – many men freeze before they can be found, or are even buried in the shifting snows. When the booming of the shells ends for a moment, one hears the squawks and cries of crows, ravens, buzzards – even owls – gathered on the bodies of the poor horses. Strange to say, they never touch the human bodies."

"*February 23*

"I have had a very interesting conversation with Wrangel. He is certainly not currently a member of the other camp, but is very friendly to me, and came today, 'to tell me his opinion of me'. I was not looking forward to what he might say, thinking of the time I accidentally slapped him last year."

CHAPTER SEVENTEEN

"I NEVER CEASE TO REGRET"

“ “Wrangel admitted that last June, after my speech at Danzig, he was one who supported my being court-martialed and imprisoned. I told him this was not news to me, at which he was very surprised. However, he went on to say that he could not cease regretting the stance he had taken at the time.

“I told him he should not think I know so very little, though he believes that I hear nothing as I am sent so few Government dispatches. He responded that the King often complains that I am so silent and never give my opinion – though it is by his order that I am silent.

“ ‘Ask Bismarck, ask Prince Hohenzollern, if I am silent. I was practically dismissed from the Ministry, and they expect me to speak up and put myself at risk again? Ask the King to show you our correspondence, and you shall know if I am actually silent.’

“That was my response to his words. He declared that since November he has disagreed entirely with Bismarck, though before that he had been his supporter. He also confirmed that there are many who continually attempt to turn Papa against me. I thanked him for his confession, that he told the truth of the contemptible plots to divide father and son, husband and wife, father-in-law and daughter-in-law, and indeed, mother and daughter, as they so often attempt to force you not to confide in your own family.

“You will remember his letter to you when we were in Scotland, when he wished to reconcile you and Papa, which we did not know what to make of.

"He has praised my conduct here and thanked me for 'helping to manage things', and says that many men who hadn't known what to make of me would be glad if I was officially at the head of everything. I wasn't sure if he only meant here in the military or as King, but he is whole-heartedly my supporter at the moment."

"*March 7*

"The headquarters moved, so we were to march through the night for several miles. This is the first of the actual marching I have experienced, and I am rather exhausted.

"We stopped at the Vonsilder Inn, or rather the Carter's Store and Home for passing farmers. Karl and I were given a room on the outer wall next to the street, but it was most miserable. The troops were passing by constantly, and when I had finally drifted off, someone knocked loudly at the window, thinking this was Wrangel's headquarters; I finally asked for a different room, and we were given one on the outer wall in the back. Several families were passing by, and we were again awakened by cries of 'Papa?' 'Where is Papa?' 'I don't want Papa to go!' 'No, Papa must stay with us!' and so on. How the appeals of these little voices recalled you *und die lieben Kinder*[33] to my mind, you can imagine.

"Finally, when they passed on, two tomcats decided it was time for a yowling match on the roof, and you may imagine the racket which followed. It was then three o'clock, and time to move on. I had had perhaps ten minutes of sleep.

"My occupation next shall be to keep Wrangel sensible and prevent him from attempting to launch an attack on the fortress of Düppel with ordinary hunting rifles."

---

33 The dear children

Berlin, March 9

Vicky sat in the little chair, placing her hand into the strap and allowing the doctor to connect the wires. "It is quite painless. I let them do it to me first, in England, already. I was not comfortable with the idea at first either."

She had finally convinced Wegner and Langenbeck to continue a treatment for Willy's arm which had been suggested when they were in England. The machine did look fearsome, she admitted, and she had been very anxious when electrotherapy, or galvanization, as the Germans called it, was suggested.

The current, however, was so low, it was not painful. She felt strange twitches convulse the muscles of her arm, and the temperature of her arm rose, but it was not unpleasant.

Wegner watched her. He still seemed to expect her to go into convulsions, or something of the sort.

"You don't think I would electrocute him, do you? He is my son, as well as the heir. Come, try it."

Wegner nodded nervously. He placed his hand into the machine after Vicky got up. His face relaxed. "I do not wish to be blamed for doing anything I might regret," he said. Vicky sighed. This was always his response to anything he didn't understand, or which was different from the protocol he was trained in.

"Willy, come here," Vicky called. She knelt by his side as they strapped his left arm into the machine. His arm twitched, and his fingers straightened after a minute or two.

"Mama, I feel my fingers!" he cried, looking at his hand.

"Yes, Willy, and you can straighten them, too," she said when it was all over. "But come, it is time to go to bed." She lifted him, nodding to the doctors, and went to her bedroom. "Can you raise your arm?" she asked, setting him down by the bed. He tried to raise his arm, and lifted it with his right arm. It reached a little higher than usual, and his elbow and fingers had much more free movement than usual. "See if you can get into bed alone."

Usually, Willy tried and tried to scramble up onto her bed, but she always had to lift him. She watched as he clenched the blankets with his left hand, struggling to find footholds.

"Yes!" they both cried as he finally fell forward into bed.

She joined him soon, hugging him tightly as he wrapped his arms around her neck, pressing kisses on her cheek. "Dear Mama, you're warm," he whispered, "but my arm isn't cold." Vicky smiled. His arm was warm after the electrotherapy. "Mama, when does Papa come home?"

"I don't know yet, Willy. We don't know when the war will be over."

"War, Schleswig, Düppel, hurrah for Papa!" Willy cried in a sort of chant, jumping up and marching comically across the bed. He jumped in the air with the "Hurrah!" and flung himself down again by her side.

✳ ✳ ✳

Berlin, March 10

"Mama, here is Papa," Willy said. Vicky glanced up hurriedly, realizing Willy had recognized Fritz's picture in the paper she was reading. "And here is Grandmama."

"Yes, Willy, and can you read me what it says? Start with Grandmama's picture."

"The – Queen's – eldest – grandson – is a fine – child," Willy read slowly. He looked up at Vicky. "But Mama, I am the eldest!"

"They mean her eldest English grandson – whose christening is today. They don't mean to ignore you, but all of England is elated at the birth of Uncle Bertie's heir. Willy, what happened a year ago today?"

He thought for a moment, and his face lit up with a smile. "The wedding!"

Vicky nodded. "Now read me what it says under Papa's picture," she encouraged.

"The Crown – Prince – shows great – spirit – after – his first battle." Willy looked up at her again. "Papa is in the fighting?" His eyes were wide with alarm.

Vicky shook her head. "It is a mistake. He was near enough to hear the battle plainly, and see an explosion in the distance, but he is not in the fighting." She gave him another picture to look at. "Willy, can you tell me about Düppel?"

"Düppel – is a hill, a mill, and a fortress."

Vicky nodded. "It is a hill, a great hill, and there is a mill on the top. Or there was." She murmured the last words to herself. Düppel Mill was away from the fortress – it hadn't had to be destroyed. Prince Charles had commanded that it be, and she had seen a photograph of the mill, dilapidated and with the blades lying on the ground. "And our troops shall bombard the fortress," she went on, half to herself. "You have done very well, Willy. But I must write to Papa now, so go to Mrs. Hobbs."

Willy kissed her again, and ran to the door. Vicky rang for the nurse, who soon appeared.

"*March 10*

"*Mein Schatz* – The christening is today, on Bertie and Alix's first anniversary. How I wish I could see my little nephew! Uncle George represents the King of Denmark, and is delighted to stand as honorary grandfather in this way.

"How I miss you I cannot say. Willy asks much after his dear Papa. He reads the papers with me – finding your picture and others he recognizes, and I have him read the captions. He has an understanding for the affairs of the day, but I can't help feeling he is far behind what we were at his age – far behind even what Bertie was. He thoroughly understands what he reads, and asks many questions, has a marvelous memory for words and things, and says he understands when I explain political affairs to him, but when he tries to speak of it independently, it is so confused I can't follow his thinking.

"After his electrotherapy, he was able to climb onto the bed on his own last night! This will be welcome news to you, I am sure, but you must admit it is a great triumph!

"Oh, but how deeply I feel it! I can never cease to regret his poor arm, and the fact that our heir is a cripple!"

"*Kolding, March 10*

"*Meine Frauchen,*

"I visited the wounded and the prisoners today. To see the men whom one has seen a few hours before, normal, healthy, cheerful, now lying in bed with such terrible injuries is desperately sad. One poor cripple, who has both legs amputated, gave me his hand and began to talk, not uncheerfully. But it is indescribably moving to see such things, especially when they do not seem upset, but take it as a duty done. I could not keep the tears from my eyes.

"I also visited three Danish officers who are our captives, Captain Dane and Lieutenants Holstein and Brandt, very nice people. I showed them the photos I asked you to send, our pictures from Bertie's wedding. I am not at all hesitant to speak of my friendship with the Danish family, and to express my sympathy and understanding for their position. Alix, I call my sister, not even adding the 'in-law', and they seem to realize my authenticity, especially after seeing the pictures.

"Karl Sigmaringen is a very good friend of mine now. At first I was disinclined to like his company, being of the opinion that he only came here out of a sense of adventure, but he takes the war seriously, and wishes for the training it gives him. He is one of the very few here with whom I can speak with absolute openness about our political views, so his company is very welcome.

"Falckenstein brought me a letter from Bismarck to Wagener, which was very curious to read. He praises me even behind my back, which makes me all the more suspicious, and I cannot help wondering what is up.

"Fritz Karl was said to have received Royal orders from Berlin, but has not been heard of here. I must go soon to Gravenstein, to sort this out."

"*March 11*

"Onkel Karl has written to me, complaining of Wrangel's 'inconsiderateness' in not informing him when this part of headquarters moved. He had also asked Graberg, who also gave a vague answer and received a reprimand. I shall explain to Onkel Karl the condition of the telegrams here. Our messages to Berlin and Vienna are coded, but there is no cipher between the individual army corps, so we cannot send our plans on in that way. When attempted, they have always fallen into the hands of Danish spies.

"Onkel Karl finds fault with everything as usual, saying everyone at Gravenstein is in a 'lethargic condition', and that Fritz Karl refuses to take part in the next battle, though the King himself has ordered it! I shall go there very soon, to see what is the matter with Fritz Karl."

"*March 18*

"What you say about Wilhelm is very gratifying, and I do not think he is at all backwards. I was only beginning to read at the age he has now reached. Very few children of his age can compare to what you and your siblings were then.

"If he does not meet your ideals, only think how little I have met my own, in many things which have happened in the last month. I have let my temper get the better of me twice – once in the affair of slapping Wrangel and once in what I said to your Mama. Many other little occurrences have also taken place which I am ashamed to mention.

"You, *meine Frauchen*, are the only ideal I have attained. Even the thought of you, though far away, makes me a different creature, and with you in my thoughts I can brave anything.

"The situation with Wrangel has gone to such an extent that I can go nowhere without his running after me. A crowd of his entourage always follows him, and so it simply draws more attention to our presence rather than protecting me as he thinks he is doing.

"I have written to Papa about Wrangel, and also of the proposal Falckenstein and others have made that I be given the supreme command instead of Wrangel. This would not do at all. No one would understand the insult to Wrangel for him to be recalled at such a point in the war, and I believe it would also deeply offend Fritz Karl for me to be so suddenly promoted – I, who have no former war experience, to suddenly become Supreme Commander just before the expected victories.

"Papa wrote most kindly to Wrangel, sending a copy also to me, thanking him for how he has introduced me into the business, but adding that he must discuss every order, telegram and letter with me.

"Therefore, I assembled the whole staff, excepting Wrangel, saying everything he orders must be brought before me, that this is the order of the King. Everyone must understand that now I am the Supreme Commander in all but name. May *Gott* bless this appointment which I am far from worthy of."

"*March 21*

"Yesterday I was with Wrangel, Fritz Karl, and the grenadiers of the 3rd Guard Regiment, on reconnaissance. We had been marching for several hours, and were very hungry. In the midst of what was obviously farmland, we came across a large, round, flat, elevated plot of quite solid ground, where the snow was blown away. Today the wind was mild in comparison with anything we had yet experienced, and we sat down here to devour our rations.

"With the heat of the noon sun, and so many bodies seated on the ground, the substance beneath us began to thaw, and we found ourselves in the midst of a farm's manure heap! You may imagine the comments made by the men. The stench was quite awful, and no one's appetite survived the assault."

"*March 25*

"I am finally at Gravenstein, where Fritz Karl was very hesitant to begin plans for a bombardment. I have promised to help him, and he agreed, the date for the bombardment being set for only three days away.

"The Johanniter corps do more than I ever expected, and I am eager to hear how they are spoken of in the papers at home. The ambulances are always ready, in the midst of the fiercest fire. Onkel Karl must really be praised for this, for we would have lost an uncountable number of men without them, and it is all organized personally by him."

"*March 27*

"The bombardment is again delayed; I really must go to Gravenstein and see Fritz Karl. Onkel Albrecht says he is always ill whenever there is to be a significant undertaking."

Gravenstein, April 3

Fritz opened the door, looking about, shivering. It was not so cold as it had been, but Spring had not yet come. Somehow, here at

Gravenstein, it seemed almost colder inside than out. The floor was covered with a thick layer of dirt, and everything was filthier and filthier as he went further in. Finally, he came to the rooms which, from the description he had received, must be the bedrooms.

There was a long hall, with curtains hung, dividing the room into many small compartments, with each man's bed and luggage, and little else.

He hurried to the second of these rooms, where he had heard Fritz Karl was. He coughed loudly as he came up, and saw the curtain move. He was awake.

"Fritz Karl? Why are you here? Why have you never even sent the message from the King, if you could not bring it? What are you –"

"Oh, so you, too, must come and barrage me with questions!" Fritz Karl had been sitting up when he first saw him, but he now lay down again, his hand over his eyes.

"But we must have the King's orders! Where are they?"

Fritz Karl looked up at him. "I have them with me, here, but you know I can't give it to you, Fritz," he said, taking something from his pocket. He looked at Fritz seriously.

"Is it in the envelope still? Drop it on the floor," he said. Fritz Karl did so. Fritz stepped on it, as he had the letter which Onkel Karl had brought him. He would open it as soon as he was outside. "Where is your father?"

Fritz Karl huddled down under the blanket, seeming to shrink inside of himself at the mention of his father. He sighed, muttering "no warmth ever seems to penetrate this part of the world." He didn't answer Fritz's question.

The boom of cannons sounded again. Fritz Karl held his head in his hands. "Oh, my head! I cannot take this nightmare any longer." He pulled the blanket over his head. "I do not know what is worse, the cannon or the sound of Abbat's *Feldjäger*[34], who is

---

34 Scout, huntsman

there" – he motioned towards the curtain to his left – "who never stops snoring! You know I cannot sleep well in the midst of all these people, and he snores up the scale and back down again! *Ach*! My nerves cannot bear it!"

Gravenstein, April 6

"I have brought you these," Fritz said, taking something out of a bundle he carried. "I wear these, and I have never been ill since the beginning of the campaign. Vicky made them. She learned how from the Scots women at Balmoral."

Fritz sat on the edge of Fritz Karl's bed. He had brought a set of woolen underclothing which Vicky had made for him.

Fritz Karl took the things from him, nodding, a brief smile passing his face. "It is very kind of you, Fritz. You do not wish to keep them?"

Fritz shook his head. "I have another set after what I am wearing." He tried not to laugh at the thought which crossed his mind. At home in Berlin, most of the family hardly ever wore warm enough clothes during the winter. Fritz did, and was teased endlessly for it. "We don't need such things," they had often said, and called him weak and effeminate for wearing them. They had carried this on here, in the terrible cold of this campaign. Fritz was almost the only one of the officers who had not been ill.

He had brought the things for Fritz Karl, but he didn't imagine he would take them. They would, of course, not fit him – the shirts would be too tight, the arms and legs far too long for him. But the look on his face was one Fritz had almost never seen in him – one of real gratitude. He wasn't even sure he hadn't seen tears in Fritz Karl's eyes before he turned away, covering his head again with the blanket.

✻ ✻ ✻

"Fritz Karl has not been at all his usual self since the defeat at Missunde and the retreat from the Dannewerke. He is gentle and mild-mannered, very concerned about the men and anxious not to send them uselessly into danger, and also kind to me. He never calls me "Fritzch", or any of his other names for me, and also makes an effort to avoid any possibility of drawing me into the web. You will understand what I mean.

"He has been ill, but his whole manner is so entirely different it is not simply because of his illness. I do not like to say more in a letter. All the other generals and commanders get quite impatient with him; he is no more 'Prinz Voran[35]', but lingers, delays, hesitates and vacillates endlessly, and is constantly in the midst of scenes of which I am not accustomed to see him on the receiving end.

"Also, he is quite afraid of his father, and for good reason. He had sent a telegram to me, informing me of a battle plan, but which was taken by the Danes, who now know the lines of our preparations, and he has had to give up the prepared bombardment."

Fritz paused from writing, unable to concentrate with the noise in the next room.

"*Feigling! Weichei! Huhn!*[36]" Each word in Onkel Karl's voice was punctuated by a loud *thud*. "One may as well call you *eine Hähnchen,* rather even than *Hühn*[37], which is too nearly a compliment to you, as you are like a little hen crying that the sky is falling! Don't let anyone see you again, crawling away like a dog with its tail between its legs!"

---

35 The prince who is always in front.
36 Coward! Wimp! Chicken!

37 *Eine Hähnchen* is specifically a hen, rather than *Hühn* which can mean chicken in general.

251

"But Papa, I am ill! Don't shout – oh, my head aches!"

"*Milchbart!*" *Thud.* "*Waschlappen!*" *Thud.* "*Memme!*"[38] *Thud.* "At times like this I thoroughly regret having you as – never mind. But I should call *you* Wimpy, Fröhtrich, *Schlapschw –*" He brought his fists down on the table twice more, but Fritz Karl cut him off.

"Papa! Please!"

"Yes! The King never dithers about as you do! Your brother-in-law has ten times your bravery! Look at what the Crown Prince has done, managing Wrangel and everyone else as well!"

Fritz covered his ears, feeling himself blush. He did not wish for praise from Onkel Karl, but it was strange to hear him praising Papa and Fritz of Anhalt – Marianne's brother – and Fritz himself – and giving Fritz Karl such a verbal thrashing, even calling him the names he often called the others.

"*Mein Schatz,*

"Things are not pleasant here, especially with the things *The Times* writes about us! Everyone acts as if I am responsible for what the English papers say.

"I cannot describe the looks I receive whenever England is mentioned, as if I could help it.

"There was a great scene yesterday. Your Aunt Adina is here, and is as *pleasant* to me as ever. Yesterday I overheard her say 'I never cease to regret that there is an Englishwoman in the family.' My blood was at boiling point in an instant as you can imagine, and I was just turning to – confront her – to see who she was speaking to – I do not know what I was going to do, when I heard Aunt Marie's voice.

---

38 Milksop … Sissy (*Waschlappen* litterally means Washrag) … Yellowbelly

" 'How dare you speak of our Crown Princess in that way! If you regret the wishes of your brother – indeed, *brothers* – our Kings, you may take yourself back to your own adopted country, which you abandon so often. Prussia loves their Crown Princess, and if you do not, you must disown Prussia, too!'

"I *did* turn then, and saw the aghast look on the Grand Duchess's proud face. I went up instantly to Aunt Marie and thanked her for her kind words. Aunt Adina may well wish to leave Schwerin, where she never even attempted to make herself popular. That will never be my feeling for Prussia. I love our country and long for its good, and no matter how much I shall always love England I will never forsake the country I have accepted as mine – any more than I could say I did not love you!"

CHAPTER EIGHTEEN

AN ENGLISHWOMAN IN THE FAMILY

Mein Schatz, how I long for you I cannot say. This separation is so long, it seems it must be a year since your departure, though it is only a few short weeks. I understand so well your being uneasy at all the flattery poured upon you, but you are to be envied in some ways. Everyone loves you; you gain everyone's appreciation! I do not have that gift. That is plainer than ever with you away. I am too English, and at home in England, I am often criticized for being too Prussian. I can never do anything right, it seems."

"Defeat – of the – Prussians," Willy read. He looked up, his little face full of horror. "Mama, have we lost?"

Vicky took up the paper. It was *The Times*, as she expected. "No, Willy. This is only a newspaper war. In – well, nearly ten years ago, about when Papa and I were engaged, England was at war with Russia. Großpapa's sister was the Empress there, and Prussia was angry with us – I mean, they were angry with the English. They – the Kreuzzeitung at least – reported our – the English victories as defeats, out of spite. Now, *The Times* does the same to us – to the Prussians."

254

"Mama, you say 'we' about English. But you do about us. I – I can't follow." He leaned his head on his hand, making a face as if it made his head ache.

Vicky sighed. "I know I do, and it must be confusing. But – I was – I am an Englishwoman. I cannot help who I was born, nor do I wish to disown my family." She lifted Willy onto her lap, turning him to face her. "You are born a Prince, a future King. But Princesses are different. They marry, and go to another country. Only if they are in a position like my Mama's is that impossible. And sometimes even Princes become a King of another country. Your Aunt Alix's brother, who is also called Willy, became King of Greece through an election. Do you understand?"

Willy nodded. "I want you to be Prussian," he said, hugging her.

"I am a Prussian, and proud to be. But I am also who I was born. I can't help thinking of England as home. It was my home for seventeen years."

"*Mein Schatz,*

"I wish you would return as Willy begins to be so naughty and disobedient, and needs to experience your authority. He absolutely refuses to let his nose be blown, and snorts like a little pig, which keeps me awake, and flails about when I try to make him. He is very obstinate also about his baths, which he declares he no longer needs."

"Come here Willy, and blow your nose," Vicky called. Willy sat against the wall, his arms crossed. His whole attitude reminded Vicky of Fritz when he wished to refuse to do something he had been ordered to do. Willy began to sink down into the space between the bed and the wall. "If you go down there you won't be able to get out again."

He rolled over. "You haven't kissed me good night, Mama," he whined.

"Blow your nose and I will. I can't sleep with you snuffling in my ear. You should also go and let Mrs. Hobbs help you take your bath; it has been far too long."

Willy scowled. "I don't need a bath. The sentries don't bath so often."

"You aren't a sentry."

"The soldiers don't bath!"

"I'm sure many of them wish they could bathe! Poor fellows, the trenches must be a dreadful place!" Vicky lay down, her thoughts suddenly far away.

Willy dived across the bed, trying to hug her, but she pushed him away. "You haven't done what I told you, Willy. Go to Mrs. Hobbs and ask her to help you."

"But I don't need a bath!"

"You're not a soldier yet, William."

Willy looked at her. She called him "William", instead of "Willy", so little, she hoped that might make an impression, but he only tried to snuggle up to her again.

"I'm a Prince!" he whispered.

"Papa is a Prince, and he longs to be able to bathe." Vicky sat up, went to her desk, and took one of Fritz's letters. "Read this, Willy – translate it if you can."

Willy studied the letter, silently sounding out the words. "Papa says it is – disgusting – there, and he – longs for –" Willy trailed off before he finished his sentence. Vicky took the letter back, glancing over Fritz's lines:

"The sanitation here is so poor, there are many revolting scenes. The trenches are the worst, but even at headquarters it is quite dreadful, though Flensburg is far better than Gravenstein. I long to be home, and to be able to take a long bath, to wash away the grime of this place from my body as well as my mind."

She returned the letter to its place, and lay down, turning her back on Willy.

Willy lay down. She glanced at him. He had turned his back on her, imitating her manner. "I don't want a kiss."

Vicky sighed, but didn't answer. He must learn to obey her. She soon dozed off in spite of his snuffling.

"Fritz?" She jumped awake, thinking she had heard his voice, but realized she had been dreaming. She heard a sniff, but it was a different kind of sniff now. She lay still, listening. *Sniff sniff.* There was a smothered sob.

She turned over, taking Willy in her arms and kissing him. "Willy, don't cry. I love you." He didn't answer, but there were no more sniffs. "Willy, don't you love your Mama?"

"I don't want a bath!" he sobbed. She sighed. She had thought – hoped – that he was crying because she hadn't kissed him goodnight. She had given in to his willfulness in the first moment of waking. He would only be more stubborn the next time.

"*April 8,*

"*Meine Vicky,*

"The second parallel trench before Düppel is finished, but Fritz Karl has declared that a third must be built before we storm. It is too far to go on open ground as it is.

"I have so little to do at times that I help the men dig the snow away, which thankfully is really beginning to thaw, and to carry the heavy materials. I do not go near the actual trenches, so you must not worry that I am exposing myself needlessly to danger.

"Fritz Karl telegraphs to Berlin to ask when the London Conference will meet, which will most likely mean an armistice. We hope to take Düppel before this."

"*April 10,*

"Mama seems concerned at my writing on no other subject but the war, 'as if I now have no other interest'. I only do so because to attempt to indulge my other interests only brings the longing for home and for you to an intensity I can hardly bear. It is better to submerge my non-military being in my soldier's existence until I know when I can come home.

"I heard she wished Papa to recall me when this bombardment was to grow serious. You, I hear, took my part. I cannot leave the army's fate in Wrangel's hands, so I must remain here as long as he does. It is hard enough to think that I shall have to leave it in Fritz Karl's hands when I do come home.

"The storm is to be on the 13th or 14th, as the second trench is to be finished very soon. As a prelude to this, the bombardment from all batteries has started today. It is astonishing how quickly one can become accustomed to such sounds, for everyone sleeps well, except for Fritz Karl, it seems.

"I have distributed the books you sent among the wounded, after adding a note to each that it was given by you."

"The storming is delayed again by Fritz Karl, and a fourth parallel trench is to be built, only three hundred paces from the enemy's nearest. Of course I will not see it; it is far too dangerous. The construction will be extremely difficult, probably resulting in as many losses of life as attempting the storm from the third parallel would cause.

"Fritz Karl asked me to come to see him alone, to show me letters from the King. Onkel Karl is not at all happy about our being on not-hostile terms and meeting alone over political matters."

Düppel, April 16

Fritz bent down as he walked through the first trench, inspecting the security. It was quite tall enough to walk comfortably here. The fourth parallel had, thankfully, been finished with very few losses, the Danish suspecting an attack from a different side and apparently barely noticing the construction.

He turned, following the zigzag of the communications trenches. He held a handkerchief over his mouth and nose. The stench in this trench was horrible. There was very little sanitation here, it being impossible to leave the trench and go into enemy firing range. He turned back. He would not go to the third parallel anyway, keeping his promise to Vicky and his parents not to expose himself. Already, when he was in the communications, there was another trench he began to follow, but he was turned back by guards posted.

"Bullets fly freely here, *Herr Leutenant;* it is not safe to walk upright." The men saluted but obviously didn't recognize him for who he was.

Fritz stood upright, stretching. He hadn't realized how confining the trenches felt, even in the places where it was safe to walk upright. He hurried to his carriage, eager to get away from the atmosphere of filth and death.

Spring was awakening around them. He told the coachman to drive on in the opposite direction of the trenches, going on until they reached farmlands which were not torn by shells and drenched in blood.

A little lamb went frisking by, another following on wobbly, newborn legs. Fritz felt tears come to his eyes watching the happy little creatures. Nearby, in another field, a man walked slowly, sowing seed. How could such peace and beauty exist so close to that world of horrors he had just fled from?

He turned his carriage back. He still couldn't be gone from Wrangel for any length of time. His eyes filled with tears again as he reached the border of the war zone. At the edge of the green farmland was a crater blasted by an overreaching shell. Just outside the crater lay the body of another little lamb, its white fleece streaked with blood.

Fritz covered his face. The sight moved him indescribably, in spite of his having witnessed far worse sights. It was symbolic of the entrance of violence into the peaceful, innocent life many of the people here obviously led.

"*Flensburg, April 19*

"I had not the time to write the last two days. It is the first I have missed, and I have thought of you nearly every minute.

"The shelling continued through last night. Vicky, I could not sleep for the thought of what would occur the next day. Very few could, I think.

"Later, I sat watching the sunrise, my thoughts with you. Now it was I who wished that we could watch the sunrise together, as you wished a few months ago at Balmoral. Can it only be a few months since those beautiful, peaceful days there? But I did not wish you to watch the sunrise I watched – the sun, rising to show the horror of war, the dead and wounded, and the slaughter soon to come.

"How such beauty and such horror coexist is beyond me. There was a slight line of light on the horizon, the sky turned a soft rose, soon turning to brilliant crimson, and the sun appeared in all his glory. But he appeared to look down on the torture the people – the Prussian and the Danish – were to inflict on each other. The beauty of the scene was soon spoiled, the smoke from the shells at times so intense as to blot out the sky.

"About eight o'clock, I joined Wrangel and many others on our way to the Spitzberge, or Avnbjorg, the high hill overlooking the scene, and out of firing range. Fritz Karl finally appeared, swinging himself into the saddle, and joined us, taking the lead. He stood out, certainly, from afar, his uniform scarlet and his boots as glossy a black as ever. Everyone else wore their worn, faded – in many cases quite filthy – uniforms, and the shine of our boots was the last thing on our minds.

"Just before ten o'clock, silence fell. The shelling ceased, giving way to a nerve-racking silence. Nothing appeared to move; there were no birds; the Danes did not show themselves.

"A minute before ten, a band in our second trench struck up a loud marching song, which the men's voices soon joined.

"Fritz Karl had sat perfectly still on his horse, his eye on his watch. Now he rose in the stirrups, drew his sword, and, at precisely ten o'clock, waved his sword so it caught the sun's rays, screaming at the top of his voice, 'Attack!'

"The cry of 'Forward!' 'Forward!' 'Forward!' went on through all our ranks and trenches. The men swarmed out of the fourth parallel and up Düppel like a swarm of bees from a burning hive.

"The Danish fired, but the first wave of bullets were not properly directed and many hit the water harmlessly. Many men fell in the first charge, but after only seven minutes, a Prussian flag fluttered above a Danish redoubt. This was torn down, but replaced quickly with several more.

"I shall not write much here of the battle which followed. The Danes were conquered with remarkable speed, and many prisoners taken – none of our men taken. Onkel Karl's Johanniter corps work wonders among the wounded, as do the people of the new organization which they call 'the Red Cross'. But no amount of surgeons can work fast enough in a time like this – and many men do not make it through the night.

"Surely with this victory Wrangel will be called home in honor, and Fritz Karl may be given supreme command."

"*April 21*

"Papa is coming tomorrow, to congratulate and review the troops on the site of the victory, and so there will be more hustle and bustle than there was in the battle. There will be many speeches, many embraces, many pompous articles to be read in the *Kreuzzeitung*, and many congratulations for things which have only robbed so many of their lives or loved ones."

"*April 23*

"Yesterday about noon I was in Papa's arms. He then greeted Fritz Karl with equal warmth, and shook hands heartily with

Wrangel. All the reviews have gone very well, everything splendidly organized by Fritz Karl.

"The survivors of the storm-troopers marched by holding our flags aloft and the captured Danish flags upside down. Papa visited the Johanniter hospital, and thanked Onkel Karl heartily for his contribution in this direction.

"There was a great alarm today when the Danish fleet was spotted in the distance. There was a deliberation between the King, Wrangel, Roon, Manteuffel, Falckenstein – and not Fritz Karl or myself.

"The plans were approved – which do not take Wrangel home! Instead, he is to go on to Fredericia, to be ready for the siege there, if the Peace Conference does not call off the war.

"I am afraid I was very blunt and rude to Manteuffel and Roon when I told them that Wrangel's stay was an impossibility, and I even lost my temper with Papa, though the day has thankfully not yet come when I speak to him as I did to your Mama in November.

"People are dissatisfied with Fritz Karl and it is clear they do not wish to make him Supreme Commander, though who should be otherwise it is not clear, unless it is to be me.

"Papa's conversation and tone made his state all too obvious; he was in great agreement with Bismarck, Roon, Onkel Karl, etc, though he was not cold to me. Several hundredweight of the Berlin atmosphere was brought into camp, to flatten me.

"As I have said, all pour flattery upon me until it is too heavy to stand up under.

"Papa has never mentioned my personal conduct, only asked me whether I thought Wrangel could remain here without me.

"When addressing the troops, Papa let his heart overflow, but I could not help cringing at so much praise for our bravery. I cannot forget that the victory had obviously been on our side the whole time, as the Danish were outrageously outnumbered, though they had fortifications to shelter behind, which we did not.

"Papa has also refused to see Fritz Augustenburg, who wished to pay his respects. Bismarck's influence is obvious here, and everyone says that the Duchies of Schleswig and Holstein shall end up annexed by Prussia instead of held safe by Prussia for their rightful sovereign.

"All of this piles on top of me, and the disappointment of not going home tips the scale, and I am feeling very low indeed."

"*April 24*

"I remain at Schleswig for a few days and then return to my post as Wrangel's nursemaid. Thankfully they have left no one behind from Berlin, so I am not more surrounded by spies and traitors than previously.

"Papa offered to send for you to Hamburg and for me to accompany him as far, but I feel it is better to remain here than torture myself – and you – with having to say goodbye immediately after meeting.

"I am angry, as you may gather. On top of everything, Onkel Karl left for Berlin this morning."

"*April 28*

"They think it fine to heap abuse on you, and say you do not share the country's joy in our victory, as you are far too English to have anything but Danish sympathies."

"*April 29*

"Fredericia is evacuated by the Danes! There shall be no siege, and the Austrians occupy it, leaving us no reason to go!"

"*May 2*

"There is to be an armistice at last! So we shall meet soon after all! How the joy overwhelms me I cannot say; I hardly know what I write!

"I am very pleased you have Affie's company. I could not keep the tears from my eyes when I read your description of how low you have been, and it came just at the time when I was angry over the decision about Wrangel. I hope I shall see Affie, and that his decoration shall be delayed until I can conduct it myself.

"Bismarck sent me a messenger with three several-week-old government dispatches. This is what I am allowed to see, and he writes nevertheless that they must be returned with all speed. I send a messenger direct to you, telling him that I wish my parcel to be in your hands in the morning, so that he will not delay and allow himself to be spied upon.

"The Austrian fleet has finally arrived. They are rather late, I believe.

"Fritz Karl indulges himself in passive, contemplative activities, and mostly remains in bed since the announcement of the evacuation.

"I shall soon be on my way to Hamburg, as you too will be, and soon we shall be in each other's arms."

CHAPTER NINETEEN

MY HEART'S BEST TREASURE

Hamburg, May 13, 1864

Vicky lingered under the trees as she walked back to the station. She could see a distant train now. She paused, watching, thinking of how long it had been since she had seen Fritz. They had been apart for nearly four months! That seemed impossible. She hoped this would be his train. He had written that two Prussian trains would arrive at that station today, and he could not say which one he would be on.

As the train pulled into the station, a man looked out of an open window, waving. Vicky smiled to herself. She had seen so many of the Austrian troops waving and kissing their hands to the ladies. Yes, this man was kissing his hand. But this was a Prussian train. The Austrians and Prussians had separated.

She looked around. There was no crowd, and she was the only lady waiting at the station. She shrank back towards the thicket uneasily. Why was a strange man greeting her so? She looked at him again. He had a long, thick beard and a tanned face, but something about his eyes seemed familiar. Yes, where had she seen him before?

The train had stopped now, and the passengers were getting out. Vicky watched several families step out, obviously recently reunited, as fathers and husbands, brothers and sons embraced their family members repeatedly in public. But the man with the long beard stood alone. He had no family with him; there seemed no

266

one there to meet him. But he stood, looking about, seeming as if he was waiting for someone to greet him.

He looked towards her again, then stepped forward, and began to walk towards her, an eager expression in his eyes. She shrank uneasily away again, but he was beside her in a moment. He raised a hand to touch her cheek. She was about to snatch herself away, but he had taken her hand. Finally, he spoke.

"*Meine* Vicky?" His hand lingered on her cheek, his thumb brushing her lips.

"Oh, Fritz!" Vicky flung her arms round his neck, tears blinding her as she felt him clasp her to him. "I – oh, Fritz." She couldn't say anything more as sobs tore through her.

"You did not know me?" His voice trembled as he leaned down and released her arms from his neck. He stood up again, gazing down tenderly into her eyes.

"You – you look – so – so different," she gasped. She touched his long beard, reaching up for a kiss and throwing her arms round him again. "I knew your eyes were familiar, but – you look so different. But I should have known, as others do too." She studied his face. "You look so serious, and –"

"And what, Vicky?"

"I – I don't want to say you look older, but –"

He nodded. "I would not be surprised if I do."

She took his hand, pressing it to her lips. "*Gott* has given *you* back to *me*," she whispered, looking up into his eyes. He smiled and kissed her again, and they hurried to the carriage. He had said that to her so many times.

Fritz was changed in other ways besides his long beard and serious expression. Vicky noticed more changes each day, indeed, each hour she spent in his company. His voice carried a tone of command it never had before; his manner lacked some of the diffidence and hesitancy which had generally characterized him. She was glad to see this; it was certainly time he came into his own strength.

There was a look in his eyes at times which told of the sights he had witnessed; he had indeed borne the hardships of a northern winter war; his face was tanned and there was a small scar on his cheek.

At night, when she was nestled again in his arms, there was something different, too. His hands, though as gentle as ever, were calloused and hardened; at times they felt sharp against her skin. His body was thinner, but at the same time, more muscular. She knew from his letters that he had grown accustomed to long marches and rides in deep snow, helping the men carry heavy materials, digging the snow and ice away from the camp, clinging onto ropes to stay together in the raging winter storms, when one could easily be blown off balance and buried in the whirling snow. He had grown stronger, but he didn't realize it, and she often winced at what he most likely thought was a gentle squeeze of his hand.

"Fritz, when you were – ah!"

"Did I hurt you?" he asked, stroking her cheek, his eyes full of concern.

"Yes, but – it is nothing, Fritz." She paused, turning over and trying to lie down comfortably. "It is only – you don't know your own strength anymore," she said, smiling as she traced a line of the muscles in his arm with her finger. "But I like this," she said, taking his hand and feeling the calluses on his palm with her fingers, pressing his hand to her lips, and stroking his long beard. "It is all you, and I love you, even if it is different from the – *you* – we knew before the war." She drew his arms more tightly around her. "I'm so glad to have you back, Fritz," she whispered, pressing his hand to her heart.

"I feel, in many ways, as if I am a different person," he said, kissing her cheek, "but here, nothing is changed, besides my exterior." He laughed, and turned to cradle her face in his hands. "War is a dreadful, terrible thing, and I shall never forget it," he said, shuddering. "Vicky, I thought of you, very often, in the worst moments. Your face was before me as we walked through the blizzard – your face before me at the moment of the storming of Düppel. I dreamed of you often, at night, lying alone on the cold ground or in the lonely farmhouse beds. I dreamed of this, too." He gently placed a hand on her abdomen, and received an answering kick.

"Baby is lively," Vicky said, putting her hands over his. "It was a comfort to feel that I had another little one to love, while you were away. Willy has kept his Mama company and has mostly been a good boy. But you need to speak to him on the subject of bathing." She laughed. "He is such an affectionate little boy; I never remember any of my brothers being quite so demonstrative as he is."

"Your Mama was not as demonstrative towards little children as you are. Did she have you in her room every morning, as you do?"

"No, though she was always a very affectionate mother, as I remember. I always felt I was the most trouble, although she always says Bertie was."

Berlin, May 17, 1864

"Papa." Vicky followed Fritz as he went up to his father, kneeling and kissing his hand. Vicky curtseyed deeply.

"I do not have time to speak much," the King said. They both looked up at him in surprise. This wasn't the greeting they had expected after Fritz's return from the war. Fritz tried again to begin a conversation, but his father waved him away.

"Never mind; he has been irritable of late," Vicky said as they got back into their carriage. Fritz frowned as they drove up to the Schloss. In the entrance, they met Prince Charles and Aunt Marie.

"I am so pleased to see you here again, safe and well," Aunt Marie said, embracing Fritz. "And you are looking much better now that you are together again." She kissed Vicky's cheek.

Vicky felt Prince Charles's eyes on her, and shrank close to Fritz, pulling his arm around her, half wrapping herself in his cloak. Prince Charles tried to meet Fritz's eye, but Fritz saluted, looking over his head.

"You've done well, Fritz." Prince Charles nodded briefly, turned and went in. Vicky looked up, and was surprised to see tears in Fritz's eyes.

"What is the matter?" she whispered.

"Fritz. They call me Fritz," he murmured.

Vicky nodded. "Is it the first time?"

Fritz nodded, swallowing and wiping his eyes. He had mentioned in his letters that Fritz Karl had also called him "Fritz", not "Fritzch", as he always had.

"Come," Vicky whispered, heading back to the carriage. "The children are longing to see you."

Vicky carefully opened the nursery door, and peered in. Mrs. Hobbs sat in the corner with Henry on her lap. Willy lay in bed, chattering away to Sophie Dobeneck. Charlotte also lay in bed, but

Vicky couldn't tell if she was asleep.

She glanced up at Fritz, her finger to her lips. She opened the door wider, and they both entered. Fritz knelt by Willy's bedside.

Vicky saw Willy look up at him, a look of confusion on his face for a moment, but Fritz said something Vicky couldn't quite hear, and they threw their arms around each other.

"Papa! Papa, I – Mama said I was a good boy. I take care of her, Papa!" Vicky stepped closer, and saw tears streaming down both their faces.

"Yer 'ighness! Yer 'ome! I didn't know you the first moment, what with yer beard and all, but it is you, in the flesh!" Mrs. Hobbs had set Henry down and rushed to Fritz's side, attempting to bow, curtsey and salute all at the same time, and finally, she too embraced him.

"How is the little one?" Fritz asked her. She returned to Henry, lifting him up and placing him in his father's arms.

"Papa!" Henry said. Vicky was glad he didn't seem afraid of Fritz. She had wondered what the children's reactions would be to his beard, but they recognized his voice.

"Papa? Papa home?" came sleepily from Charlotte's little bed. Fritz turned, kneeling down.

"Ahh!" Charlotte screamed, pulling her blanket over her head. "Hobby! Where's Papa!" she screamed. Mrs. Hobbs hurried to her side, lifting her in her arms.

"Hush, my liddle Princess, this is yer Papa," she said, turning to Fritz. Charlotte covered her face, hiding against Mrs. Hobbs' shoulder, sobbing. She laid her back down and shrugged, turning to Vicky and Fritz.

"Hi don't know what to do with 'er. Must you keep the beard? She might not know you with it."

***

May 20

"Vicky?"

Vicky turned at Fritz's voice, staring for a moment. She smiled. "This is how we know you," she said, throwing her arms around him. He had shaved, and again wore mutton-chops rather than a full beard. "Though I thought you very handsome the other way."

"I will go and see if Charlotte knows Papa now," he smiled. "Do you wish to come?"

Vicky nodded, and they went to the nursery.

"Papa home! Papa home!" Charlotte squealed, clapping her hands as Fritz knelt down before her. Her face beamed with smiles as he took her up in his arms.

Willy looked up at them. "I knew you, Papa. You can't hide you. Papa?" He ran to Fritz, reaching up to take his hand. "Why don't the guards salute me? They always did before."

Fritz looked down at his little son, ruffling his hair. "They are obeying orders."

"What orders?" Willy asked in English. Vicky smiled, stifling her laughter. He said the word indistinctly, so it sounded more like "odors" than "orders", but she must not laugh at such a moment. It was important for Willy to see that she took Fritz's words seriously. "Why would they have orders not to salute me?"

"They are not to salute an unwashed Prince," Fritz said solemnly, crouching down to look Willy directly in the eye. "Wilhelm, go and ask Mrs. Hobbs to help you with your bath. Then you can go outside, and see what happens when you obey your parents."

Willy nodded, but grimaced as he looked up at Vicky. He

turned, hanging his head, and went up to Mrs. Hobbs, who waited at the doorway. "Bath, Hobby," he said in a subdued voice.

June 9

Vicky stood outside the station house, just off of the red carpet which was rolled out. Behind her stood Fritz, Abbat, Prince Charles, Prince Albrecht, and all the other Princes of the family – Fritz Karl of course being absent. All were dressed in Russian uniform. It was nearly eleven o'clock at night.

Finally, she saw lights in the distance, and soon the train's whistle sounded as it drew to a halt. All the Princes stood to attention, saluting as the door opened.

Vicky looked up at Tsar Alexander as he stepped off the train. He was tall and slender, and very like the Prussian family. The woman who followed him was very tall – not very much shorter than he, and had something about her face which strangely reminded her of Alice.

"Mon cousin." He stepped up and kissed Fritz on both cheeks, as Vicky knew the custom was in Russia, shaking hands with all the Princes and embracing Fritz. He turned to Vicky. A sudden shyness seemed to creep into his manner; he stared awkwardly at her for a moment, and turned away. She heard him murmur something, and heard the word "Victoria." She smiled. She probably reminded him of Mama. Mama had been a little younger than she was when he was in England.

June 10, 1864

"Vicky?" Vicky struggled to open her eyes. It was early in the morning. She looked up. Fritz knelt at the bedside, gently shaking her awake.

"What is it, Fritz? Must you go so early again?" He shook his head. "Was I – I wasn't having bad dreams," she yawned. His expression reminded her of when he woke her when he could tell she was having nightmares.

Fritz took her in his arms, rubbing her back gently. "We need to speak of something serious."

Vicky yawned as she lay her head on his shoulder. "I will try to stay awake."

"There is to be tea and dinner this evening with the Russian family," he began. He paused, looking her in the eye.

"There is nothing unusual about that."

"It is to be at Glienicke." He paused, still looking her in the eye. "Do you think – do you feel – I don't know if we could –" He didn't finish his sentence, beginning over and over again.

"Yes, Fritz. You will be with me, and there will be many people about. I am well enough, and in those circumstances, I will not feel uncomfortable."

Fritz nodded, kissing her forehead. "*Gut.* I was thinking of this a great deal, but I wasn't sure what to ask you. I hoped it would not be necessary to refuse during the Russian visit, though Alexander himself would understand. He is all too aware of Onkel Karl." Fritz's expression hardened. "But still, I would not have liked you to have to refuse the first dinner during the visit."

Glienicke, Potsdam, June 10, 1864.

Vicky clutched Fritz's arm nervously as they passed the Lions' Gate at Glienicke and walked up the staircase. She had been to a few balls and dinners at Glienicke before, but the balls and their accompanying dinners were usually given at the Casino, a small building nearer the river. She had never been inside the Schloss here.

From outside, Glienicke Schloss was quite unpretending. It was a large – though rather small for a castle – boxy yellow building with green shutters. Inside, it was equally different from the other castles. The ceilings were fairly low, and each room's walls were a solid color. There was a blue room, a dark green room, a rose room, several white or very pale tan rooms. She knew the bedrooms were a lighter – though not pale or bright – green. Fritz had told her so.

The smell of cigar smoke lingered heavily on the air, and under it another scent – something Vicky couldn't identify.

The other guests were waiting in one of the tan rooms, and rose as Vicky and Fritz came in. Prince Charles entered from another door. He offered his arm to the Tsarina, and they all entered the dining room in a procession.

The dining room was a large, red-walled hall with portraits of Prince Charles and his wife on the walls. The chair cushions were red as well, the same shade as the walls.

Vicky sat down, glad to be seated between Fritz and the Tsar. Aunt Marie sat on Fritz's other side, and Abbat next to her. Vicky was so thankful that they had made the arrangement that she sat with them at the events and dinners, and not with Prince Charles, who sat between the Tsarina and Aunt Elisa.

"You are so like your mother," the Tsar said in French, glancing at her with a little smile.

"She sends her kindest greetings," Vicky replied, smiling back. "I am certainly very interested to meet you," she murmured. "I only wish it was in a more agreeable setting."

He pursed his lips, glancing across the table at Prince Charles. He nodded briefly. "We will not speak of such subjects here. How is your Mama? I feel deeply for her in her sorrow."

Vicky stood at Fritz's side. "I'm tired," she whispered.

The dinner was over, and everyone stood or sat about in groups, talking. The Tsar stood nearby, talking with Aunt Marie, but watching Vicky when he thought she wasn't looking at him. Prince Charles sat at the far end of the table, talking with two of the gentlemen of his household.

"What?" Fritz asked, leaning down to hear her better. The buzz of conversation was rather loud, and the mysterious, unidentifiable odor had seemed to grow stronger. It smelled sour and strange, but Vicky still couldn't identify it.

"Do you wish to go? Or to sit down?"

"I'll sit down if you'll stay with me."

Fritz nodded, and they sat next to each other on the red sofa at the edge of the room.

Dessert was served, and shortly afterwards, a door opened, Frau Kampmann entering with the little girls. Vicky glanced across the room at Marianne. She was engaged in conversation with another lady and hadn't seemed to notice her children's appearance.

The little girls stood close together, Mariechen's arms around Ebi and Louischen, their hands intertwined. They remained in the doorway, looking about nervously, and only went to meet the guests after several encouraging nudges from Frau Kampmann.

They reached the sofa where Vicky and Fritz sat, and all three looked up, smiling briefly. Vicky watched them as they made their way into the center of the room, and went up to Prince Charles. He bent down and kissed the girls on the top of their heads. They were about to go on, when he took Ebi's hand, pulled her back, whispered something in her ear and gave her a biscuit from the table.

Something made Vicky's spine prickle as she watched, a nervous shiver passing over her as Ebi looked up, her face transformed. She broke away from Mariechen's grasp and went round the room again, smiling, nodding and holding her hand out to be kissed, in the manner of a young lady being trained for the "cercle", rather than the small, shy child she had been a moment before. She passed by Vicky and Fritz without looking at them this time, not even nodding.

Frau Kampmann took her hand as she passed by her, and ushered the children out again. Louischen and Mariechen turned back, Mariechen meeting Vicky's eye with a brief, shy smile.

Suddenly, everyone rose. Vicky looked about, realizing they were forming the procession again. She stood, taking Fritz's arm, and walked with him, feeling rather sick. *I didn't eat anything, it can't be that*. Fritz had told her long ago never to eat or drink at Glienicke. At one moment she had almost forgotten and taken a sip of water, as she was feeling rather sick, but Fritz had noticed and stopped her. She was far past the morning-sickness, and didn't usually feel this way anymore.

She followed Fritz where he led her, feeling more disoriented than ever. They came to a small door before which stood two very tall men with drawn swords. Prince Charles nodded to them, and they stood aside. He quickly unlocked the door, and all of the men and some of the women had to stoop to enter. The next room was paneled in mahogany, with two large, low chandeliers.

Vicky shook her head and began to look about. This was Prince Charles's collection room. Jeweled weapons hung on the brown walls, glinting in the light of a hundred candles. More lay in display cases, nestled in crimson velvet. Old guns – rifles, muskets

– swords with beautifully encrusted hilts, shields with gilt designs she longed to study more closely. Almost everything had a touch of turquoises about it, or if not that, a sparkling, shining sapphire.

Vicky shivered. This was enticing, now that she was here. She remembered her second dinner in Berlin, when she had first sat next to Prince Charles, and he had asked if she would "come and let him show her his treasures." She had declined, as Fritz and Mama cautioned her to go there as little as possible.

She looked up at the small, glittering knives, and froze.

There it was. An elegant white-bladed dagger with a swirling V set in sapphires.

It was the dagger which Fritz had given to his father on his ninth birthday, then being set with a W, and which had been reset for Fritz to give her.

It was the dagger Prince Charles had taken from her in the laundry.

It was the dagger which he had tried to trick her into taking back, in an attempt to make her accept his power.

It was the dagger whose flat she had felt the sting of if she didn't do what he said.

Vicky moaned involuntarily, covering her face and pulling Fritz's cloak around her. It was intolerable to be tormented like this in front of the room full of people, and even more intolerable that she had felt Prince Charles's gaze on her. She could feel it without even looking at him.

She felt Fritz's arm go around her, and tried to walk with him, though she couldn't see. In a blur, she heard him excuse himself and her. The sound of voices and footsteps faded, and she sensed they were in another room. She felt Fritz lift her carefully, and walk on, her face still covered by his cloak. He spoke softly as he walked.

"*Meine* Vicky," he murmured. "We must have you out of this

place. I should not have let you come here. I will soon have you home."

At last, she felt a breeze on her face. It was a relief to breathe fresh air, and no longer smell the cigars, no longer to have her nostrils filled with that heavy, sour odor. She could tell they were near the bright lamps outside. Fritz spoke to someone – and she felt herself being laid down on a cushion. She felt Fritz lift her head so it lay in his lap.

Potsdam, Neues Palais, June 10, 1864

Fritz gently lifted Vicky's head and stepped out of the carriage. "Carry her gently," he said to the footmen. A sort of stretcher was fetched, and they hurried inside.

Fritz followed closely behind, directing them to lay her gently on the bed. He was thankful to see that her eyes were open, and that they looked clear and alert.

"What happened, Vicky? I should not have taken you there, but what happened? You seemed well all through the dinner."

"Yes, Fritz, but – my head!" She put her hand on her forehead and groaned. "And the smell – that sour smell – I have smelled it in certain rooms in the Groß Schloss, and at San Souci, when the King was dying. What is it?"

Fritz shrugged. "I smelled nothing sour. I only smelled the vile cigars." He went round the bed and lay down beside her, taking her hand and stroking her cheek. "What was it? What made you hide your face and nearly faint?"

"The dagger," Vicky said, her voice coming out hoarse and trembling. "He – he had it there. I – I am glad – I saw it – because – I was –" She began to shiver and moan again.

"Hush, *meine* Vicky." He gently wrapped his cloak around her, stroking her forehead.

"I was beginning to become fascinated," she finally said. "I wanted to study the things there, and felt a desire to return. It was unreasonable. At the same time I knew where we were, but it was a strange, separate thought. But then I saw – my dagger, and –" She shuddered again, her eyes taking on the strange, blank expression which was all too familiar.

Fritz lay down by her side. "*Meine* Vicky. *Ach*, how I wish we had not gone." He shook his head. He had known it might cause this, but Vicky had insisted she was strong enough to go.

"You saw what happened with Ebi, too, didn't you?" Fritz jumped at the sound of Vicky's voice. She had recovered much more rapidly than she had in the past. "That made me feel very uneasy, too."

"I know. I want Marianne's girls to have our children as their friends, but we must be careful for our children's sakes, and our own," Fritz said. "A little child could make a mistake so easily, in the midst of their play, although we have told them."

June 18

"The left wing, and the crown," Onkel Karl called, simultaneously raising his pistol and taking aim. *Bang! Bang!* The artificial eagle swung wildly for a moment, then everyone could see that the left wing was torn away, but the crown still remained.

A new eagle was hung, this one being too badly torn apart. Many more took their turns, some hitting the target they called, some missing wildly and firing into the thicket beyond.

There were only two men left in line. Each made a bad shot,

having only chosen one target. A footman stepped forward to remove the eagle, but Vicky stepped forward, taking position before the target. The footman hurried away, laughing to himself. More laughter was heard in the crowd. Vicky glanced back at Fritz, her face flushed.

"The Crown and the Scepter," she called, raising her pistol. *Bang! Bang!* The whole crowd was silent. The eagle swung violently, and the footman stepped forward to examine it.

"The eagle is missing its crown and its scepter," he announced loudly. The silence was unbroken.

Abbat threw his cap in the air. "Three cheers for our Crown Princess!" he called.

Fritz tried to join in the cheers which followed, but his voice wouldn't come out; he felt choked with emotion. He gazed at Vicky, his heart bursting with pride. The crown and the scepter were the most difficult targets; no one else had called the scepter, and only Onkel Karl the crown, which he had missed.

Several men came up to shake hands with Vicky and Fritz, who stood hand in hand. "You have a wife to be proud of," one man said to Fritz. "I wouldn't like to cross her."

"You beat us all!" One of the very young recruits had come up, gazing admiringly at Vicky. "I wonder what Papa will say to the contest being won by a girl!"

Fritz turned, looking about in the crowd. Onkel Karl stood at the other side of the clearing, a look on his face as if he had swallowed a very bitter pill.

June 23

"Denmark refuses the conditions, and begins hostilities again,"

Vicky read aloud. She looked up at Fritz. "Dividing at the Dannewerke was suggested, allowing Denmark to keep two thirds of Schleswig. And yet they refuse it? They have refused all the suggestions, so the war goes on." She took Fritz's hand. "I am glad Moltke is in charge now, and not Wrangel, so you do not have to return."

Fritz nodded. "Moltke is an expert strategist. I was not able to take in even half of what he taught me while he was my aide-de-camp."

June 29

"Victory at Als, and this will be the end of the war." Fritz turned to Vicky. "The end of the war on *this* day," he murmured.

"This day?" Vicky looked up from her painting, puzzled. "What is peculiar about this day?"

"Nothing. It is Onkel Karl's birthday."

August 3

"Peace is signed, and Fritz Karl will be home tomorrow," Fritz said, looking up from his papers as Vicky came in. "They cede the Elbe duchies. It only remains to be seen if Bismarck will keep his word, and we hold them for Fritz Augustenburg, or if they are to be absorbed into Prussia, as so many people say."

"Surely they will not do that! The whole of Germany would be in an uproar if they did so."

Fritz shrugged. "Austria hopes to obtain access to the seaports somehow. I don't see how that will happen if it becomes an independent state. And many strategists declare we must keep it, and build a canal, so we may have naval access without having to round Denmark."

"But that is absurd. Prussia is not a naval power!" Vicky laughed. "The very thought is a funny one. And Austria keeps her fleet in the Adriatic. That is why they took so long to arrive during the war! And besides, your Papa received Fritz and Ada so kindly. Surely he does not mean treachery."

"Perhaps Papa does not, but Bismarck does, I am certain."

Marmor Palais, Potsdam, August 6

Vicky met Marianne at the top of the stairs.

"Oh, I wish I hadn't invited you today," Marianne said, wringing her hands and looking tearful.

"Why?"

"He isn't away, as I said he would be," Marianne murmured. "You don't have to come, if you don't wish."

"I do not want to disappoint you, nor to not have the visit with you I promised myself," Vicky said, taking Marianne's arm and squeezing her hand. Marianne nodded, and led the way to the dining room.

The girls sat at the table grouped around Marianne's chair as they often did when Vicky came to tea, but they sat silently, not talking as they often did when alone. Vicky looked about the room. At the distant end of the table sat Fritz Karl, a wine glass and several bottles on the table before him. He took a long, slow drink, and then looked up at Marianne and Vicky, who had seated themselves between the little girls.

"Why did you wish to deprive me of such a *lovely* visitor, Marianne," he said, just loud enough to be audible. Vicky felt his eyes on her, but she didn't look up.

"Aunt Vicky, you never come here when Papa is home," Mariechen whispered.

"Your Mama thinks it better I do not, usually, but we expected him to be away today."

Mariechen nodded. "I know; he has much to do still, with correspondence about the war, and he was to go on the hunting party to Todensrode, but I believe the Duke of Brunswick had a fall and couldn't be a comfortable host."

"Do you have any new drawings to show me?"

Mariechen nodded again. "Yes, Aunty, but I would have to go and fetch them, and I don't know –" She glanced at Fritz Karl.

Vicky nodded, turning to Marianne, who sat stiffly, not looking up or speaking. "Will you not try to –"

"It is no use," Marianne whispered, and Fritz Karl looked up again at the sound of her voice. She shook her head, and continued her silence.

"My feet hurt," Louischen said loudly, holding her bare foot up above the table.

"Hush," Marianne whispered, motioning her to put her foot down, but Fritz Karl had looked up again.

"Why don't you even keep the brat decently dressed, Marianne. If you are to have these useless girls, you ought to –"

"I think my feet are too big now," Louischen said to Vicky. "I can't fit them in my shoes anymore."

"That simply means you need new shoes, Louischen," Vicky said, looking at the little girl's foot which she again held up above the table. "Your feet aren't too big."

"Papa said they were," Louischen said, a quiver going over her little face.

"She doesn't need new shoes until the construction is finished" Fritz Karl said. "We have enough expenses without *that*." He spat out the words.

He acts as if he was being asked to build another palace for the girls, rather than ensuring I am capable of caring for them, Vicky remembered Marianne saying another time he had refused a simple request which should have already been available in the household.

"Do you wish to come to the Neues Palais?" Vicky whispered to Marianne as they both rose.

"I don't see how we can, with him in this mood, and at home," Marianne whispered, tears coming to her eyes.

"I will see that Louischen has new shoes, and –"

"No, you will not!" Fritz Karl had stood and strode across the room toward them, wine glass in hand. "I am the master of my house, and I–"

A shadow fell across them, and Fritz Karl's face changed. Vicky and Marianne clung to each other, neither wishing to turn their backs to Fritz Karl, but wondering who was there.

"I am only here on a friendly visit," came in Fritz's voice, and Vicky breathed a sigh of relief. Louischen clung to her, but her grip relaxed slightly at the sound of his voice. Fritz stepped forward, between them and Fritz Karl. "I am here on a friendly visit, and wish it to remain so," he said, sitting down. He kept his eyes on Fritz Karl, who returned silently to his seat.

"My report was over quickly, so I came to find you," he said to Vicky, putting his arm around Ebi and stroking her hair as she leaned her head against his shoulder. "I saw that Fritz Karl was home," he said, lowering his voice, "and thought it better I come in unannounced."

"Yes, Fritz," Vicky whispered. "Things seemed about to get ugly."

Fritz Karl looked up again, beginning to speak without addressing anyone directly. "A man can't come home without finding unwelcome guests being invited to his house. A man can't be master in his own house." He rose again, his step unsteady, his eyes unfocused as he stared at Fritz. He stepped forward, his hand hitting the back of a chair, and the wine glass falling to the floor with a loud crash.

"How dare you!" he shouted at no one in particular. "Louise, come and get me another glass." Louischen stood, looking at Vicky and Marianne and then at him with wide, alarmed eyes. She gazed at the floor, covered with shattered glass, and at her bare feet. "Obey me!" Fritz Karl shouted again.

Vicky saw Louischen step forward, a look of agony in her eyes before she even reached the broken glass. Marianne rose, her face flushed with anger, her mouth open to speak, but before she did, Fritz rose, put a hand on her shoulder and shook his head, and stepped forward, scooping Louischen up in his arms as he stepped across the room to another table where several wine glasses stood. He returned, placing Louischen in Vicky's arms and depositing the wine glass on the table before Fritz Karl.

Fritz Karl rose. He stepped forward. "How dare you interfere in my household? I think I have made it clear enough that you are not welcome here, you and your–"

"I will not be rude to you, if you are not rude to me," Fritz said, his voice calm and steady. "I have just given you the glass you asked for. You have, in the past, come to *our* house, and 'interfered in *my* household,' as you say. I do not call it rude to protect an innocent child from one who would compel her to harm herself." Fritz rose, holding out his hand. "*Guten Tag.* I see we have outstayed our welcome. But you will kindly give your permission for Marianne and the children to visit us? They are very welcome at the Neues Palais."

Vicky saw Fritz Karl's fist clench; his whole arm trembled. "How dare you come between me and my wife and children? No, you cannot invite them; they do *not* have my permission to go *anywhere*!" He snatched the wine glass from the table and smashed it against the back of the chair. "And you cannot leave this place until–" He stepped toward the door, leaning down to pick something up.

Vicky glanced down. There were his spurred riding boots, a coat tossed aside, and – in his hand, his riding whip. He held it threateningly as he stepped forward so he was in front of the door.

"You will not do anything foolish," Fritz said, but his voice was tense this time. Fritz Karl stepped back, beginning to raise his hand, but his movements were clumsy; he was thoroughly drunk. He stepped on something, and stumbled.

Vicky looked up again, but the movement was too fast for her eyes to follow. Fritz held the lash of the whip tightly. Fritz Karl regained his balance, and glared at him, struggling to pull it out of his grasp, but Fritz stood firm, quite towering over Fritz Karl. Fritz still wore his boots, while Fritz Karl had taken his off.

"I will certainly not abandon those I care about in your company when you are in this state," Fritz said. "They will accompany me, or I shall ask my father to place them under my protection permanently." He stood still, watching carefully as Fritz Karl finally gave up the tug-of-war, and releasing his hold at the same moment Fritz Karl dropped the whip.

"You won't get the King's permission for that," Fritz Karl muttered as he stalked out of the room.

Louischen burst into tears as the door slammed. "Aunty, my feet – they hurt before, but now –" Her voice trailed off as she tried not to sob. Vicky looked at her feet. There were several flecks of blood. She had stepped on the tiny shards of glass, although Fritz had rescued her before she had gone any further.

"Come, girls, before he comes back," Marianne said, taking Mariechen and Ebi's hands and hurrying to a door at the opposite end of the room. Vicky followed, carrying Louischen in her arms, as Fritz followed slowly, continually turning to look back. "Come this way," Marianne said, and they went through a different corridor than Vicky had ever been in.

"Here," Marianne said, opening another door and hurrying on.

"Are we going to the Grotto?" Vicky asked. The Marmor Palais had an underground dining hall which was only used in particularly hot, dry years.

Marianne nodded, and then shook her head. They went on, passing through the Grotto, and then into another room. Marianne waited till Fritz had joined them, and closed the door she had just opened, locking it behind them.

"Where are we going?" Ebi asked, looking about. Marianne turned toward the distant end of the room, going forward, and lifting a curtain. She felt the wall, and put the key into the keyhole of a door Vicky couldn't see. It appeared as if part of the wall came away, and the opening was just tall enough for Vicky to go through without stooping. Marianne passed through, still holding Ebi's hand.

Vicky followed, kissing Louischen's forehead as she gave a whimper of pain. Her foot had bumped the doorway as Vicky carefully stepped into the dark passageway. She looked back as Fritz stooped to come through. Marianne went back to lock the door.

"It gets higher further on," she said, as they began to walk again. The passageway was very short at first, but soon opened up.

There were several forks in the passage, but Vicky followed Marianne's lantern, which she had picked up at the entrance of the tunnel. It was cold and dark, with damp arched brick walls, very different from the Palace corridors.

"Here we are," Marianne said. "Be careful; it is a winding stair," she said, holding the lantern carefully as she went around and around.

Vicky handed Louischen to Fritz. "I must take my time," she said, letting the others go up ahead of her. She was already exhausted. "I shouldn't be climbing spiral staircases in my condition." Her time was drawing nearer; she expected the baby within the next month.

Finally, Vicky reached the top of the stairs. Marianne had unlocked another door. A few more steps, and they came out into what appeared to be a small guard house. When they were all out, she turned, locked the door, and breathed a long sigh. She turned to Fritz.

"*Danke*," she murmured, squeezing his hand. "I don't know what would have happened –" Her voice was choked with emotion.

Fritz nodded, and embraced her. "I am thankful we were present, except – our presence was what provoked him so."

"No. It would have happened anyway; it always does when he is like that." She shuddered, hugging Mariechen and Ebi to her.

Fritz nodded, a sad smile on his face. He turned to Vicky. "I was wondering if you would have a chance to meet Fritz Karl as he was during the war, or if he would already be like this again." Marianne looked up at him, a strange expression on her face.

"You mean – when he is not hypnotized?" Vicky asked. He nodded. "I thought that was what you meant. And – do you mean to hint – is he only a coward when he is so – or is it something else? Are you hinting –" She whispered in his ear.

Marianne shook her head. "Please, do not speak of this in front of the girls," she said, but Fritz nodded to Vicky. Maricchen covered her ears, as she always did when her mother said she didn't wish the girls to hear something. Ebi leaned against Marianne, looking tired, and didn't seem to take notice of what was being spoken of.

Louischen looked up from where she had hidden her face on Fritz's shoulder. "Ef-feminate." She said the word slowly. "Ef-feminate. Fem-in-nin." She looked at Vicky. "It means – like a woman?" Vicky nodded. "Purple," Louischen said seriously, nodding and hiding her face again.

Marianne was about to speak, but Fritz interrupted her. "I do wish it was possible to get Papa to place you under our protection permanently."

Marianne sighed, shaking her head. "Saying it to Fritz Karl wasn't a step in that direction. He will tell his father, and it will be more impossible than ever."

"But we must not stand here talking," Vicky said, stroking Louischen's forehead. "We must get home and get something for these poor little feet."

Marianne's eyes filled with tears, and they went out of the guard house. Vicky looked about. "There is one of our carriages, and Hedwig in it. Come."

"Is that better?" Vicky asked Louischen, kissing the tears off her cheeks.

"Y-yes," Louischen sobbed. Several tiny glass splinters had had to be removed under a magnifying glass. Her feet were bathed and bandaged.

"I will make sure you have some new shoes," Vicky went on, stroking her hair and sitting by her on the bed.

"No – no!" Louischen cried, a frightened look crossing her face. "I couldn't wear them at home, because he would–" She broke off, covering her face with her hands.

"He would what? Louischen, tell us," Vicky said, clasping Marianne's hand and exchanging an alarmed glance with her.

"He would burn them. And he wouldn't – just burn, but burn a little, and make me wear them when they are hot. He did that with the gloves you gave me – the pretty ones you made – the last time he was so bloody angry."

"Louischen!" Vicky cried, and looked at Marianne. "I suppose that is something *he* says?"

"N-no," Marianne said slowly, "that is not one of *his choice* expressions. I do not understand where she picked it up. And besides, she only says it in English, so it doesn't make sense."

"Louischen," Vicky said, turning back to the little girl, "why do you say he is so 'bloody' angry? Don't you know that is not a nice thing to say?"

Louischen looked up, puzzlement showing in her eyes. "How else am I to describe it? – Oh, do you mean, it is one of those – *red* words – like Papa uses?" Her eyes filled with tears. "I don't want to!"

"Describe what? If you don't mean it the way I thought you were saying it, there is nothing wrong."

"Papa's voice is always red, and a little liquid, but – when he is so angry – I see the blood running – dripping – I saw it on my feet when he was staring at them, before he even broke the glass."

Vicky nodded. "There is nothing wrong in saying that, if you mean it descriptively. Only don't let other people hear you say 'bloody' like that. It doesn't sound nice, and it is considered what you call a 'red word'." She paused. "Louischen," she said, as Fritz took Louischen, "tell us all about your – the colors you said different words are? Are there other color words besides red words?"

"Oh, yes," Louischen said, a smile slowly passing over her face, as she snuggled in Fritz's arms. "There are pink words, and yellow words, and green words, and brown words, and blue words, and black words, and orange words," she said slowly. "I like the first three best. The others –" She paused, a painful look coming over her face as she seemed to stifle a sob. "But you don't know? You really don't know, Aunty?" She looked up at Vicky, and then at Fritz too.

"*Nein*[39]," Fritz said.

"It seems so strange. Mama and Ebi and Marie don't see it either. Why do I see it when no one else does?"

"Well," Vicky said slowly, "you have been given a little – no, a big gift."

Louischen looked around. "What? When?"

"I mean this way you see things. You can tell the truth of what people feel about each other, and what words mean, how people use them, and so on, can you not?"

Louischen nodded.

"Tell me what you mean by some of the different color words," Vicky said, stroking her head.

"Milk is a pink word. I remember you thought I meant the milk was pink." She shook her head. "The word 'milk' is pink. Some words are a color, but not always," Louischen said slowly, her face furrowed with concentration. "Mama, and baby, and words like that are often pink, except if someone uses them unpleasantly.

"Those words –" She paused, a tremor passing over her and making her catch her breath before going on. "Those words Papa uses so much are – red words. But you knew what I meant by that. I don't have to say them, do I?"

Fritz shook his head, kissing her forehead. "No, Louischen," Vicky said gently. "We know what you mean."

"Those are red words – they look like blood, except – when Papa's friends are there, they use those words, when their voices are green, and that – confuses."

"Green means happy, doesn't it?" Vicky asked. Louischen nodded. "They think they are being playful, but are using nasty words. I know what you mean. What are yellow words?"

Louischen smiled. "Words," she paused, thinking. "When we can't say the word. How you say things you don't understand – is

---

39 No

yellow. When we say things strangely, like a baby." Vicky smiled. It was funny to hear such a young child say such a thing, but Louischen spoke so fluently so early.

"Do I speak English in yellow?" Fritz asked, smiling.

Louischen nodded, giggling.

August 14

"Cake! Cake!" Henry gazed delightedly at the candles, and Vicky had to hold his hands to keep him from trying to grab them while they were still burning.

"To think he is already two," she whispered to Fritz, shaking her head. And Willy – Willy was quite a big boy now, and sat at the table between Vicky and Fritz today. It was his first formal dinner.

Marmor Palais, September 1

Vicky walked carefully up the stairs. *This must be my last visit before the baby comes, I can't be going up and down all these stairs constantly.* She knocked softly at the door of Marianne's sitting-room. There was no answer. She went to another door, and knocked, but again, there was no answer. She paused, thinking. *I know I saw Fritz Karl go out this morning, and he hasn't come back. I was quite sure Marianne was home.* She was turning to go and ask Countess Alvensleben if Marianne was at home when there was a sound in the corridor.

"Oh, Vicky, I was going to come over and see if you could

come and help me!" Marianne cried, coming around the corner and throwing her arms around Vicky. "I don't know where to look anymore!" She burst into tears.

"Marianne, what is it? Where to look for what?"

"Ebi!" Marianne cried, struggling to control herself but bursting into fresh tears. "Mariechen is in the schoolroom and Louischen is in the nursery, but Ebi is not with either of them. You know I didn't like the idea of separating the girls, but I didn't know how to refuse! It is time for the elder girls to have more lessons, but I want them all to be together. Oh, my poor Ebi!" She broke off, wringing her hands.

"What – where might she be?"

"Fritz Karl came to the schoolroom this morning and told her to go with him. Mariechen tried to go to, as I have always wished them to stay together, but he was – he didn't wish it, and he went away with her - I don't mean went away; she never left the house, but he actually went away about half an hour later and Ebi is gone! I don't know where to look anymore!"

"Haven't you gotten anyone to help you?" Vicky looked at Marianne, her heart full of sympathy, but it seemed strange for her not to have asked for help before this. "What time was it?"

"It was ten this morning, Mariechen said."

And he left at half past ten, and now it is two in the afternoon, Vicky thought. *Wherever that poor girl is, she has been there for over three hours.*

"No one would listen to me when I tried to ask for help – you know how they are; I can't ask for anything and receive a respectful response. Even from my own ladies! Either they seem never to hear me or they are frightened of him or they are so rude – and I cannot bear that just now!" Marianne burst into tears again. "And I can't hear well enough to hear if she is crying somewhere!"

"Let me go and speak to Mariechen, before we do anything else. When do you expect Fritz Karl to come back?"

Marianne shook her head. "Not for two days."

Vicky nodded. "Good." She hurried to the schoolroom, Marianne following.

Mariechen sat at her desk reading when Vicky opened the door. "Aunt Vicky?"

"Mariechen." Vicky held out her arms and embraced the little girl, kissing her cheek where there was a large, painful looking bruise. She knelt down as she often did when she talked with her. "Mariechen, tell me what you know about Ebi."

"Papa–" Mariechen's voice caught as she began to speak. She was obviously trying not to cry. "Papa came here at ten this morning, an hour after we had begun our lessons. Fraulein had just left the room for a moment to fetch another book, and he stormed in, very upset about something – I couldn't quite make out what – and took Ebi by the arm and shouted that she must go with him. I tried to follow, as Mama always told me to never let Ebi out of my sight, but – he – he –" Her voice broke and she hid her face against Vicky's shoulder.

Vicky rubbed her back, speaking softly and gently to try to comfort her. "I'm here, Mariechen. Mama is with me. No one else. You can tell us what happened."

"Papa – Papa" – Mariechen put her hand up to her head – "my head still aches – but he took Ebi and slammed the door. I had put my hand out, and it nearly caught my fingers. I – I felt as if I had been knocked down, and as if I couldn't move or think. When I could, I went out, but I couldn't find them anywhere, and I saw Papa's carriage drive away. The coachman said it was only him – she hadn't left the house. Großpapa's carriage was there also, but I didn't see him, either, though I saw and heard him and Papa in the courtyard this morning, arguing and shouting. I wasn't near enough to hear what about. I saw him leave too."

Vicky glanced at Marianne, and then looked Mariechen in the eye again. "You are certain you saw your Großpapa leave?" Mariechen nodded. "Did he leave before or after your Papa?"

"After – about eleven o'clock."

"We must search," Vicky said, looking at Marianne. "Where is Louischen?"

"In the nursery, where the girls all sleep still," Marianne said.

"Let me go up and fetch her. I think she might be useful."

"Aunty Vicky!" Louischen threw her arms around Vicky the moment she opened the door. "Aunty, I'm so lonely here. Why can't I go to the schoolroom?"

"Hush, Louischen," Vicky whispered. "Ebi is missing and we're trying to find her. I would like you to help."

Louischen nodded, running down the corridor. "I know where she might be," she said, and darted into another room.

Vicky followed her, surprised when she passed the doorway Louischen had disappeared through. It was a beautiful little room with a large stained glass window, with several flowering vines growing up around it. Louischen stood, gazing upward, seemingly lost in thought.

"Ebi isn't here," Marianne said, taking Louischen's hand and leading her out of the room. She had calmed down a little while Vicky was talking with the children.

"Louischen," Vicky said as a young man – one of the footmen – approached, clicked his heels, and went on, "I want you to ask that man to help us search."

Louischen ran back to the man, who walked on as if he didn't see her. She said something in a loud whisper Vicky couldn't quite hear, and he stopped and looked at her, kneeling down to hear what she was saying.

"*Meine Schwester* is missing and we want you to help," she said in German.

The young man nodded. "I ought not to speak while I am on duty, but I will help you find the little Princess."

Vicky saw the grateful look Marianne gave the young man. He

was really quite a boy, but he had looked older when they had first seen him. Since Louischen's first whisper his face had changed and seemed to come alive, looking young and cheerful.

They went on through the corridors, coming to the large halls which were used for balls and dinners. They entered another corridor on the other side of the hall, one of the backways used by the servants. Vicky paused, watching Louischen. Her little face was screwed up in concentration, but she seemed to be trying to smell something.

"It is very blue – so blue I can't see the yellow – yes!" She ran forward to the door of a closet at the end of the corridor.

"Here she is!" she called.

"How do you know? Can you hear her?" Marianne asked, picking her up and hugging her.

Vicky went to the door and knelt down, pressing her ear to it. "I don't hear anything. Are you quite certain, Louischen?"

"She is so sad, how can anyone not see it?" Louischen asked. "I can even smell it," she murmured, her expression changing again.

Vicky turned to Marianne. "Do you have a key which will open this?"

Marianne sighed. "They will have one downstairs in the kitchen." She turned to the footman, but then back to Vicky. "I would ask him to go," she whispered, "but if anyone else meets him and speaks to him, he might not remember."

Vicky nodded. "I'll stay here. Let Louischen stay too."

Marianne hurried away. Vicky sat down, holding Louischen and singing softly.

"Aunt Vicky?" a voice called from inside the closet.

"Ebi!" Vicky felt tears rush to her eyes at the sound of her voice. "Ebi, Mama is going to fetch the key to get you out of there."

"The blue is gone – or changed," Louischen murmured to

herself. "I can see her again – yellow – bits of blue, now green, and pink. I am so glad!"

Vicky let Louischen talk on, unsure of what she meant. She had tried to ask Louischen to explain herself many times when she talked this way, but she seemed to think everyone must understand.

"Only, I can see it through doors and in the next room. No one else seems to be able to except for Großpapa," was all she had said.

Vicky continued to sing, but her voice caught as she heard Ebi stifle a sob. She felt a tear drop on her hand. Louischen was looking at the door, her gaze intense, tears pouring silently down her cheeks.

"Vicky? Am I in the right place?" Marianne called, and then hurried around the corner. "I don't go in the back corridors very much, so I don't know my way. I wish I hadn't taken so long." She put the key in the lock and it turned silently. She opened the door.

"Mama!" Ebi cried, but didn't rise. Marianne knelt down, throwing her arms around her daughter and bursting into tears.

"Ebi, I – I didn't know what had happened to you, *meine Liebling*[40], my treasure," she sobbed.

"Papa – I – I don't know," Ebi said softly. Vicky looked at her. Her face wore a somewhat blank expression.

"Don't you realize how long you have been in there?" Vicky asked, stroking her head.

"It hasn't been more than a few minutes," Ebi murmured, as Marianne lifted her up.

The clock struck three. Ebi's eyes widened. "It was only ten."

"Have you been asleep?" Vicky asked. Ebi shook her head.

"I – I don't know. It was as if your singing woke me, but – I don't think I was asleep." Ebi spoke slowly, her step slow and stumbling as they began to walk down the corridor. "Papa came to

---

40 My darling

the schoolroom, and said he wished me to go with him, but – how did I get here?"

September 15, 2 a.m.

"Oh," Vicky groaned, waking at a sudden pain in her back. She turned restlessly. It had been so hard to get comfortable to sleep the last two weeks. The pain returned.

"Fritz?" She turned to him, sitting up, shaking him gently. "Fritz?"

"Vicky?" Fritz yawned enormously, blinking up at her.

"I – we should tell Wegner; the time is come. But I think I can sleep more," she said. "But I am quite certain."

Fritz nodded, and got up, going into the next room to send for Wegner. He came back into the bedroom, sitting down to wait, attempting to suppress another yawn.

"Your Highness?" Wegner entered, bowing and clicking his heels as Fritz rose.

"The baby is coming, but my wife says she is comfortable enough to sleep more. But please, send for the others and be sure they are here within the hour," Fritz said.

Wegner nodded and clicked his heels again, and Fritz closed the door, returning to bed. "Are you comfortable?" he asked Vicky, bending over her to kiss her before he lay down.

"I could do with the extra pillows I have in my dressing-room," she said. Fritz brought them for her to arrange. She sighed, and smiled up at him. "Yes. I can sleep for a while."

Noon

"Wah! Wah!" The baby screamed as Fritz held him. He laid the little boy in Vicky's arms, putting his arm around her.

"A third son," he said, feeling his face glow.

Everything had gone very quickly, and the doctors left after only a few minutes. The maids remained to change the sheets and make sure Vicky's needs were met. Finally, Fritz and Vicky were alone together, but there was a knock at the door. Fritz went to open it.

"Mama!" Wilhelm ran to the bed, as did Charlotte, eager to see their new little sibling.

"Here, be careful, but you may hold him," Vicky said, taking Wilhelm's arm. His face seemed to glow as he looked down at his little brother.

"Baby! I want to hold him!" Charlotte cried. Fritz took the little one and gently placed him in her arms, and then took him again, climbing onto the bed by Vicky's side. Mrs. Hobbs stood at the door. Fritz nodded to her.

"Can Georgiana see 'im? She came just for that," Emma said. Vicky nodded.

Georgiana was the housekeeper who took care of Vicky and Fritz's suite of rooms; she was Emma's sister. They both came up to the bed, Georgiana crooning as she took the baby. "Now take them to bed," Vicky said, nodding to Georgiana and kissing Wilhelm and Charlotte. Emma lingered.

"Do you wish me to stay, yer 'ighness?" she asked. "Where is the wet-nurse?"

Vicky laughed. "There is to be no wet-nurse this time. I am perfectly capable of nursing my own child, and performing my duties as a Princess at the same time, no matter what Mama and Queen Augusta think." She smiled at Emma, and looked down at her little son. She had the blankets pulled up, so that she could nurse privately, even while the doctors and other people were still in the room. "But I would appreciate it if you would set up the cradle and things I have there," she added, nodding towards her dressing-room. "Here," she pointed to a spot about ten feet from the bed. "I want my baby to myself this time. I don't mean I do not appreciate all you do," she said, as Mrs. Hobbs turned away. "We are very grateful for all you do for the children."

September 18

"Yes, Papa, and I wish to ask Wrangel to be a sponsor," Fritz said, stroking the baby's head.

Vicky smiled at her father-in-law. "We wish to ask the Emperor and Empress of Austria. So he shall have the names Franz, Friedrich, and –" She looked back and forth at him and Fritz.

"Sigismund," the King said.

Fritz nodded. "I should like that name to be in our family."

Vicky grimaced. "It is such an odd name, and will sound – but never mind. I can call him Siggy." She had been going to say the name "will sound odd in English", but it would be rather rude to give that objection to a historical name the King and Fritz both liked.

September 29

"Nine years," Fritz wrote in his diary. "Nine years since our engagement, and how much pure, sweet, domestic happiness God has given us."

Vicky lay in bed, pressing her baby to her heart. "My precious little thing," she whispered. She had never felt so content as she did now. She felt so at peace at night, with her little son in her arms. She never felt restless and inclined to cry, as she had after the births of her other children.

"I am happier than ever before, though I hardly know how that is possible," she whispered to Fritz when he came to join her. "I never knew I could love someone – it is not that I love him *more* than the others, but – I love him in a different way. Even when I nursed Willy and Henry, it was so infrequent and brief that it was not like this. He is my heart's best treasure, besides you, of course." She snuggled in Fritz's arms, looking up at him. His gaze was fastened on Baby's little face. The little one looked up, their eyes locking. Vicky smiled. She was glad Fritz didn't seem put out by her having the little one with her at night.

September 30

"No one took notice of Mama's birthday besides her children and her sister," Fritz told Vicky when he came in. "I went to see Aunt Marie. She was quite offended about it."

"Your Mama is not here. How can we know that no one

wrote?" Vicky asked, looking up from where Baby lay sleeping in his cradle.

Fritz shook his head. "She arrived yesterday. She wishes to see her grandson, of course. I took your message, which you said to write to her."

"Have she or your Papa said anything about our journey to Switzerland?"

Fritz shook his head.

October 8

"Papa says we cannot take the children, and must turn the baby over to a wet-nurse. He also says we may only remain away for six weeks at most, and preferably four, instead of the two months we asked for."

Fritz looked up to meet Vicky's eye. She looked up. "I would rather not go at all!" she cried.

Fritz sat down beside her, putting his arm around her. "I will speak to Papa again. He must change his mind."

"Yes, do, please, or I really would rather not go."

October 18

"Franz Friedrich Sigismund." Vicky listened to the clergyman's speech. The christening was almost over, and she had her baby in her arms again. "God bless the dear mother, our Crown Princess, and the child."

The group began to disperse, everyone forming into smaller groups, and the buzz of conversation grew louder. Vicky saw Fritz Karl across the room. He had never joined the group around the font. He stood, leaning against the wall, his arms crossed, a scowl on his face. Vicky sighed. He had done so at the christening of each of her children. She tried to imagine how he felt, as the birth of yet another son pushed him, who had once been near becoming the Crown Prince himself, yet further down in succession.

Fritz's father had as a young man sought to give up the throne to marry Elisa Radziwill, the woman he loved. Prince Charles, it had seemed, would be the next King after his childless eldest brother. Fritz Karl had been fourth in line for the throne – not so extremely close, it seemed, but if Prince Wilhelm, as Fritz's father was then, renounced his claim, he would have been very close indeed. Everyone was always certain Friedrich Wilhelm the fourth – the King Vicky had only met briefly a few times in her first two years of marriage – would never have children. With Prince Wilhelm out of the way, Prince Charles would have become King after the deaths of his father and brother.

As a child, Fritz had told Vicky, Fritz had always refused to listen to lessons about the line of succession. "I could never understand how the deaths of my family could be a subject of education," he had said. Apparently, Fritz Karl had had a similar issue. It was not until a shared lesson, when Fritz was eleven and Fritz Karl fourteen, that they had both truly come to realize their respective positions.

Vicky felt a hand on her shoulder. She had been so absorbed in her thoughts that she hadn't noticed that almost everyone had gone. It was Fritz.

"Vicky, Papa says we may take the baby with us, and stay away as long as we like. We still cannot take the elder children, but at least he has relented about this."

"Has he relented about the wet-nurse?"

"He says we are to take a wet-nurse, but that causes no difficulty." He looked down, his mouth twitching as he tried not to laugh.

Vicky nodded. "I shall take a wet-nurse, certainly." She laughed. "That doesn't mean I will give her that occupation."

Fritz nodded. "Did you hear the other news?"

"What? I was thinking about other things, not listening."

"Onkel Karl has an appointment as Governor of Mainz. That means he is to be away from Berlin during the season for three years." He met Vicky's eye again. "It is an honor he cannot refuse. You remember Papa held this position when I was a boy."

Vicky threw her arms around him. "That is wonderful news! And to think this news comes on your birthday." She looked up at Fritz, trying to smile, but she couldn't tell what expression her face showed.

Fritz nodded. "It has been a pleasant day, every time it has come around since '60. You have succeeded in your wish – your wish that it would not be a bad day on our calendar."

"I said it was wonderful news," Vicky said, squeezing Fritz's hand, "and it is good news – for us. But it means he is to be near Alice. Mainz isn't far from Darmstadt. And Vivi too."

Fritz nodded, his face growing serious. "May *Gott* keep them safe."

CHAPTER TWENTY

A MIDNIGHT VISIT

October 21, 1864

Vicky leaned over the cradle she had moved for the night into her dressing-room. It would be the second night she hadn't brought Baby to bed with her, and the first night to leave him in a different room. She had nursed him about an hour ago, and hopefully, he would continue to sleep peacefully for some time.

Vicky opened the door of her dressing-room, peering into the bedroom. A candle flickered on the table, but it had burnt low, and would soon go out. Moonlight streamed in through the window. Fritz saw her. "I came home early last night from the theater, but you were already asleep," he said. "The performance was – disgusting." Fritz had gone to the theater the night before, and had said he had something to say about it in the morning, but he had been out all day. He sat on the edge of the bed, his head leaned on his hand, as he often did when embarrassed. Vicky slipped over to the bed, laying her nightgown at the foot, and slipped under the blankets. Fritz hadn't looked up. She shivered at the touch of the blankets on her bare skin; it was getting quite cold now.

"Why did you go to the theater last night, if it was so offensive?" she asked.

"I thought it was to be something else. Someone had sent me a paper, advertising the play. It was torn out of a larger page. I didn't think about the fact that the day of the week and the year were torn off. I notice that now when I examine it. It is last year's advertisement, when they actually had something decent." He turned to look at her, sighed and rolled his eyes, and let her take his hand.

"What was performed?"

"The cancan," he groaned, covering his eyes again. "I would never have gone to such a thing! And it was worse than it is in Paris! It is just what Onkel Karl delights in. I should simply give up going to the Vic– to *that* theater. I will not sully your name by association."

Vicky felt his hand clench. She took his fist, loosening his fingers, pressing his hand to her lips. The Victoria Theater was a new theater built the year after they were married. It was named in her honor, but it had been taken over by someone who was a very good friend of Prince Charles. Occasionally, however, there was a good play, so Fritz had not given it up entirely.

"I know you would never go to such –" Vicky began, but paused, watching his face. He had been blushing from embarrassment; now, she saw his face flush again, but his expression was very different. Her nightgown, lying on the bed, had caught his eye. He turned, leaning down over her.

"Never mind," he whispered, their lips meeting. Vicky raised her head to return his kiss. He ran his hand up her arm. "I don't see how anyone could imagine a man would wish for such entertainment if he had such a wife as you," he murmured in her ear, his mustache tickling her neck. His lips touched her throat; his fingers ran along her chest just above the blanket. He drew it down, and she wrapped her arms around him, pulling him to her and kissing the top of his head, feeling his breath warm against her breast as his hands lingered caressingly. "Vicky," he murmured, his voice intense, in a way which always reminded her of the first time she had heard him pronounce her name in that tone – the evening when Papa had fallen asleep while chaperoning them while they were engaged.

Just at that moment, the candle flickered out, and – there was a knock at the door.

Fritz sat up hurriedly. "Rosa?" Vicky called, getting up, slipping on her nightgown and dressing-gown and going to the door.

"*Ihre Hoheit, ein Brief für sie[41]*," Rosa said, setting a note on the little table by the door and curtseying.

Vicky closed the door and went to the window. She looked at Fritz. "Should I open it right now or –" She slipped off her dressing-gown again, the moonlight showing her silhouette through her nightgown.

"See who it is from, since it was sent at such a strange hour."

Vicky sighed and lighted a lamp, opening and glancing at the note. "There is no address on the envelope; it simply says "*Die Kronprinzessin*", and the crest is cut from the top of the pages." Vicky leaned closer to the lamp. "Here is one where the edge of the crest is visible – yes, I believe it is from the Marmor Palais."

"The handwriting looks disguised. It looks as if it could be Marianne's, but–" Fritz joined her. Vicky glanced up at him, shuddering and clutching his arm. "Look at this. It is asking us to go to the little house Wally and Marie used to live in. At this hour of the night? It says to come immediately." Vicky looked up at Fritz, clinging closer to him.

"You think it is not from Marianne?" he said gently, putting his arm around her. She nodded.

"Let us look at it carefully," Fritz said. "It could be some sort of trap, but if it *is* from Marianne, we must go! What extremity might she be in which would make her send this?"

"Examine it; Fritz, I will call Rosa again," Vicky said, putting her dressing-gown back on and stepping out.

"Count Seckendorff gave it me, and said it was from Princess Friedrich Karl," Rosa said as Vicky opened the door again.

"Go and fetch him. Yes, now, immediately," Vicky said hurriedly. She closed the door and turned to Fritz. "She is quite

---

41 Your Highness, a letter for you.

certain it is from Marianne, and she says Count Seckendorff brought it directly from her."

"I should say it is from the scent, also. It smells like – yes, here is something." Fritz looked into the envelope, tipping it into his hand. A pressed cherry blossom and a pine needle fell out. "You know how Louischen is always doing that." There was a knock at the door, which he answered. He whispered to Vicky, "Get dressed, hurry."

Vicky closed her dressing room door and dressed hurriedly, hearing Fritz speak in a low murmur. It was always strange to hear him and Count Seckendorff converse. Their voices and accents were so similar; it was almost as if it was only Fritz speaking to himself.

Vicky came out, and Fritz's dressing room door closed. Count Seckendorff stood at the door. "The Prince wishes me to accompany you," he said, bowing to Vicky. "Princess Friedrich Karl gave me the note herself, and seemed in great distress."

"Rosa, fetch two of the men we can trust – you know who I mean – whoever is awake, and tell them to meet us in the courtyard."

"A carriage will be faster than the night train which has already left," Fritz said, and hurried forward.

The carriage was prepared by the time they reached it. They started immediately.

The moonlight shone on the river as they walked towards the house. Vicky was glad they didn't have to carry lanterns. If it wasn't Marianne, she didn't want to be carrying a light which would show where she was.

"Hush, girls, I believe they are coming, and then we can go."

Vicky took a deep breath and let it out very slowly, hearing Fritz sigh also. It was Marianne, after all. They hurried forward, Seckendorff and the others going back to the carriage.

"Marianne, what is the matter? Why are you – where are you going?" Vicky hurried forward, watching Marianne pacing up and down, and a man lifting a trunk into a carriage which was draped in black, every shining part of the carriage and harnesses covered. The wheels, too, were rubber, and would sound quietly on the pavement. Marianne was dressed in deepest mourning, as was the coachman.

"I must go – we must go," Marianne said, her voice trembling. "Please, don't wake Ebi," she said as Vicky went to the carriage.

"Aunty!" Louischen threw her arms around Vicky's neck and clung to her. Vicky stood, kissing the little girl's forehead as tears came to her eyes.

Fritz came up and took Louischen in his arms, kissing her forehead and whispering something in her ear. She laughed through her tears and kissed his cheek. Vicky was surprised. Louischen was very frugal with her kisses.

She turned back to the carriage, sitting down inside.

"Goodbye, Aunt Vicky," Mariechen said softly, squeezing her hand. "I – I hope we will see you again, but Mama says that isn't very likely."

Vicky didn't know what to say, and embraced her silently. The girls, too, were dressed in black, but in thin, almost threadbare, cheap cloth. Ebi was asleep, her head leaned on Mariechen's shoulder. Vicky bent over her, kissing her forehead very gently. She looked at her sweet little face, and at a large bruise on her cheek. Her heart ached as she turned away.

"Vicky, take her. I wish to speak to Marianne a moment." Vicky took Louischen from Fritz, and walked up and down, very softly singing her favorite lullaby.

"Aunty, why are we going away?" Louischen looked up at her, her big eyes even wider than usual as she blinked through her tears. "I don't want to leave you."

"I don't know, Louischen, but your Mama is trying to keep you safe. Trust her. Uncle Fritz and I will always love you and pray for you."

Fritz and Marianne came towards her, Marianne struggling to keep back her tears. Fritz took Louischen again.

"Oh, Vicky, I don't know what to say!" Marianne sobbed, taking her arm. Vicky walked a little way with her, and turned toward her.

"Why are you going?"

"I – he – oh, my poor Ebi! I cannot stay and –" Her voice broke and she sobbed aloud.

Vicky threw her arms around her, wondering what to say. "Fritz and I will do anything to help you. Where are you going?"

Marianne shook her head. "I – I cannot tell you. I – you must be able to truthfully say you don't know – that I didn't tell you. You know he can tell."

"So this is something about Prince Charles, and not only Fritz Karl?" Vicky murmured. Marianne suddenly tore her arm from her grasp, hurrying to the carriage.

"We must go, while it is still dark. I am so thankful there has been no snow yet, so that does not make us more visible."

"*Gott* be with you, *am wiedersehen*[42], Marianne," Fritz said, squeezing her hand. His voice trembled; he, too, was attempting to hold back tears.

"*Auf Wiedersehen.*" Marianne had climbed into the carriage, but turned to look at Fritz, then at Vicky. "Though that may not be in this world."

Vicky kissed Louischen again, and squeezed Mariechen's hand.

---

42 Till we meet again

She closed the carriage door, and the coachman spoke to the horses.

Vicky took Fritz's arm as they stood together, watching the carriage drive away, and slowly turned, walking back to their own carriage.

"Did she tell you anything? Why are they leaving?"

"I only know it is something to do with Ebi, and that she doesn't want to tell us more because Onkel Karl will wish to know where they have gone." He paused, looking at Vicky. "You know he can tell if one tries to evade the answer."

"Yes," Vicky said, shuddering. "Where are they going, I wonder?"

"She will probably go to Anhalt. And –" He paused again. "And Onkel Karl will probably have some scandals to deal with, if she succeeds."

"You think she wishes to bring a case against him?"

"Certainly." Fritz nodded, squeezing Vicky's hand. "Only, I don't know if it is possible. If it is something to do with the girls, the case must be made by the father, and Fritz Karl –"

Vicky shook her head, shuddering again. They had reached the carriage, but before they got in, she turned, throwing her arms around Fritz. "If only she could be as happy as we are!"

Thank you for reading "Under a Cloud"
Reviews are appreciated at Amazon or Goodreads

ABOUT THE AUTHOR

Luv Lubker has lived in the Victorian era half her life, making friends with the Bronte sisters and the extended family of Queen Victoria. Now she knows them quite as well as her own family.

Born in a cattle trough in the Appalachian mountains, Luv lives in Texas - when she comes to the modern world.

When she isn't living in the Victorian era, she enjoys being with her family; making and eating delicious raw food, riding her bike (which she only learned to ride at 25 though she ridden a unicycle since she was 7), and watching animals - the passion of her childhood.

Visit Luv Lubker's Historium Press Page
or Author Website

www.thehistoricalfictioncompany.com/hp-authors/luv-lubker

www.therivalcourts.com

Preview of "Under the Sword"
Book Three in the Rival Courts series

✳✳✳✳✳✳✳✳✳✳

PROLOGUE

Potsdam, Brandenberg, October 21, 1864

The carriage drove on, almost silently, the padded wheels making soft noises in the grass and autumn leaves. There had not yet been any snow. Everything was black; every shining part of the harness was covered; the coachman was dressed in dull black. Four cloaked figures sat inside, a young woman dressed in deepest mourning, her face buried in her handkerchief, and, huddled next to her, were three little girls. A single small trunk sat behind them.

"Mama," the eldest girl said, "Where are we going?"

"I – I do not know yet, Mariechen. We must arrive in Anhalt if we can, and I shall decide further then."

"Is Charlotta in the trunk?" the youngest girl asked quietly, as if speaking to herself.

"What do you mean, Louischen, how would she be?"

"The little girl in the glass over my bed. I always kiss her goodnight. And I didn't... before we left." The little girl tried to control a sob.

"Oh," the other girl groaned, rubbing her eyes. She had fallen asleep between the other two. "Mama, can we not stop? I think I'm going to be sick," she murmured.

"No, Ebi, we must go on, as far as we can tonight. And I want

314

you to be very careful when we do stop. Stay together, and don't call each other by your names – but do not use your titles either. We must think of some other names to use. We don't want anyone to recognize you."

"But, we will go home, won't we, Mama?" Louischen looked up at her, her big eyes filling with tears again. "Will we see Aunty Vicky and Uncle Fritz again before we go on? Why were they crying when they came here? Why were you crying, Mama?"

"*Ach, meine lieblings*, what can I tell them?" the woman sobbed to herself. She thought of the goodbye which had taken place a couple of hours before, when she had embraced her friends and cousins, the Crown Prince and Crown Princess, for what might have been the last time. "*Gott* be with you, *am wiedersehen*, Marianne," Fritz had said, with the kindly look he always had for her as he squeezed her hand, but there had been sorrow in his eyes at the same time. Vicky had thrown her arms around Marianne impulsively, and kissed the little girls goodbye, clinging particularly to Louischen.

Marianne looked down at her three daughters with a lump in her throat; three such small, pitifully helpless morsels of humanity. Ebi, thankfully, had not been sick. Marianne's heart twisted at the sight of her sweet little face as her head leaned on her sister's shoulder, her mouth dropping open as she drifted off again.

She sadly shook her head. *No,* she thought, *you will never see Aunty Vicky and Uncle Fritz again.* She covered her face with her hands. She could never bring her little girls back to Berlin as long as her husband and his father lived.

HISTORIUM PRESS

www.historiumpress.com